DAVIS WEST

Witness in the Wings

ISBN 979-8987915622

ISBN 979-8987915615 (ebook)

Wolfheart Press

Alpine, CA 91901

CONTENTS

INTRODUCTION

After writing his first book, *Reunion* (a memoir of camaraderie and trauma about a twenty-year-old sailor who lost all his navy friends in the WWII battle with the Japanese kamikaze), the author was searching for his next story and turned to me, his Jewish partner, for ideas. We had met at the San Francisco Opera in 1968 where he was the master head painter. For many years he painted all the scenery on that opera stage. I witnessed his mastery from the wings in my minor role as an apprentice designer and keeper of the archives. The opera's designers and directors came to San Franciso from Europe and their trends in stage design over the twentieth century were filed in these archives. The execution of those multi-faceted designs over the decades was in the hands of the author of this book. When I first met him I was in awe of his skill and dedication. At that time no woman could be involved in the painting of scenery due to an all-male union. I decided to attach myself to this crew of former WWII veterans who had returned from battles with both the Germans and the Japanese, worse for wear, bitterly scarred, and prejudiced in particular against the group they called the "Krauts."

These men had won the war, but in the world of Opera, German culture and music had become the latest trend. The works of Richard Wagner now dominated the San Francisco Opera's repertoire. The German-born manager of the San Francisco Opera brought in German directors, designers, choreographers, and German-speaking secretaries. What was once the province of whimsical Italian artists creating beautiful evocative scenery for the romantic and soaringly sentimental Italian love stories of Verdi, and Puccini, favorites of died-in-the-wool opera lovers, was now being turned into a cold, dark colorless setting where lights, not paintings, made the stage. The prior sets for the Italian love stories had been a painter's challenge and an opportunity to master the chiaroscuro and painterliness of illusionistic rendering.

The foundational training of the author of this book came from Eugene Dunkel, a master painter from the Bolshoi ballet who was a pioneer of early scenic painting in New York and founder of the first major American scenic art studio. He mentored Davis West and transmitted his energy and stylistic brushwork to him and later to me as West's mentee, who became his wife and his widow.

When I began my career as a would-be scenic painter, sitting on the stage of The San Francisco Opera House was the ghost ship for "The Flying Dutchman" an opera written by Richard Wagner who it has been said, imagined the doomed captain of that ship to be "the wandering Jew," a character who had lost the right to live among civilized men, who deserved to be forever at sea, welcome in no port. Wagner was a virulent antisemite. His music from the opera Die Valkyrie was played as captured Jews of Europe were marched into the gas chambers of Auschwitz, Belzec and Dachau.

I witnessed from the wings how the imperious German director, who had been sponsored by the German San Francico community and society for the advancement of German culture in the U.S., flaunted his authority over these American veterans by stomping around and barking orders like an SS Officer. You could cut the resentment he created with a knife. That is why when my husband asked me, "What should I write about now?" I said, "Write your world, the stage world you commanded when we met; write what it was like when the world of color and dream-like canvases turned to black and white and the stark wreckage of what I saw on that stage—a bloody ragged ship—when I first entered into your world. Write about what you learned from me, your Jewish woman with her own inherited fear and disdain for those Nazi murderers, having come from Polish immigrants who barely escaped the holocaust. You hated them for your reasons, and I hated them for mine. Put the two together and write a story about what you had to live through and relive when they took over your dynasty on that opera stage."

Although Davis L. West and I, Catherine Hand, lived and worked together for 30 years, our backgrounds could not have been more different. He had gone to battle and never recovered from the psychological trauma of seeing all his friends die, whereas I, a baby then born in 1942 of Jewish heritage, had no firsthand knowledge of war. My first encounter with real German Nazis was in 1960 in Mexico City, when my mother offered to take me and my 11-year-old little brother on a summer study trip to Mexico. Our guide invited us to the apartment of a supposedly retired German ballerina and her cohort, who turned out to be a former SS anti-partisan Nazi General. This chilling encounter in which my mother and her children were invited for the sole purpose of robbing her I told of in a short story that I later wrote titled, The SS

Anti-Partisan Squadron Commander and The Silver Slippers, which appears in the epilogue of this book.

Years later I was a young woman witnessing the acting out of German foreign directors on an American stage where their brutality was on display in their behavior. The witness created by the author of this book is a fictional version of me. She is a concentration camp survivor of Belzec, who having been tortured is missing two fingers, and the witness who can identify the German director as her concentration camp torturer. From that point on, the author takes the reader on a wild hunt with agents of the Israeli Mossad in an attempt to kidnap these Nazi criminals and ship them off to Israel to be tried as murderers like Adolph Eichman.

In real life, the author my husband followed me when I went to live and work in Israel. While there he met Israeli people who'd become my friends, and some of them, whose names have been changed, feature as Israeli Nazi hunters in this story.

To learn more about my first encounter with a Nazi, see my short story in the epilogue. The encounter I describe inspired the placement of a medallion at the center of the proscenium on this book's cover. This medallion hung on the neck of the SS (Schutzstaffel) General who terrorized me, my little brother, and my mother (a holocaust escapee) when he held sway over us, dangling its gruesome image over our heads.

Catherine Hand
Editor and Widow of Davis West

PROLOGUE

B lack threatening clouds slowly drift across an endless sky. The ocean is dark and restless. Silhouetted against the deep indigo background, the hulls of two ships are seen in the distance, their rigging cutting the scarlet sky above. Center stage, the Dutchman's ship looms over the jagged wharf and humble structures of the Norwegian fishing village where all is still dark. But from within the ghostly ship emanates a weird green glow which reveals a shroud of black netting draped over the blood red sails.

The scene is set behind the grand drape. Stagehands stand ready in the wings and the chorus silently awaits its cue. Behind the drape, house lights go down. The prompter enters his box. The conductor enters the pit, climbs to the podium and taps his baton. His follow spot is extinguished and now the only light visible in the house comes from the director's table positioned in the center of the third row. His blocky features ghoulishly illuminated by the dim reading lamp, the renowned German director Paul Berger sits flanked by his two assistants.

Amber lights are adjusted to a warm gold on the grand drape and the conductor raises his baton. The music erupts from the orchestra pit filling the house with warning sounds of impending doom. The grand drape slowly rises revealing the ominous scene to the rhythm of chanting seafarers. Suddenly the director heaves his bulky frame up from behind his table and his imperious, thickly accented voice rings through the opera house.

"Stop! Stop! It won't do."

White light floods the stage and the auditorium. Instruments are silenced, color drains from the scene and from the faces of the performers as the feared director lumbers down the aisle and up onto the stage's apron.

The frightened stage manager runs out from the stage right wing to meet him. "Yes, Maestro, what is it?"

Berger, muttering to himself in German turns to the little man. "The prop crew. Where are these men? Call them at once. Something must be done with the ship. This is no musical revue. Black, we must have more black!"

ONE

There were a lot of other bars I liked better than the Courtroom Bar, but it was close to my office, and they poured a good drink. My business wasn't exactly booming. I hadn't had a decent case to work on in months and this was another slow Friday afternoon, so I closed up shop and took a walk.

The San Francisco fog had started to roll in over the neighborhood of Twin Peaks as I pushed through the swinging doors and looked for a stool at the crowded bar. The opera season was about to open and quite a few of the customers worked on stage across the street at the opera house. I glanced over the crowd and recognized two stagehands sitting at a booth to the right of the entrance. One of them was Earl McGuire, the head carpenter at the opera—known as Mac to his friends. His red face beamed as he looked up, squinted through his glasses, and motioned for me to join them.

I maneuvered to the booth and slid in next to him. "Haven't seen you in here for quite a while, Mac. You must be putting in some hours over there at the opera."

Mac reached for the dice box and smiled. "Those damn krauts. They're keeping us busy all right. Just when we think we're all set and have our moves worked out smoothly, the God damned German director wants to make major changes." He turned to the fellow sitting next to him. "You know Mike, don't you?"

I didn't but held out my left hand and shook Mike's right one. "I've seen you in here a few times. I'm Vince DeLucca."

"Mike Cannon. Glad to meet you, Vince."

Mac pounded the dice box on the table. "One flop high dice for a drink." He looked at me. "OK with you, Vince?"

I nodded my approval. The waitress took our order and when the drinks arrived, I paid her for them.

"Thanks, Vince." Mac raised his glass. "Well boys, here's to Ben. God rest his soul."

Mike lifted his glass as well. "I'll drink to that. I still can't figure it. Ben never took drugs that I knew of."

Mac smacked his lips, "Well, you never know about some of the guys you work with."

I was having a hard time following the conversation. "Who is Ben?"

Mike replied, "He was the assistant prop man at the opera. Two nights ago, he was found dead in the basement below the stage. We heard it was an overdose, but what the hell he was doing down there, I don't know."

Mac waved for the waitress to order more drinks, but she was busy with someone else. "Yeah, it's too damn bad. This is the first time anything like this has happened since I been working at the opera. Pretty sad, I'd say."

I wondered if the death of one of their union brothers had anything to do with the call I received earlier today. It was from the business agent of the stagehands union asking for a meeting tomorrow morning. I wanted to ask a few questions, but figured I'd wait until tomorrow, then I would know for sure what it was all about.

Mac started in on a tirade about the German directors on the stage of the opera. "Christ! These last two seasons have been rough. We're not used to taking orders from a bunch of Germans. We have a hell of a time understanding them. Most of them don't speak English." He held up his open hand and touched each finger in succession. "We've got German stage directors, German lighting designers, German conductors and German scenic designers, not to mention all of the singers. Christ! It's like we're putting on the Berlin Opera."

"Yeah, and what about this afternoon?" Mike added. "Here we were trying to set up a scene on stage for lighting when they yell like hell because the scenery's not set in time for them to play with their stage lights. It didn't used to be that way. Somebody's going to get hurt if they don't wise up."

Mike belted down his drink and looked at my empty right sleeve. "Say, Vince, don't think I'm being nosy, but how'd you lose your arm? Was it in the war?"

Mac frowned at Mike. "For Christ sake, Mike! That's the man's own business. You damned sure are nosy."

I smiled, "Hey. It's no big deal. I took a dose of shrapnel at Anzio, so now I'm stuck with an empty sleeve."

"There you go," said Mike. "See what I mean? The lousy krauts, they got you in the war, and now after the war they're still giving us hell on stage."

Mac looked for the waitress again. "Let it rest, Mike," he growled. "It would be a different story if we weren't getting paid."

"I'll take the Italians anytime," said Mike. "They know how to put on an opera. I remember when—.

The waitress plopped down three drinks. Mac looked up surprised, "Damn! That's fast. I didn't even order yet."

She pointed to the bar. "They came from that gentleman over there."

They turned to look, and Mike yelled, "Ey, Jer! Come on over."

The big man spun off the stool and walked to our booth.

"Jer, meet Vince DeLucca," said Mac. "Vince, this is big Jer. He paints all of the scenery over there at the opera."

I could see why they called him big Jer. He was well over six foot and appeared to have at one time been an athlete. He shoved in next to Mike and set his drink on the table. Glancing at my right sleeve he held out his left hand and smiled. "How you doing, Vince?"

I took his firm grip and said, "I'm doing OK. So, you do all of the painting for the operas? It must be very difficult to paint on such a large scale."

Mike laughed. "Yeah, and the stuff is getting even larger since we've been doing these German operas. Jer, how are you painters holding up? I noticed you and your boys putting in overtime at night. Are you behind schedule?"

Big Jer pondered on the question. "You might say we're a little behind. We've had a few changes and some additions."

Mac tapped his empty glass on the table. "We got our share of changes, too. I wish the bastards would make up their minds."

"Enough of talking shop," said Big Jer. He looked over at me. "What do you do, Vince? You don't work up at the opera front office, do you?"

"No. I'm not with the front office."

Mac put a hand on my shoulder. "Vince here is a private eye."

"Is that right?" said Big Jer with a look of surprise. "I've never run across a real private eye before. Must be an exciting job. How long have you been in that game?"

"Not too long. After I got out of the service, I took on a part time job with a friend of mine as an insurance investigator. Not very exciting, but it kept me busy. Two years ago, I opened my own agency and since then I've been able to keep my head above water. Mostly routine, nothing that you might call thrilling or dangerous."

"Hey, Vince, did Joe Bender call you?" asked Mac.

"Yes, he did. Do you know what it's about?"

Mac looked over at Mike and said, "Yeah. Ben Koslo's death. I don't know the particulars, but since the police closed the case, the union body voted to look into it. I knew you were an investigator and had your office around the corner, so I mentioned your name."

"What did Bender say when he called you?" asked Mike.

"Not much. We set up a meeting for tomorrow morning."

"About the funeral, Jer," said Mac" Are you going? It's this Sunday afternoon."

"Yeah, I'll be there. I liked Ben. He was a good man. I wonder how Julie is taking it?"

"Christ!" exclaimed Mike. "They were only married for six months, then this had to happen. Shit, let's have another round."

Mac looked at his watch and nodded. "We've got time for one more before the rehearsal." He picked up the dice box. "Jer, see if you can catch the waitress."

One flop high dice was not my game, so I stood up and said my good-byes.

Mac pounded the box down, rolled out the dice and looked up at me smiling. "Ey, Vince, we'll be seeing you at the theatre."

It was dark and foggy as I walked up Grove street to my office. I took a deep breath of the night air and wondered why they needed an investigator if the police had already closed the case on Ben Koslo's death.

TWO

At 8:00 the next morning, I stopped in at New Joe's for scrambled eggs and Italian sausage. After a couple of cups of coffee, I walked down Jones Street and stopped in front of the building where the union office was located. I went up one flight of wooden stairs, stopped at the first door on my left and knocked.

A loud voice yelled, "It's open." I turned the knob and entered. Behind a counter was a heavyset man bending over a desk, looking squint-eyed at some papers he was holding.

"Goddamn typing is getting smaller every day." he said and looked up. "What can I do for you?"

"I'm Vince DeLucca. I've got an appointment with Joe Bender."

"Oh yeah, he's in there." He pointed to an office in the back. "Go on in. He's expecting you."

I walked around the counter and approached the office. The door was open. Sitting behind a large oak desk was exactly what I thought a union business agent would look like: grey suit, shirt collar open, slightly bald and chewing on a cigar. The telephone rang. He looked up and pointed to a chair as he grabbed the phone. "Bender, Local 16."

He reached across the desk for a pencil. "Next Thursday?" Tapping the pencil on the desk he looked at me while listening to the voice on the line. He started to write. "They'll be there...eight carpenters, two props and four electricians...Curran Theatre, 8:00 Thursday morning." He lowered the receiver and finished his scribbling on the pad. He took the cigar from his mouth, leaned back in his chair and gave me the once over. "So, you're Vince DeLucca?"

"That's right."

He got up and walked from behind the desk and shook my left hand. "I'm Joe Bender. I don't know exactly how to begin. I never had the occasion to use a P.I. before." He moved back to his desk, looked at his watch and sat down. "I've got a meeting uptown in forty-five minutes, so I better get to it. I suppose you've heard about the death of one of our union guys at the opera."

I nodded hoping he would get to the point.

"Ben Koslo, the assistant prop man was found dead in the basement below the stage at 2:00 AM Thursday morning by an old colored man that runs one of the elevators out front. The body was slumped over a table. Beside him was an empty syringe. The police were called, and the body was removed. The autopsy showed a massive overdose of heroin. They figured another druggie OD'd and let it go at that. Well, we don't buy it and neither does his family. The union body had a meeting and voted unanimously to investigate the death. Mac at the opera house recommended you, so I called."

I leaned forward in the chair. "You mentioned his family. Who notified them of his death?"

"I did, by telephone. His mother and father took it hard. They couldn't believe it. I called his wife but couldn't get hold of her. In fact, from what I hear she can't be located. Ben's folks don't even know where she is. Maybe she took a trip or something, who knows."

"What about the syringe... did they check for prints?"

"Yeah, I called the chief of detectives, and he confirmed that the prints were definitely Ben's."

I leaned back thinking that this was going to be a token investigation just to satisfy the family and some of the union members. I had never investigated a death before and I felt that it would be a waste of time, but even wasted time meant money and I needed money. "So, you want me to see if I can find out something that will disprove that Ben took an overdose by accident. Is that it?"

"That's about it. What do you say, will you take the job?"

I held off on answering. "You know, of course, if it wasn't an accident, then what we're talking about is murder."

"Yeah, I know it's ridiculous. Why would anyone want to murder Ben? But we feel that it deserves a little more looking into than what the police did. No matter what you find out, at least we tried to do something."

I stood up and said, "All right, I'll take a crack at it, but you and the family might not like what I turn up."

Bender frowned. "You mean it could get dirty and maybe prove Ben was a drug addict?"

"It's possible."

Bender picked up the pencil and started to write on the pad of paper. "Anything is possible, but it has to be done. Now to the terms. I don't know what you guys get paid, but we can't afford too much. In the movies, the guy always asks for two hundred a day plus expenses. We can't go that high, so at the meeting we figured a flat fee with a limit of three weeks. Can you take on the job for five hundred a week and expenses?"

I tried not to look pleased. He couldn't know that this would be the first paying job offer I'd had in three months. "Yes. I think I can live with that."

"Fine. I had a few ideas on how to go about this. I was going to put you on as a permit man to work with the crew at the opera, but—pardon me if I'm blunt—you need two arms to work on the opera deck. We couldn't pull it off. They would think I was nuts if I sent a one-armed man there to work."

"Don't give it a second thought, Joe. I don't need two arms to do my job, just a lot of answers to a lot of questions. That's all."

Bender seemed relieved. "OK, then it's all settled. Jimmy Fallon is the union steward at the opera. He will introduce you around. You'll have access to all parts of the opera house day or night. If you ask questions up at the front office, you might not get a hell of a lot of cooperation. I believe they think Ben's death puts a black mark on management. Most of the fellows working on the deck were good friends of Ben and they'll gladly answer all of your questions." Bender glanced at his watch, stood and said, "I've got to get moving." He stepped forward and shook my hand. "Thanks, Vince. No matter what you find out we appreciate your help. Is there anything else you need before I leave?"

"Yes, a couple of things."

"Yeah, what're they?"

"The address of Ben's folks and a small cash advance."

THREE

I had always wondered about what went on behind the scenes at the opera house. Now I was going to get a first-hand glimpse of the working parts that produced grand opera. I've never been an opera fan. The few I had seen bored the hell out of me, but I'd always been curious about how they did the staging and scene changes.

I whipped my Volkswagen into a parking stall next to the big gray granite building on the corner of Franklin and Grove and walked up the large oval driveway. To my left was the stage entrance. I pulled open one of the big glass doors and went inside. There was a glassed-in booth where the doorman sat at a desk. Ahead of me was an elevator and to the left, a door that probably opened to the backstage area.

The doorman set his coffee cup down, looked up from his newspaper, leaned out through the door of the booth and growled, "Can I help you?" He looked angry as if my presence had disturbed his morning coffee. He wore an old Stetson tipped sideways on his head, large horn-rimmed glasses and a cigarette hung below his large black mustache.

"I'd like to see Jimmy Fallon. My name is Vince DeLucca."

His mustache stretched wide when he grinned. "DeLucca! Ey, gumba! I'm Al Ferrigno." He stood up and came out from his cage. "Wait here. I'll go get Fallon." Then he disappeared through the door to my left. At the end of the hallway to the right of the elevator I could see a door with a sign that read, 'Green Room.' I was thinking about that sign when Al Ferrigno returned. Behind him was a small red-faced Irishman wearing a baseball cap with buttons pinned across the front above the visor.

Ferrigno proudly presented me as if I was one more Italian to add to the ranks of the opera house. "This is Vince DeLucca. Treat him right or you don't get any more of my mama's lasagna." He stepped back into his booth and sat down.

Fallon held out his right hand. I reached over and took it with my left. He noticed my missing arm as he said, "Joe Bender called me. Jesus! I didn't think you'd be here until Monday. I'm Jimmy Fallon. You don't waste any time, do you?" I could tell Jimmy could use a drink. He seemed nervous and on edge. He kept looking up at the clock over the elevator. "We'll be breaking for lunch in a half hour. Come on backstage. Now's a good time to meet some of the boys. We'll be between changes soon."

I followed Jimmy through the door onto the stage.

"Watch your step, Vince."

It was dark and I couldn't see anything but a blue glow coming through a big backdrop hanging in the air. I kept close to Jimmy as we walked along a handrail to a small table at the back with a dim lamp set on it.

Jimmy said, "Grab a chair. They'll be through with the lighting rehearsal in a few minutes."

My eyes were slowly adjusting to the surroundings. I noticed what looked like hundreds of ropes hanging from the darkness above. The ropes wound around pully wheels attached to a fifty-foot-long vertical iron rail stretching high above. There were several men lined up by the ropes. A man's voice on the intercom cracked through the silence. "Take out foliage border one and two. Take out foliage legs. Take out back drop and raise the left and right-side tabs." The men standing by the rail grabbed the ropes and started to pull. The scenery went up like someone had released a window blind. I could hear rolling units rumbling offstage. The lights came on and the stage was empty.

I looked over at Jimmy. "What the hell just happened?"

He smiled and said, "We just struck a scene. After lunch we'll set another one for lighting."

It was a fascinating bit of business. I inspected the iron rail and what I had thought were hundreds of loose ropes from above turned out to be an intricate hanging mechanism. Each line wound around pulleys and were counterweighted to raise and lower back drops and heavy scenery.

A large burly man with a black beard approached us. He pulled off his gloves and threw them on the table. "Who have we got here, Jimmy? Don't tell me you're gonna give me a one-armed flyman?" He grinned at me. "No offense fella."

Jimmy slapped him on the back. "This big rowdy is Hersh Conley, the flyman. Hersh, meet Vince DeLucca. He's going to be around for a while asking questions about Ben's death."

Hersh's smile faded. "Ben was one of the good guys. Can't figure him taking drugs. I damned sure didn't know about it if he was. Just can't figure it."

'Mac' McGuire and his assistant walked over to the rail. "Hello, Vince. I said I'd see you at the theatre, but I didn't think it would be this soon. Did you introduce him around, Jimmy?"

"I didn't get the chance yet, Mac. He just got here."

Hersh slipped on his coat and said, "Hey, Micky, Mac! How about lunch?"

"OK with me," said Mac. "Let's drop over to the Courtroom and grab a bite. Want to join us, Vince?"

"No thanks. I really would like to look around a bit."

"Suit yourself. OK, boys. Let's go tip a few."

Mac and Hersh walked along the rail to the door followed by Mike and a clearly thirsty Jimmy Fallon. The backstage area cleared out fast. I noticed the front curtain was down and I could hear the orchestra rehearsing in the pit. So far I hadn't asked anyone any questions, but I'd already received an answer from Hersh the flyman. He doubted that Ben was taking drugs. I walked across the stage and discovered the prop room. This was where Ben had worked as assistant to the head prop man. Two men were sitting at a table eating lunch. I figured I might as well introduce myself. Both looked up as I stepped into the doorway.

The thin bald-headed one asked, "Can we help you?"

"Yes, maybe you can. I'm Vince DeLucca."

"Oh yeah. Bender said you would be coming around. You're going to look into Ben's death."

"That's right. Are you the head prop man?"

"Yes, I'm Denny Bernard and this is Jim Woods. I suppose you want to know a little about Ben."

"Yes, I would. Anything you can tell me."

Denny wrapped up the rest of his sandwich and put it in a bag. "Well, Ben was my assistant for three years and a damn good one too. He worked hard. Everyone liked him and as far as drugs is concerned...it's not likely. I was with him day and night and never once was there any indication that he took drugs. I'm telling you... what did you say your name was?"

"Vince."

"I'm telling you, Vince, the man didn't take drugs. That's why this whole thing is a big mystery to all of us. We definitely would have known if Ben had the habit."

"Did he do any serious drinking?"

"Hell, he drank a little. Who doesn't, especially in this crazy business, but he never overdid it." Denny looked over at Jim. "Not like some guys I know."

I turned to Jim. "Did you know Ben well?"

"Sure, I did. Believe me, he never took drugs. Hey, a lot of us smoke a little grass and drink a little booze, but the hard stuff? No way. Nobody could hide it working on stage with these guys. As far as I know Ben played it straight."

I turned back to Denny. "Joe Bender told me Ben had a wife."

"Yeah, Julie. A hell of a nice gal. They were married about six months ago. I couldn't reach her by phone. I wanted to tell her how sorry I was. In fact, I tried Ben's folk's home, too. I thought she might be staying with them after the...uh...after his death. Ben's Mother told me she hadn't seen or heard from Julie since the... since it happened."

"Didn't you think that was strange?"

"Damn right I did, but I figured she had her own way of mourning for her husband. Maybe it was to go off by herself, I don't know."

"When's the last time you saw Julie?"

Denny thought for a moment. "She was here the same night Ben died. I remember because I couldn't find him during the second act change, but later I went out front and he and Julie were sitting in the orchestra."

"Had he ever missed an act change before?"

"No, never." Denny scratched his head. "You know, come to think about it, he was acting sort of strange all through the third act."

"In what way?"

"Well, he stayed off by himself and wouldn't talk to anyone, like something was bothering him. I don't know. All I know is, he wasn't like the old Ben."

"Did you notice anything else that happened during the rehearsal that might have something to do with his strange behavior?"

"Yeah, I did, now that you mention it. Maybe he had a fight with his wife. I saw Julie talking to Ben in the wings, then she just walked off. Looked like she was mad or upset about something. I asked Ben if anything was wrong. He said she was just tired, so he sent her home. Then a damn strange thing happened. We had just made the change into the last act of the Dutchman."

"The Dutchman?"

"Yeah, you know, the ghost ship of the Flying Dutchman. The German director Paul Berger stopped the rehearsal and was on stage yelling about something, so Ben and I came out of the prop room to see what was going on. The guy was having a fit. Berger said something had to be done about the ship, like draping it with more black gauze or net to make it look more ghostly. Wait, he didn't say ghostly. What did he say? Oh yeah, he said, 'I want it to look dead and terrifying.' It was then that Ben said something to him that didn't make any sense to me at all. He said, 'Like Belzec?' The director looked at him with a strange expression on his face, then turned away. I didn't know what the hell to make of it."

"Did you say 'Belzec'?"

"Yeah, at least, it sounded like that. What do you think it means?"

"I haven't the slightest idea. Maybe it's a Polish word for ghosts. What happened then?"

"Well, we did what the man said and draped the ship with more black gauze, then the rehearsal went on."

"So, right after you set the last act, Ben went off by himself and wouldn't talk to anyone."

"Yeah, that's about it. The whole thing didn't make any sense. After the rehearsal, we were going over to the bar for a drink. I looked for Ben, but he wasn't around, so I figured he'd gone home."

"You've helped me a great deal. Thank you for answering my questions."

I started to leave when Denny asked. "What do you think? Does it look like some kind of foul play?"

At that point, I couldn't help but have the feeling everyone was over-reacting to Ben's tragic death. "Let's give it a couple of days, Denny. It's too early to say for sure." As I passed through the prop room door, I heard Denny say with a snicker, "A Polish word for ghosts. That's a good one."

I walked upstage behind a big blue cyclorama that curved around the stage from end to end. Looking up I could see a bank of lights extending the width of a long bridge that appeared to be suspended from cables overhead. I wondered what it was, then I heard my name being called from above. Leaning over the end of the bridge thirty feet in the air was black-bearded Al Ferrigno. "Ey, Vince! Come on up. I want you to meet the guys. Go in the elevator and press 1F." He swung in from the bridge and disappeared.

I went to the elevator and pressed the button 1F. After a few seconds the elevator stopped, and I pulled the door open and stepped out onto the upper level. Before me was the paint bridge and the lights that I had seen from the stage far below. To my right, sitting around an oval wooden table, were six men.

Al Ferrigno stood up smiling. "Vince, meet Big Jer the scenic artist." I nodded, remembering him from the Courtroom Bar yesterday afternoon. Ferrigno slowly walked around the table and pointed. "The

24

rest of these guys make up the scenic crew. We have Tommy Doyle, Earl Sudderth, Phil Cohen, and..." He put a hand on the shoulder of the man nearest to him. "This is Bruno Guffanti. Gentlemen, I give you Vince DeLucca."

Tommy Doyle laughed, "Mama Mia! Another Italiano."

Ferrigno turned, facing Doyle. "Not just another Italiano but an Italian private eye."

Big Jer was amused. "Don't mind these guys, Vince. It's all in fun."

Doyle said in a loud voice, "Fun? You think it's fun to be surrounded by Italians everyday of your life? Christ! We got Ferrigno, Guffanti, Ferugio, Molinary, D'Angelo, Agnini, Fagoni, Baccaloni, and now we got DeLucca."

Bruno poured me a cup of coffee and put a hand on my shoulder. "Don't take Doyle too serious. To hear him talk, you might think he doesn't like Italians. Truth is, he doesn't even like the Irish."

Al Ferrigno sat down and grabbed his coffee. "You talk about Italians... Hell, we're up to here with the Irish. Look who we got working here. We got McGrath, McGuire, O'Neill, O'Leary, Conley, Fallon, Corcoran, and Doyle."

Earl Sudderth sliced a piece of salami with his pocketknife and handed it to Bruno. "That's not all we got. What about all the Germans?"

Big Jer frowned. "Jesus, Early, did you have to bring that up? Doyle bent my ear for hours yesterday yapping about the Germans."

At the mention of Germans, Doyle stood up, put a comb under his nose in an impersonation of Adolph Hitler, and started a comic routine in a thick German accent. "Talk about Germans? It's a Goddamn invasion. We got more krauts here than they had in the Bulge. Look who we got. First there's Herbert Glaz, head of the whole shooting match. If he's not a kraut, he sure acts like one. Then we have that fat bastard, Paul Berger, straight from Hamburg or Munich. There's the old gal, Elsa Streich, the scenic designer. She probably made lamp shades during the war. What about Kert Reiner and Otto Muller? Then of course we have Berger's two assistants, Otto Kurtz and Fritz Kranke. Two weird ducks. If they're not SS men I'll eat your hat. Mein Gott! They've made a beachhead and are taking over. You'd think we lost the war. It's too bad we can't bring a bunch of Japs over to help the krauts put on the opera. Hell of a way to win a war and—

Big Jer pulled Doyle down into his chair. "That's enough, Tommy. We get the idea."

"Sounds like you don't like Germans, Tommy," said Bruno.

"Don't like them? I hate them. Same as the Italians and the Irish." Tommy Doyle looked over at Phil Cohen. "What about you, Philsy. Do you like krauts?"

Phil smiled and said, "I've got nothing against them personally except that they killed six million Jews."

Tommy laughed, "Is that all that's bothering you, Philsy?

Al Ferrigno stood up and walked to the elevator. "Never a dull moment on the scenic bridge. I've got to get back to work. See you guys at the three o'clock coffee break."

Big Jer lifted himself out of his chair. "Let's go, boys. It's time for us to do a little work too."

Doyle lit up a cigarette and said, "See you, Vince. Maybe next time I'll tell you some of my war stories." He looked at my empty sleeve. "Maybe you'll tell me some of yours." He turned and went out onto the paint bridge.

I went toward the elevator thinking I hadn't been able to learn much from these characters so far, but I knew sooner or later I would. Big Jer moved up next to me and said, "You're welcome to stay up here if you want. I know you wanted to talk about Ben. I'm afraid we didn't help you very much. Why don't you meet us after work at The Courtroom. We'll have more time to kick it around then."

"That's fine with me. What time do you quit work?"

"At four-thirty. What do you say we see you over there about quarter to five."

"OK, Jer, I'll be there." I pressed the elevator button and rode it down.

As I stepped out of the elevator toward the stage entrance Al Ferrigno stopped me. "Vince, what did you think of the scenic crew? Crazy bunch aren't they?"

"They seem to enjoy themselves all right."

"Wait until you see them after hours in the bar. Then they really enjoy themselves."

I smiled and walked out through the front entrance on the way to my car, thinking, so far this day had been interesting, but I wondered if I had earned my money.

Back at my office I checked the mail and my answering service. There were the usual bills and no calls. So far, I had learned one thing from the people I had talked to. None of them believed that Ben had willfully taken drugs. I stretched out on the small couch and tried to figure out a plan of action. First, I'd have to talk to the man who found the body, then take a look at the place where the body was found. A talk with Ben's folks and his wife would be important. The telephone rang. I lifted the receiver. "DeLucca Investigations."

"Vince, this is Joe Bender. I just found out something I think you ought to know. I talked to Ben's folks, and they still haven't been able to locate his wife. They called the police and reported her as a missing person. Mrs. Koslo was pretty damn upset. She said the police told her it was too soon to report a missing person. They said after five days they would do something. It may be nothing, but I thought you'd want to know."

"Thanks, Joe. Like you said, it may be nothing, but we'll know for sure tomorrow at the funeral."

"Yeah, that's right. If she doesn't show, it's for sure that something's not right. Are you thinking there's a tie-in with Ben's death?"

"Could be, Joe. It damn well could be."

"OK, Vince. Keep me informed. How are the boys down at the opera treating you? Mac told me you were there today."

"Yes, I was. They're a good bunch and very cooperative."

"I'm glad to hear that. Oh, by the way, the services are being held at Unger's Mortuary in Daly City, and then it'll move on to the cemetery. Gotta rush. Goodbye, Vince."

I sat on the edge of the couch and wondered if Julie's disappearance really had anything to do with Ben's death. If so, this was turning out to be another kind of ballgame.

***

At a quarter to five I walked into the Courtroom Bar. The place was half-filled. Louie the bartender waved and pointed to the booth near the window where Big Jer was sitting with Bruno Guffanti.

I sat down while Jer rolled the dice and said, "How you doing Vince? Grab a dice box, we'll roll for a drink." The drinks came and I paid. "You don't have much luck with the dice do you Vince?" Jer downed half of his vodka and looked at me. "OK, Vince. How can we help you?"

"Well, it would be a big help if you could give me some background about Ben's wife. Do you happen to know her?"

Bruno looked up from his drink. "Sure, we know her. It was Jer that introduced her to Ben. Why do you want to know about Ben's wife? Do you think she had something to do with his death?"

"I don't know. I might be grabbing at straws, but she has disappeared. No one seems to know where she is and that seems very strange to me."

"I wouldn't take it too seriously if I were you," said Bruno. "She'll probably show up just before the funeral."

I was about to ask another question when in through the doors came Tommy Doyle wearing a tan trench coat with the collar turned up. He wore a hat with the brim pulled down low over his brow. He stepped up to the bar, snapped his fingers and in his Bogart voice he said, "All right, Louie, set up another round for the boys and make mine a VO on the rocks."

"Yeah, who's going to pay for it?" Louie answered as he continued wiping a glass.

Doyle tipped his hat back on his head. "Why they are, naturally. You know I don't carry any cash with me." He turned and faced the table. "Well, if it isn't the Italianos, Guffanti and DeLucca. Where's your friend, Fignuts Ferrigno?"

Big Jer pulled him down on the seat. "Sit down, Doyle. Where the hell did you get that outfit? You look like Sam Spade."

"That's the idea. I borrowed it from wardrobe. I'm going to give Vince a hand on this case. You know, there's a lot of things to investigate over there at the opera house. Like who stole the pound of coffee that I brought in three days ago? And why does everyone get a parking ticket out front except Bruno? What does Earl Sudderth do when he goes to the bathroom for a half hour? Where does Soggy Wagner hide his bottle? And who wrote, 'Doyle is a fag' on the shithouse door?"

The waitress set their drinks down on the table and waited.

"Pay her, Doyle." said Bruno.

"Me? Pay her?"

"Hell, yes. You ordered the drinks, so pay her."

Doyle looked over at Big Jer, "I seem to be a little short. Can you ...?"

"Goddamn it, Doyle! Someday you're going to surprise the hell out of all of us and pay for a round. Christ! You don't even make an attempt to search through your pockets when the drinks come."

Doyle grabbed his drink, turned it up, then set the empty glass back down on the tray. Listen, if you guys had a wife like mine with three screaming kids you'd be broke too."

Jer shook his head and dropped a ten spot on the tray. Surprise me, Doyle. Just once lay out a twenty and shock the hell out of us."

Doyle turned his attention toward me. "Vince, are you married?"

"No, can't say I am."

"Well, think twice before you do. They keep you broke all the time."

Two hours and six drinks later Doyle was still on a roll, and I had forgotten all of the questions I was going to ask. Finally, there was a lull in the conversation. Doyle had relaxed and stared deep into his empty glass with a silly smile on his face. Maybe now was the time to find out something.

"About Ben's wife," I said. "Who introduced her to Ben?"

"I did," said Jer. "I first saw her about a month before they were married. She wasn't what you'd call beautiful, but she damn well could have been if she fixed herself up a little bit. She looked sorta sad and out of place. The boys and I usually have a few drinks and dinner after work then come back to watch the rehearsal. She was standing by the stage door talking to Peterson, the night doorman. Evidently, she wanted to come in and watch, but Peterson wouldn't let her in without a pass." Jer lifted his glass and drained it. "I felt sorry for her.

She seemed like a real nice gal, so I talked Peterson into letting us take her in with us. She was thrilled. We went out front through the Green Room and sat about twenty rows back in the orchestra. I tried to talk to her, but she was too interested in the opera. She never took her eyes off the stage. Finally, we got bored and were ready to leave. I asked her to join us for a drink, but she wanted to stay."

Doyle raised his head. "Can you imagine her not wanting to have a little drink with a great bunch of guys like us?"

Jer continued. "When I got up to leave, she held out her hand and thanked me for bringing her in to watch. That's when I noticed she was missing two fingers. We left her there and went to the bar. I mentioned her missing fingers and Doyle had to make some kind of joke about it. He nicknamed her three-finger Julie."

Doyle spun his empty glass on the table. "Well hell, how did I know Ben was going to marry her."

Bruno nudged Doyle in the ribs. "Shut up and let Jer finish the story."

"Julie became a regular almost every night there was a rehearsal. She must have loved opera. One night, Ben came over to where we were sitting to discuss some of the new props for one of the shows, and I introduced him to Julie. They hit it off from the start and got married a month later. That's about it. Needless to say, we didn't call her three-finger Julie anymore."

Not too much of what Jer had told me was useful but it was a start. "Jer, I'd like to talk to the man who found Ben's body. Do you know his name?"

Bruno spoke up. "Old Julian Bagely. He's always at the opera house. Ask Ferrigno, he'll find him for you. He's quite a character. He'll be there tomorrow."

I reached for my drink and thought about three-finger Julie. So far, I had a dead man who died of an overdose of heroin, and nobody believed it. His wife with two fingers missing on her right hand had disappeared. Where did I go from here?

Doyle shattered my thoughts as he pounded the dice box down on the table. "How about one more for the road?"

I'd had my one for the road. It was time to go.

After leaving the bar, I walked to my car. I still had a couple of hundred left from the advance Bender had given me that morning. I figured I'd treat myself to a big steak and a bottle of good wine. My apartment was in North Beach just around the corner from Bonito's restaurant on Lombard Street, so I drove home, parked in the garage and walked to the restaurant. It had been a busy first day on the case. I had learned just enough to make me curious. There might be more to this thing than what was on the surface. I would have to dig a little deeper, but now, I needed some food then a good night's sleep. Tomorrow I would talk with Julian Bagely, then go to the funeral.

***

At 8:00 Sunday morning I was at the stage door of the opera house. The back doors were locked so I looked through the glass. No one was there so I walked around to the front on Vanness Avenue, went up the stairs and tried those doors. They were all locked too. I looked through the windows and saw a janitor mopping the marble floor. I tapped on the glass with my keys and caught his attention. He came to the door and pushed it open a foot.

"Yes, what do you want?"

"I was told I would find Julian Bagely here this morning. I'd like to talk to him if I may."

The janitor looked off to his left and said, "We're not supposed to let anyone in. Does Julian know you're coming to see him?"

"No, he doesn't, but would you tell him that Vince DeLucca is here about the investigation of Ben Koslo's death."

The janitor nodded and opened the door. "Come on in. You'll find Julian in that little alcove just beyond those double doors there to your left."

I thanked him and tried not to step on the wet marble as I tiptoed down the hall hugging the wall. I came to the alcove and saw an old black man sitting behind a small table. He was wearing a black suit with a red carnation in the lapel and slowly turning the pages of a large leather-bound book.

"Mister Bagely? May I have a few words with you?"

He looked up and said in a slow deep voice, "Yes sir. Julian Bagely at your service."

"I'm Vince DeLucca. I've been engaged to investigate Ben Koslo's death."

Julian slowly turned his head from side to side. "Terrible, terrible thing. That young Mister Ben was such a nice man. Terrible."

"I understand, Mister Bagely, that you found the body."

Julian stood and walked out around the table. "Yes, Sir. I did. In the orchestra room. I knew he was dead soon as I turned on the lights."

"Turned on the lights? You mean the room was dark when you found him?"

"Yes, sir. Black as burnt cork it was."

Julian's suit was so worn that it was shiny, especially at the knees. There were black smudges on the collar of his white shirt. His partly bald head had what looked like black shoe polish rubbed onto it.

Despite his strange appearance, I had a feeling Mr. Julian Bagely was going to be very helpful to me.

"Mister Bagely. Did you tell the police about the lights being off when you found the body?"

"No, sir. They didn't ask me. There was plenty more to tell, too, but they didn't ask. I knowed Mister Ben didn't kill himself."

"How did you know that, Julian?"

"It was a feeling I had in my bones. I just knew, that's all."

"Did you see or hear anything before you found Ben's body?"

"Yes, sir, I did."

"What did you see, Julian?"

"I didn't exactly see anything, but I heard something."

I waited for him to go on, but it was obvious he wouldn't speak unless asked a direct question.

"What exactly did you hear?"

"Well, sir. Right next to the elevator in the basement is the trash room. After cleanup out front, I come down and go through the trash. I find all sorts of things."

"What sort of things, Julian?"

"Well, sir. I find programs that are still tied in bundles. One time I found a silk scarf. There's always something to take home."

"So, at 2:00 AM, Thursday morning you were going through the trash?"

"Yes, sir."

"What kind of noises did you hear?"

"It sounded like chairs being dragged across the floor. The musicians had all gone home hours before, but I thought maybe some had come back to pick up something they forgot."

"How long did the noise last?"

"Just a minute or two, then I heard the footsteps."

"Tell me about the footsteps."

"They went by the trash room and turned down the passageway that leads under the stage. By the time I crawled out of the trash bin, they were gone."

"Then you went to the dressing room and turned on the lights?"

"Yes, sir. And there was poor Mister Ben leaning over the table face down. I don't know why, but I knew he was dead."

"Julian, these footsteps that you heard, did it sound like they were running?"

"No, sir. They was walking."

"Did it sound like it was more than one person?"

"Yes, it did. Sounded like at least two."

I knew that with this new evidence, the police just might reopen the case. Or would they? Why didn't they ask Julian these questions at the time the body was found? Why were they satisfied to let it go as an accidental death?

"Julian, would you show me where you found the body?"

"Be glad to, sir. Just let me get my keys and we'll go down to the basement."

He reached under the table and unhooked a ring of keys. I followed him as he limped down the marble hall to then oak door with the sign that read 'Green Room'. He tried several keys before he finally found the right one. The door opened into a medium sized room. The walls were painted light green. Against the walls were cushioned seats and chairs. On a table in the center was a vase filled with brightly colored fresh flowers.

I was curious. "Julian, what is this room used for?"

He spoke with pride. "This is the Green Room. Some of the visiting artists have champagne parties in here. Just small get-togethers before the curtain."

We walked through the room to another door at the far end. Julian opened the door into a hallway that led to the stage door and the elevator. Now I knew where I was. This was the same elevator that had taken me up to the scenic bridge. We stepped into the elevator and Julian pressed the basement button. One floor down, the doors opened to the passageway where Julian had heard the footsteps.

He pointed to his right. "That's the trash room there." He limped down the hallway to a brown metal door marked 'Orchestra Dressing Room'. He opened the door and turned on the lights. Metal lockers lined two of the walls. In the middle of the room, was a long wooden table with several bentwood chairs set on either side. Julian hobbled forward and touched the middle of the table. "This is where I found Mister Ben laying over the table."

I stepped up to the table. There were a lot of initials carved into the wooden top. "Julian, can you show me exactly where Ben was sitting and what position his arms were in?"

"Yes, sir. I'll show you." He moved to the table and sat down in the third chair from the end. He leaned over the table and lay his head sideways on the top. Spreading his arms he said, "This was the position Mister Ben was in when I found him."

"And where was the syringe?"

Julian lifted his head but kept his arms in place. "It was lying right there between his arms."

I moved closer to the tabletop and inspected the area on each side of Julian's arms. The carved initials on the tabletop were old and had turned brown, all except one. The scratch resembled a swastika. The scratch marks were fresh enough that they could have been made within the last week. We walked back to the elevator. I studied the passageway running off to my right and asked, "Is this where you heard the footsteps?"

"Yes, sir. It is."

It appeared to be a cement tunnel about six feet wide. Steam pipes were attached to a low ceiling and running water flowed in a gutter on the floor. I looked down the long dark passageway and could see a dim light at the far end.

"Where did you say this tunnel goes?"

"It goes under the stage and the courtyard then ends up in the City Administration Building where the War Memorial Trustees have their offices."

"Thank you, Julian. I think I've seen enough."

Julian took me up to the stage door entrance and let me out.

I turned and said, "You have been a great help, Julian. Much more than you know."

FOUR

In a day and a half, I had found out quite a lot about Ben's death. Enough to make me think I might have stumbled onto something. I thought I had been spinning my wheels until I talked to Julian Bagely. The footsteps just before he found the body, the tunnel under the stage, the lights turned out in the orchestra room and the Nazi symbol scratched into the table. Julian seemed to be telling the truth. Some might think an old man who wandered around in the basement of the opera house looking for treasures in the trash at 2:00 in the morning would probably have an overactive imagination, but I believed him. If I could prove that Ben was responsible for scratching the swastika into the tabletop, then I would really have something. If it was true, what was he trying to say? If it was murder, what was the motive? With all of the stories I had heard about the Germans taking over at the opera, anyone could have scratched that symbol in the table, but if Ben had done it, it could have been his last dying effort to etch a message into the wood of the tabletop.

I got into my car and headed for the Bayshore freeway south to Daly City. I wanted a close look at Ben's body. Twenty minutes later,

I pulled up in front of Unger's Mortuary and parked behind a black hearse. It was too early for the services and that was OK. The fewer people around the better. I went up the walkway, through the white double doors, and entered a cool hallway filled with baskets of flowers and ferns. At the end of the hallway was the chapel. A tall gaunt man in a black suit smiled as I approached him.

I said, "I'd like to pay my respects."

He ushered me into the chapel and said, "Surely."

There were white pews on either side of a carpeted aisle. At the end of the aisle was an open casket surrounded by more flowers. I walked down the aisle to the casket and there was Ben's body laid out in a dark blue suit with his hands folded across his chest. He looked like a manikin. They had put coloring into his cheeks and sprinkled him with talcum powder. I turned around to see if I was alone and was relieved to see that the man in the black suit was facing the front doors with his back to me. Now was the time for me to make my move. I stepped up to the casket and lifted Ben's right hand. It felt cold and the arm was stiff. Talcum powder rubbed off on my fingers as I closely inspected his fingernails. Under the broken nails of his forefinger and thumb were small slivers of light-colored wood. It was true. Ben had scratched the swastika into the tabletop. I wondered what else the police lab had overlooked before they sent the body to a private mortuary. I lowered his hand and stepped back from the coffin. Now I had found some hard evidence. Put it all together and it seemed to indicate that Ben was murdered. Now the big question. Who murdered him and why? As I walked back to my car I had a strange feeling that Julie wouldn't be attending her dead husband's funeral.

There were quite a few things that bothered me about this case. If he was murdered, Ben would have had to be held down in order for his murderer's to inject him. Julian had said that he heard a noise like chairs being dragged across the floor. That would support the theory that a struggle had taken place. And then the footsteps going down the passageway. It could have taken more than one assailant to hold Ben down. But after he was injected and left to die, he was still able to scratch the swastika in the table. I needed to find out more about the effects of heroin. How long could a guy last after being over-dosed?

I still had plenty of time before the funeral party would head to the cemetery. I left the mortuary and drove to Malloy's, a bar that was close to the cemetery where Ben was to be buried. I figured I'd have a couple of drinks and a corned beef sandwich, then I would call Milt Shepard. He worked as an intern for the city health department. I remembered that he was working with drug related cases, so he would be able to fill me in on the heroin business.

Sunday afternoon at Malloy's was something to see. Being so close to the cemeteries, a lot of the patrons came to the bar to cry in their beers after visiting the graves of their loved ones. I pushed in between two customers at the bar and ordered a scotch and water, tall. The old guy to my right looked up at me with red eyes. He noticed my missing arm and said, "My boy is buried over there. World War Two." He gave me a dirty look. "At least you came back alive."

The other fellow to my left leaned over in front of me and said, "Now, Patty! Don't go taking it out on this gentleman here. He can't bring your son back and you know it."

I grabbed my drink and turned to look for a pay phone when the old Irishman put a hand on my shoulder. "Don't pay any mind to what Patty says. He comes here every other Sunday, rain or shine to put flowers on his son's grave then he tries to drown his sorrows with whiskey. He don't mean no harm."

I smiled, slid off the stool and went to the pay phone at the end of the bar. Finally, I got the number for the City Health Department from the operator, dialed it, and asked to speak to Milton Shepard. After a two-minute wait he came on the line. "Hello. Shepard here."

"Hello, Milt. This is Vince."

"Vince, it's been a while. What are you up to. Still spying on wayward husbands?"

"No. Haven't had one of those in a long time. Have you got a minute? I need your help."

"That's about all I've got. What can I do for you?"

"I'd like to know how long it would take to kill someone if you injected a massive dose of heroin into their blood stream?"

"Hell, that's a tough question to answer. It depends on so many things."

"What kind of things, Milt?"

"Well, the condition of the victim before the injection and How many cc's of heroin were used. We've had a few who OD'd and died three or four days later."

"Then what you're telling me is that after an overdose, a man wouldn't die in three or four minutes?"

"No, not minutes. Hours maybe. It takes some time to completely immobilize a person, then coma, and finally death. What's this all about, Vince? Has it got something to do with a case that you're working on?"

"Yeah, it does. I'll let you get back to work. Thanks, Milt."

"Glad to help. Take care, Vince."

I hung up the receiver and thought that there was a possibility that Ben could have been knocked out before he was injected. Later he could have come to, and before going into a coma, scratched the swastika into the tabletop. If there were any marks or bruises on his head they surely would have been noticed by the police lab, but they didn't notice the wood splinters under his nails, so maybe they missed a head wound also. The police probably figured it was an open-and-shut case, so they didn't go out of their way to find anything suspicious.

I went back to the bar and ordered a draft beer and a corned beef sandwich. In an hour, it would be time to go to the cemetery. The pieces were starting to fit together. If three-finger Julie didn't show up at the cemetery, that would add another piece to the growing puzzle.

Gray banks of fog were rolling in over the San Bruno hills as I arrived at the cemetery. I stood back about forty yards in the trees and observed the funeral party. Seated in front were Ben's mother and father. The rest of the family and friends stood behind them. Among the group were several of the stagehands, including 'Mac' McGuire, Big Jer, Mike, and Denny the propman. If Julie had been there she would have been seated with Ben's folks. She obviously wasn't there. When the group started to move away from the grave site, I walked through the trees to the driveway where my car was parked. It was important that I talk with Ben's folks, but I decided to wait until later on in the afternoon when they would be alone.

At 3:30, I telephoned and was invited to come to their home. They knew that I was working for the union to clear up Ben's death and agreed to answer my questions.

It was 4:30 when I arrived at the Koslo home in the avenues close to the beach. They asked me in and offered me a cup of coffee. I knew it was a bad time to ask questions, so I tried to be delicate. "Mrs. Koslo. I didn't see your daughter-in-law at the funeral. Do you know where she is?"

She raised her eyes, red from weeping and said, "We haven't seen or heard from her since last week when she and Ben were over to dinner.

I can't imagine where she is. We called everywhere and no one has seen her." She twisted the handkerchief in her lap. "I don't know. It's not like her at all. I fear something has happened to her."

"What makes you think that, Mrs. Koslo?"

"Well, she's always been so close to us ever since she and Ben were married. She lost her parents, and we were like her second family. It's just not like her. She would never leave without saying something to us, especially now." She was on the verge of tears.

I addressed Mr. Koslo. "Sir, could you tell me something about your daughter-in-law's background? Such as where she came from before she moved to San Francisco?"

Mr. Koslo looked at his wife and touched her hand with his. "She was from back East I think. Ben told me that she lost her parents in Europe during the war. One of those German death camps in Poland. I think it was called Belzec."

That name was familiar. I had heard it yesterday from Denny the propman. "Did you say the name of the camp was Belzec?"

"Yes. I believe that was it. Somehow, Julie survived the camp. Poor girl. She never once mentioned anything about her experiences in the camp and I didn't ask, but I think that's where she lost her two fingers. We felt so sorry for her. She had been through so much as a young girl. We can't imagine where she could have gone."

"What was Julie's family name before she married your son?"

Mister Koslo lit up his pipe and said, "She told me that her father's name was Bronski. He was an official with the water department in Warsaw."

"Then Julie wasn't Jewish."

"No. She came from a Polish family."

"Then why did they kill her parents and take off her fingers?"

"That I cannot answer, Mister Delucca. In those days during the war the Germans gathered up all those that opposed them and killed Poles and Jews alike."

"Mr. Bender told me that you called the police and reported her missing."

"Yes. We did. Tomorrow we are going to call again. They must try to find her."

I knew it was hard on them answering my questions, but there were still things I had to know. "Mrs. Koslo, do you know how long Julie has been missing?"

"No, I can't say for sure, but I believe she's been gone since the night Ben died. We've called the house several times. There's no answer." She lowered her head.

"Sir. Would you happen to have a picture of Julie?"

Mr. Koslo stood up and went to a table by the window. "This picture was taken on their wedding day."

He handed me a framed photograph. Julie stood a head taller than Ben. She was dressed in white and carrying a bouquet of flowers in her gloved hands. She was very attractive, but as Big Jer had said, she showed no expression of joy. She was a beautiful bride wearing a mask of sadness. I handed the photo back to Mr. Koslo. "Sir, has anyone been to your son's home since he died?"

"Not that I know of. We intend to go over there as soon as we feel up to it."

"Would you mind if I took a look around the house? Maybe I can turn up something about your daughter in-law."

"No, not at all. If you can help us find her, we would be indebted to us. Ben lived in the Twin Peaks area on Terra Ceda Drive. The number is 776, up on top of the hill. Please, if you find out anything, let us know. I have an extra key here somewhere." He searched through his pockets. "Yes, here it is." He handed me the key.

"Thank you, Mr. and Mrs. Koslo. I am sorry about all of this."

As I walked out to my car, I felt sort of empty. There wasn't too much I could do to help ease their pain. Belzec, the name of the death camp added one more painful piece to the puzzle.

***

There was a dense fog at the top of Terra Ceda Drive. It was dark and the numbers on the houses were almost invisible. Finally, the number 776 appeared out of the fog, and I parked the car and approached the dark house. It was a tract home, probably built fifteen years ago. Every house on the block looked alike. They were all stucco with a bay window above the garage. A flight of cement stairs went up to an enclosed porch and wood-paneled front door. I took out the key, slipped it into the lock and opened the door. I stepped into the dark hallway, turned on the hall-light and closed the door. The living room was to my right, the bedroom and kitchen to my left. I hoped to find a clue to Julie's disappearance. I started with the kitchen. There were several dirty dishes in the sink. A cold coffee pot was sitting on the stove. On the kitchen table was a package of meat wrapped in white butcher paper. A sticker on the package had the name of the butcher shop and the address. I wrote it down in my notebook. In the bedroom I found a woman's clothes scattered on top of an unmade bed. The drawers of the dresser were pulled out and emptied out on the floor. I opened the closet door. Shirts, suits, slacks, and coats were all untouched, but all of the woman's belongings were removed and thrown on the bed. Was it possible that Julie had packed some bags and left in a hurry, leaving most of her wardrobe behind in such a disarray? But she wouldn't turn her handbags and purses inside out just to pack a bag. It looked to me like someone had been searching for something.

The bathroom was next. I noticed that the door lock had been broken, as if it had been forced from the outside. On the floor in front of the toilet was an open lipstick tube and in the toilet bowl was a wad of red toilet paper. The mirror above the sink was smeared with lipstick. It looked like someone had tried to wipe it off in a hurry. A picture developed in my mind. Julie was locked in the bathroom. She wrote something on the mirror with lipstick. Someone broke in and wiped the mirror with toilet paper, then threw it in the toilet bowl. I stood close to the mirror and studied the red smears. I couldn't make out the words. Most of the lipstick had been wiped off. On the upper left-hand corner, I could see the distinct lines that had been franticly scrawled on the mirror. The letters H and E were clear, but the rest was too vague to read. Following the E, it could be an S or L. Probably the word 'help'. Unfortunately, I couldn't decipher much of the words. Maybe the crime lab boys could do it with chemicals, but I had no idea what to do. I tried to visualize what had happened. Someone had frightened Julie. She ran into the bathroom and locked the door. She must have known who her attackers were and after the assailants wiped the mirror they left the premises taking Julie with them by force. I thought it possible that she might have left other messages. I carefully gave the bathroom a going over, but there was nothing more. I walked down the hall to the living room. The curtains were closed. A couch sat in front of the bay window with a coffee table in front of it across from a fireplace. There were ashes in the hearth. I knelt down and pushed my fingers through the ashes. Someone had recently burned papers in it. Nothing of them could be salvaged. On my way to the front door, I noticed a wall table in the hallway with a telephone and a pad of paper. Something was written on the paper. Just as I reached for it, the telephone rang and scared the hell out of me. I was reluctant to answer, but I thought it could be Mr. Koslo calling me, so I lifted the receiver. "Hello?" There was no answer." Hello! Who is this?" Whoever it was hung up. It could have been a wrong number or maybe someone checking on Julie. I held the paper in the light and saw a name and telephone number written on it. 'Wolf Kotchman 665-3384.' I put the paper in my pocket, walked out the front door, locked it, and made my way through the fog to my car.

As I opened the car door, I looked up and noticed lights on in the house next door. Maybe they might know something about Julie. I walked up the stairs and rang the front doorbell. The porch light went on and the door opened. A man in his early forties stood in the doorway. In his hand was a mixed drink. He slurred his words through a drunken smile. "What can I do for you?"

I stepped into the light. "My name is Vince DeLucca. I'm a private investigator looking into the disappearance of Julie Koslo, your next-door neighbor. I'd like to ask you a few questions."

"You're a private eye? You got to be kidding. You're selling something, right?"

"No. I'm not selling anything. I just want to ask you a few questions."

"OK, come on in buddy and have a drink."

I stepped into the house. He closed the door and led me to a bar in the living room. He poured himself a stiff one and said, "What'll it be? Bourbon, scotch, or gin?"

I could have used a drink, but I thought I'd better get my questions answered before the guy became incoherent. "Thank you, but I'll pass."

"OK, Buddy." He looked hurt. "So, what kind of questions do you have in mind?"

"When was the last time you saw Julie Koslo?"

"Who?"

"Koslo, the woman that lives next to you."

"Oh her." He took a slug of his drink and thought. "Let's see, when did I?" He looked up. "Hell! I don't even know the people next door. What's the story on the broad? Did she take a sneak?"

"Something like that. Do you remember seeing her in the last four days?"

"Yeah...no...not exactly."

"Which is it, yes or no?"

"Well, I don't know if it was her, but I saw three people leave the house and get into a car out front."

"When did you see them?"

"When? You mean what day?"

"Yes. What day and what time was it?"

"Jesus! You sure want to know a hell of a lot." He took another drink and plopped down on the sofa dropping his glass on the rug. "Don't bother about it. When the bitch comes home, she'll clean it up. Let's see, where was I? You wanted to know...Oh yeah, it was last Thursday." He looked up at me with a sheepish grin. "You want to know how I knew it was last Thursday, right? Well, I'll tell you. That's the night my wife goes out with the girls, or so she says. I was waiting for her to show when I heard this loud banging coming from next store. I went to the window and a minute or two later I saw them walking to the car."

"What time would you say it was?"

"Hell, I don't know. It was late, I can tell you that."

"Was it around midnight?"

"It could have been. I don't know. It was like pea soup outside, just like tonight." He lowered his head as if he were exhausted. "I don't know who the hell they were."

"Could you see what kind of car it was?"

"Car? Hell, I told you it was like pea soup."

He had given me all I wanted to know. I thanked him and started for the door.

He raised his hand and said, "Say, how about that drink, buddy?"

I closed the door and went to my car.

There was swirling fog on the top of the hill. I had a hard time trying to stay on the right side of the road. I figured I'd go home and get some sleep; it had been a busy day. Or maybe a night cap at Bonito's first and then bed.

The fog cleared as I came down off Terra Ceda Drive. It was then that I noticed a pair of headlights behind me. I sped up and the lights stayed with me. I slowed down and they laid back. It looked like a tail to me, so I turned left into a side street, made another left at the end of the block then pulled to the curb. I turned off my lights and waited. The tail didn't show. Either I had lost him, or it was all in my imagination. I jammed the car in gear and took off. At Vanness Avenue, I thought I saw the same lights again, but there were several cars on the street so I couldn't be sure. I turned right heading for North Beach. A pair of lights turned with me about two hundred yards behind. Once again, I made a left and a quick right, parked without lights and waited. After waiting a few minutes, I said the hell with it. I headed for home, parked the car in the garage and walked to Bonito's.

I had a strange feeling that I was being watched. Julio, the bartender greeted me as I walked in. "Where you been, Vince? You must be on a hot case."

"Yeah, it's a hot one all right. Let me have a cognac and black coffee."

"Coming right up, Vince."

As I sipped my cognac, I decided that I'd imagined the tail. I was exhausted. A guy was liable to see things when he got too damn tired.

After finishing my drink, I said goodbye to Julio and started walking to my apartment. Halfway home, I heard footsteps behind me. I turned around but saw no one. As I went into the entrance, I heard them again. I opened the iron gate, stepped in and waited. The footsteps stopped just short of the gate. This was no coincidence. I had to find out who it was. I slowly went out through the gate and quickly turned the corner. The sidewalk was empty. I was playing a game of cat and mouse with a ghost.

I went back through the gate and up the stairs to my one-bedroom apartment. After pouring myself a small cognac, I leaned back in my leather chair and reviewed the last two days. A lot of people wouldn't believe what I had found out. I knew I had to call Joe Bender, but would he believe what I had to tell him? Tomorrow morning, I figured on paying a visit to the butcher shop. Maybe the butcher had seen Julie. Then I would call the number I'd found on the pad at Ben's house. I wondered what kind of name was Wolf Kotchman?

My eyes were heavy. I dozed off wondering if I was really being followed, and if so, by whom and why?

FIVE

The butcher's name was Abe Shoiket. He had a small shop close to Terra Ceda Drive. It was 11:00 Monday morning when I parked in front of his shop. Bells chimed as I pushed open the door. The place smelled like a Jewish Deli. A high glass counter displayed special cuts of Kosher meats. Behind the counter was a chopping block and hanging on hooks from the side were knives and a meat cleaver.

A large round-faced man with a gray beard came through the door at the end of the counter. He looked at me with a friendly smile, rubbed his hands together and asked, "What is your pleasure, Sir? Today we have a nice...."

I put up my hand. "Excuse me. Are you Abe Shoiket?"

He looked surprised, "I am."

"I'm Vince DeLucca. I'm investigating the disappearance of Julie Koslo." At the mention of Julie Koslo, his eyes narrowed, and his smile faded. "Do you know Julie Koslo?"

He quickly answered, "No. I don't know."

I knew he was lying. "Are you sure? She buys her meat from you. She was here last week."

"A lot of people buy meat from me. Maybe I know her, maybe I don't."

"Mister Shoiket, think back. Last week, Julie Koslo bought a package of meat here. She lives only a few short blocks away."

"I don't know any Julie Koslo."

"Shoiket, is that Jewish or Polish?"

"Take your pick, young man. Is there anything else you wanted?"

The conversation was winding down. I knew he was suspicious and holding back the truth. "Yes. I'd like one of those pickles you have in the jar."

He took the lid off the jar, removed a pickle with tongs and wrapped it in white butcher paper. "That will be eighty cents."

I handed him a dollar and as he reached over the counter to hand me the pickle, the sleeve on his left arm pulled up revealing tattooed numbers on the inside of his forearm. I hesitated taking the pickle and he saw me looking at the tattoo. Quickly, he shoved the pickle into my hand and pulled down his sleeve. I thought I'd take a shot in the dark. "Mr. Shoiket, were you ever in Belzec?"

There was a pained expression on his face. "Why do you ask these questions?

"Because Julie Koslo was in Belzec during the war, and I think you two know each other."

He nervously grasped at the meat cleaver. His voice was almost pleading, "I don't know her. I want you to leave." He stepped closer to the counter. "Please leave now!"

I slowly backed out through the door. "I'm sure we'll be talking again, Mr. Shoiket."

Now I knew the connection between Julie Koslo and Abe Shoiket. Next, I would give Wolf Kotchman a call and try to find out what part he played in all of this.

As I drove away from the butcher shop, I noticed a gray ford sedan about four car lengths behind me. I had seen that car this morning just after I left the apartment. I pulled to the left and made a U-turn. The gray sedan followed. There was no doubt about it. I was being tailed. Sooner or later, I would have to find out who it was. I made a left and pulled into a gas station. The gray sedan passed me by and continued on down the block. I was tempted to give chase but thought better of it. I figured I'd give Wolf Kotchman a call instead. While they filled my tank, I went to a phone booth and dialed the number. I was surprised when I heard who answered the phone. "Shoiket's Butcher Shop."

"I have an important message for Wolf Kotchman."

Shoiket hesitated before speaking, "There is no Wolf Kotchman here. You have the wrong number." He hung up.

Now there were two more pieces to the puzzle, but where did they fit? I decided that before calling Joe Bender, I would do a little probing into the front office at the opera. I intended to ask a few questions about the German director and whatever else I could find out that might tie the German regime at the opera to Ben's death.

***

On my way to the opera house, the gray sedan was once again on my tail. Whoever it was knew his business. He stayed a safe distance behind me and when I slowed down he fell back and got lost in the traffic. The tail disappeared when I drove into the parking lot at the opera house.

Al Ferrigno greeted me at the stage door. "Hey, Vince! How's it going with the investigation?"

"It's coming along, Al, but I need a little assistance. Maybe you could help me."

"Sure. Name it, Vince."

"I need to talk to some of the people in the front office. How do I go about that? Do I need an appointment?"

"Well, that depends on who you want to talk to. If you want to talk to the Maestro, I guess you have to make an appointment with his secretary, but as far as the others are concerned, you might as well walk right in and start talking."

"Thanks, Al. Where are the offices?"

"Press 3D. It's one floor down from the paint bridge."

A few seconds later, I opened the elevator doors and stepped out onto a long corridor covered with a bright red carpet. There were several office doors. All but one was closed. I walked down the hall to the open door and peeked inside.

She was the only one in the office. I stood in the doorway and watched her as she sat behind a desk vigorously punching the keys of a typewriter. I studied her features. Her shiny black hair was cut short. It framed her olive complexion nicely. She had a delicate mouth; the lips slightly tinted a pale pink. Her nose was small and delicately chiseled and her eyes black and intense. She was wearing a light gray low-cut dress and around her lovely neck she wore a strand of pearls.

She was aware of my presence and stopped typing. Her dark eyes flashed as she looked up at me. 'OK, Buster. You've had a good look. Now, what is it you want?"

I stepped through the doorway, stood in front of her desk and was about to introduce myself when she said, "If you want to see someone, you've come at a bad time. They're all out to lunch." She continued typing.

I looked at my watch. "Bad timing on my part. How come you're not out?"

She held her fingers over the keys, looked up at me with irritation and said, "Why don't you come back in an hour or two. The whole damn bunch will be here then." She resumed her typing. She definitely seemed antisocial, or maybe it was me. I thought I'd try again. "Don't you eat lunch?"

Removing her fingers from the keys, she sighed, leaned back in her chair, looked up and said, "Look! I've got to finish this masterpiece. As far as lunch is concerned, I'll be out for a long time if you'll just let me finish typing my resignation."

"Your resignation? Are you going to quit your job?"

With a look of determination, she leaned forward and pounded out another line, slammed the carriage over and yanked the paper from the typewriter. "You got it." She quickly signed the bottom of the paper, then took her coat and purse from a closet, turned, and looked me in the eye. "Now, how about buying a girl a drink?"

When we arrived at the stage door, Al Ferrigno was beaming. "EyVince! I see you met Maria."

I said, "No. I'm afraid I haven't had the pleasure."

"Well, I can fix that. Maria, this is Vince DeLucca. Vince, meet Maria Martinelli."

She looked up at me, then she faced Al. "You know this guy?"

"Sure I do." He leaned close to her and whispered, "He's a private eye working on a case right here in the opera house."

She looked back at me. "Really? Well, he doesn't look much like a private eye to me."

I smiled and said, "How do you do, Maria Martinelli, and what do you think a private eye should look like?"

She shrugged her shoulders. "I don't know. It's sort of strange, that's all."

"You mean you never have seen a one-armed private eye. Is that it?"

"No, that's not it. I just never have met a real one, all I meant. Let's forget it, shall we?"

"I will if you will."

Al tipped his hat on the back of his head and said, "Are you sure that the two of you haven't met before?"

She forced a smile. "Al, I quit my job. I'll be back tomorrow to straighten out my desk and pick up my things."

"Hell, Maria. I'm real sorry to hear that. You've been here quite a while. You threatened to quit before. I guess the Germans finally got to you."

"You got it, Al." She held her fingers up to her forehead, "I'm fedup up to here. Your private eye friend has offered to buy me a farewell drink." She walked toward the doors, then turned around and said, "Well, Vince. Do I get that drink or not?"

She seemed like a tough one, but I wondered just how tough she was. From what I could make out she had worked in the opera office for some time. It appeared from her abruptness that she was angry and felt she had good reason to quit. My poking my nose into her office and asking questions probably didn't help her situation, but if she was going out to have a drink, it might as well be with me. I thought she might be able to help me find out something about the German contingent. I especially wanted to know about the German director. If I could break through that hard exterior, I would have an inside track to information from the front office. But then, there was another reason why I wanted to talk with her. I sort of liked her.

I offered to take her to the Courtroom Bar, but she didn't want to go there, so I suggested a quiet little place a few blocks up on Franklin

Street. Maria agreed but insisted she take her own car. I figured she wanted to be independent and that was fine with me.

The Safari Cocktail Lounge was empty. A bartender stood behind a black Formica bar cutting lemons. Frank Sinatra's hit record 'Summer Wind' was playing on the juke box.

"Is the bar okay, or would you like to sit at a table?" Maria walked to the bar and gracefully slid onto a stool. I judged by her silence that she didn't want to talk. I moved in next to her and asked, "What would you like to drink?"

She searched through her handbag, then looked up. "Damn! Have you got a cigarette?"

I handed her one of mine and struck a match. She leaned forward to get the light, took a deep drag, and exhaled a plume of fine smoke across the bar top. Then she turned her head toward me and replied, "It really doesn't matter, as long as it's strong."

She was uptight and seemed nervous. I knew exactly how to take care of the situation. I ordered two double Beefeater Martini's, straight up. When the drinks came, I raised my glass and smiled at her. I figured I'd wait until she was ready to talk. It didn't take long. Two sips of the Martini and she started to loosen up. "What is your last name?"

"DeLucca."

"Oh yes. Vince DeLucca. Did you know that the Italians are on their way out at the opera?"

"Yes. I've heard that from some of the boys that work there."

She lifted her glass and took another sip. "I'm Italian. Did you know that?"

"I assumed you were, with a name like Martinelli."

She finished three quarters of the Martini, set the glass on the bar, and gazed into it smiling. "It's crazy you know, Vince?"

"What's crazy?"

"Well, I worked there for five long years. In all of that time, I never had any trouble, and everyone was pleased with my work. My boss was a grand old Italian gentleman. He was highly respected. Most of the directors, the conductors and the singers were all Italian." She reached for her glass. "Then the Germans moved in and my troubles began. The office staff was slowly cashiered out and replaced with Austrian, Swiss and German girls." She drained her glass and continued. "I saw the writing on the wall, but I stayed on and refused to be pressured out. The offices were enlarged, more desks and more secretaries. The files were removed from my office and in a short time most of my workload was taken away from me and placed in the hands of the other secretaries. It's like I couldn't do anything right, and soon I felt like a fifth wheel." She banged the glass down on the bar, breaking the stem. "Oh my God! I'm sorry. I didn't mean to do that." The frowning bartender came over and picked up the pieces of glass. I ordered two more. Maria put her hand on my arm and smiled apologetically. "I don't know what got into me. I've never done anything like that before."

It was obvious that she didn't drink much. She didn't know what had gotten into her, but I did. It was a double Martini. I figured it was time for me to ask some questions, but she had other ideas. Her conversation continued to flow.

She removed the toothpick with the olive from her second Martini and studied it. "You know, Vince. If I had to do it all over again I would do it the same way. The only thing that hurts is that they won't miss me." She chewed on the olive as she sipped her drink. "Well, I should care. I can always find another job somewhere. Everyone needs a good secretary." Her body relaxed on the stool. Her shoulders lowered, lengthening her slender neck. The tension in her face softened and she started to smile as she raised her glass. "Thank you, Vince, for being so nice." She took another sip, lowered the glass, and looked up at me.

"What about you, Vince DeLucca? Are you in the market for a damn good secretary? Do you have a secretary?"

"No, I don't. Someday I will. When my business gets better."

"Al told me you were working on a case at the opera house. Is it a secret, or can you tell me what it is?"

"I'm investigating the death of one of the stagehands, Ben Koslo."

"Oh, yes, I heard about it."

"Did you know Ben and his wife Julie?"

"Not really. I saw them on stage during the rehearsals."

"What was your impression of Julie?"

"A lovely girl. She didn't say much and followed Ben around like a scared rabbit. These past few days I noticed that she seemed rather tense, as if she had a lot on her mind. Now, with Ben gone, she must really feel lost. Accidental overdose of drugs, wasn't it?"

"That's what the police think."

"And you don't?"

"No. I don't buy it."

She took another sip of her Martini and laughed. "This is crazy! I've quit my job and I'm sitting in a bar drinking double Martinis with a one-armed detective. The police believe the death was an accident, but he doesn't buy it. Where do we go from here detective DeLucca?"

The way she said detective DeLucca made me feel good. It was true. I had been asking the right questions and getting some answers. The more I found out, the more I realized that I'd become involved in something big, a lot bigger than I could handle. But like the tiger's tail, somehow I couldn't let it go. She didn't know it, but Maria was going to fill me in on the very same people who had forced her to quit her job.

I looked at her and said in a stern voice, "Maria Martinelli."

She arched her back, looked very serious and tried to hold back a smile. "Yes Sir. Detective DeLucca."

"Would you be interested in helping a broken-down private eye solve a big case?"

"Are you serious?"

"I'm very serious. Will you help? There is a strong possibility that the German regime at the opera is responsible for Ben Koslo's death and the disappearance of his wife, Julie."

"Certainly, I'll help, but you're not telling me all of it. Why do you think the Germans had anything to do with Ben's death? Did you say his wife has disappeared?"

"Yes. I can't tell you anymore right now but trust me. As soon as I pin this thing down, you'll be in on it."

She put her hand over mine and said, "I do trust you. What do you want me to do?"

"I need some inside information about the German staff at the opera. I'd like to know who they are and what they talk about when they are in the office? I especially want to know about the director of The Flying Dutchman."

"I can tell you their names, but very little about what they talk about." She looked down at her drink. "Maybe I could have stayed on the job if I spoke German."

"You mean, they speak German all of the time?"

"Yes, most of the time. All of the secretaries speak German and English. I was just one of the few who spoke Italian. Two of the assistant directors pretend not to understand English, but I know they do, and they probably speak it as well. Do you want me to give you their names?"

I took out my notebook and pen. "Please. I would appreciate it."

"OK. From the top, of course there's Herbert Glaz, the general director. His office is at the far end of the hall. His door is always closed. He took over when Giuseppe Morelli retired. That's when the Germans marched in. The director of The Flying Dutchman is Paul Berger. He's the nervous sort. Very excitable. He rants and raves about everything, including the singers."

"Does he speak English?"

"Yes. He speaks it very well."

"Where did he come from?"

"I believe I heard that he came from Hamburg. He has two assistant directors, at least that's what he calls them. They follow him around like puppy dogs. Real sweethearts those two. The big one is Otto Kurtz. A frightening character. He has a large bald head and small beady eyes. He must be at least six feet six tall, looks like a wrestler. Then there's Fritz Kranke. He's a little smaller, but this one has a grin on his face all of the time. Not a nice grin. He looks like the cat that's just cornered the mouse. They both came from Hamburg with Berger. There's Kurt Reiner. He's a scenic designer from Berlin and there are a few more that came from Stuttgart, Munich and Nurenberg. The place is loaded with them."

"Can you tell me any more about Paul Berger?"

"All I know is that he has a big reputation in Germany. After the war he became a great opera director, or so they say."

"Do you happen to know what he did during the war?"

"No, I'm sorry. I don't know. You seem more interested in Berger than the rest of them. Do you have a reason?"

"Yes. I have a good reason. Do you think it would be possible for me to meet with him? I'd like to ask him a few questions."

"I could give you the number of his secretary. Maybe you could make an appointment with him. Believe me, you're going to need a little luck. He doesn't answer questions. He asks them."

"You make this guy out to be a tough cookie. I take it, you don't like him."

"You got it. He makes you feel like two cents when he talks to you. I suspect he doesn't like Italians, so watch out." She looked at her wristwatch. "Look at the time. I must be going."

"Would you like one for the road?"

"No thanks, Vince. Two doubles was quite enough for me, but I would like a cup of coffee."

She went to the lady's room while I ordered two black coffees. She returned to the bar and said with a smile, "I'm sorry I was such a pill when we first met." She put her hand on my arm. "You deserve better." She sat down and reached for her coffee. "You're a pretty smart man Vince DeLucca. A couple of drinks, a little conversation and I feel much better. Thanks."

"My pleasure, Maria, and thank you for the information."

She set the cup down. "Now I really must be going."

"Before you go, I've got two more questions."

She slipped off the stool, looked at me and said, "OK, DeLucca. Shoot."

"If you are going to help me on this case, it would be very important that we get together soon, like tomorrow night at nine for dinner. Will you join me?"

She smiled sweetly and asked. "Where?"

"Do you know where Bonito's is?"

"Bonito's! I sure do. My ex-husband works there as a bartender."

"Julio is your ex-husband?"

"Yes. We've been divorced now for three years."

"Then I guess you wouldn't want to go there."

"Don't be silly. Our marriage didn't work out, but we parted friends. What was the other question?"

"Well, when we first met you seemed hostile, and I was wondering why you wanted to come with me for a drink?"

She picked up her coat and handbag and slowly walked to the door, then she turned around and said, "Yes. I'll join you for dinner and as for the second question..." She started to walk backwards. "I wanted to come with you for a drink because I like you." She backed through the entrance smiling and was gone.

I thought Maria was one hell of a gal, straight and direct. The two Martini's might have helped her along, but she definitely had a way about her.

***

The information Maria had given me would prepare me for the meeting with Paul Berger. It was 4:00 in the afternoon, but I figured I might as well call Berger's secretary. I remembered what Maria had said. I was going to need a little luck. I went to the phone in the men's room and dialed the number. A harsh woman's voice answered. "San Francisco Opera. Paul Berger's office."

"My name is Frank Carson. I write a theatrical review for the San Jose Sun, and I'd like to interview Mister Paul Berger. I understand he is directing the opening night opera, the Flying Dutchman."

"That is correct, but you will have to go through our publicity department to get an interview. Mister Berger is a very busy man." She hung up.

I stood by the telephone and thought, so much for trying to be clever. The direct approach is the only way to get results. I dialed the number again. The same woman answered. "My name is Vince DeLucca. I'm a private investigator looking into the death of one of your employees. His name is Ben Koslo. I'd like to set up a private meeting with Mr. Berger tomorrow morning at 9:00. Would that be convenient?"

"Would you hold a moment?"

I held the receiver between my shoulder and head while I tried to light a cigarette but I didn't have enough time.

"Mr. Berger will see you tomorrow, but the only time he has open is at noon."

"Oh, I'm sorry. That's unfortunate. I have an appointment with some members of the opera board tomorrow at 11:30." I figured I'd throw that in. Maybe he would rather talk to me before I talked to the opera board.

"Would you hold again?"

I finally got the damn cigarette lit just as the woman came back on the line. "Mr. Berger will see you at 9:00 tomorrow morning."

"Thank you." As I hung up the receiver I smiled and said to myself, "I thought he would see it my way."

I left the parking lot and headed down Franklin Street. I kept a sharp eye out for the gray sedan that had been following me for the last two days. There was no sign of it, but I felt I would be seeing it again. I knew I should call Joe Bender and tell him of my progress on the case, but I decided to wait and call him tomorrow after my meeting with Berger. The best thing I could do now would be go home and get some rest. Tomorrow I would need my wits about me and like Maria had said, a little luck.

As soon as I put the key in the lock, I knew something was wrong. On the floor in front of the door was the toothpick that I had placed between the door and the jam this morning. Someone had picked the lock. I opened the door and turned on a light. The living room looked untouched. The bedroom was the same, nothing had been moved. I came back into the living room and plopped down in my chair. Glancing around the room I noticed books had been rearranged in the bookcase. It looked as if someone had taken a few of the books out then tried unsuccessfully to put them back the same way they had been before. I checked my desk and found it had been disturbed, but my gun was still in the drawer. Someone had definitely been searching for something. I had no idea who it was, or what they were after. I figured I'd find out sooner or later.

I went to bed and lay there thinking about my meeting tomorrow morning with Paul Berger. What had started out to be a routine investigation had developed into a complicated case with numerous characters, and one in particular seemed to play a leading part. I started to review the characters as my eyes grew heavy. My last lingering vision was of Maria.

SIX

At ten minutes to nine the next morning, I drove into the parking lot at the opera. The weather had turned foul. Heavy rain whipped by a brisk wind from the bay pelted my wind shield. As I walked through the stage door, Al Ferrigno greeted me. "Ey, Vince! How did you and Maria hit it off? Those Sicilians are tough, but once you break the ice, they come on strong."

I walked to the elevator and said, "We hit it off just fine, Al. I have an appointment with Paul Berger at 9:00. Has he come in yet?"

"Yeah, a half hour ago. Him and his two watch dogs. Those guys are weird. If they had Italian names, I'd think they were Maffiosos. You know where the offices are."

I still wasn't sure what I was going to say to this fellow Berger. I figured I'd play it by ear. The elevator stopped, I opened the door and walked to the office where I had met Maria and asked one of the girls where Paul Berger's office was. She directed me two doors down the hall. I stood in front of the closed door and knocked. The door opened immediately. A rush of strong perfume filled my nostrils. A tall blonde woman with a square jaw inquired curtly, "Are you Mister DeLucca?"

"Yes. I am."

She pointed to an adjoining office. "You can wait in there. Mister Berger will be with you soon."

I carried the scent of her perfume with me as I stepped into the dark office. Then I saw them...two men silhouetted against the closed window blinds sitting side by side on a bench. The one on the right was huge. The light from the window reflected off his large bald head. He had small angry eyes that gleamed in the semi-darkness. He was wearing a dark suit which seemed much too small for his large frame. His big hands rested on his knees. This had to be Otto Kurtz. Maria hadn't exaggerated his appearance. The other one was smaller like she's said. He had unusually large ears that protruded outward from his square head, made even more square by a crew cut. His nose was crooked, and his mouth twisted into a sneering smile when he saw me. He also wore a dark suit. I figured he must be Fritz Kranke. They both kept their eyes on me as I glanced around the room.

There were two chairs in front of a large oak desk. Photos of opera scenes and singers covered the walls. I looked back at the bench in front of the window. The two men watched me in silence. I could hear the sound of a chorus rehearsing coming from the floor above, but somehow the music didn't ease the tension. I figured I'd better say something, introduce myself, discuss the weather, anything at all. I sat down in one of the chairs in front of the desk and said, "You fellows waiting for Mister Berger?"

Fritz, the one with the twisted grin said in a heavy German accent, "Ya, vee vait." The big one just continued to bore into me with his piercing eyes.

The office door opened. I turned to look and there standing in the doorway with his back to me was a large rotund man in a gray tweed suit. He was yelling in a high-pitched voice at someone in the outer office. His German accent was not so pronounced as that of the grinning German sitting on the bench and he was obviously displeased.

"I will not accept it! This is grand opera! Time and again I tell you and I show you, but you refuse to learn. I don't care about your contract. I will replace you if you do not follow my instructions. You need more work before becoming a director. I cannot teach donkeys." He turned and entered the office slamming the door.

Otto promptly stood up, clicking his heels. Berger scowled, "Sit down, dummkopf! Why must you hide in the dark like moles?" He switched on the lights.

If Berger ever smiled, I thought his face would crack. Thick-lensed, black-rimmed glasses perched on the bridge of his heavy Roman nose, magnifying his eyes to twice their normal size. His thin brown hair hung to the base of his neck and a straggly mustache covering his upper lip drooped to a short patchy goatee. He looked down at me. "So. You are the investigator, DeLucca."

I noticed a tinge of contempt in his voice when he said my name. I stood up and held out my left hand. "Vince DeLucca. I take it you are Mister Paul Berger." He looked at my empty right sleeve and made no attempt to shake hands. Maria was right. We'd just met, and he already tried to make me feel like a worm.

He stepped around the desk, put his pudgy hands on the desktop and stared at me. "That is correct. I am Paul Berger. My secretary said you were investigating the death of one of the stagehands. Why do you want to talk to me? What possible connection would I have with the death of a stagehand?" He sat down at his desk and waited for my answer.

"Probably no connection at all, but the night of the man's death, he started acting strange after talking to you during the rehearsal. That's why I thought I would ask you. I thought maybe you might remember something that could have caused his strange behavior."

He smiled, "I know nothing about any stagehand's strange behavior. I am too busy with my work to worry about stagehands."

"Mr. Berger, think back. It was last Thursday, about 10:30 PM, during the last act of The Flying Dutchman. You were displeased with the ghost ship. You asked the prop man to make changes. Ben, the assistant prop man said something to you and you walked away. Do you remember?"

He glared at me from behind his magnified lenses. "I remember well the changes on The Dutchman's Ship. I don't have conversations with stagehands. I tell them what I want, and they do it. No questions asked. Where did you get this information? Who told you about the ghost ship? You said the assistant prop man said something to me. You seem to know more about this than I do. What did he say to me? Was it about draping the net over the ship?"

"No. He said just two words."

"I see, the assistant propman was a man of few words. What were his two words?"

"He said, 'like Belzec'."

If it hadn't been for the sound of the chorus rehearsal coming from the floor above, you could have heard a pin drop. At the mention of the word 'Belzec,' Berger froze. Fritz and Otto leaned forward on the edge of the bench, poised like large cats waiting for their master's command.

Berger's eyes remained on me. His thin lips tightened into a slight smile. "Mr. DeLucca, did it ever occur to you that this could have been just another of the many vile remarks that we foreigners must endure when we come to work in this country? Don't think we haven't heard the stage crew talking about us." He spit out the quoted words as if he were retching. 'The krauts, the Nazis, the SS has taken over, the master race is giving orders.' We've had to forgive this crude American mentality, but when does it end? The war has been over for nine years. Do you think it is right that we must continue to suffer these indignities?" His voice was plaintive in his appeal. "The war caused pain and suffering to all of us. Your arm, was it the war?"

I nodded and said, "Anzio."

"And do you still hate the German soldiers who took your arm? When does the hatred end? I served with the 9th Panzer Division. Right or wrong, I fought honorably for my country. Now, after it's all over, all I want to do is live in peace and carry on with my work."

He sounded convincing, but I didn't buy it.

"Please, Mr. DeLucca. Don't make more of this than there is. Let it rest." He sat back in his chair holding his hands together like a reverend after a sermon. Fritz and Otto also leaned back and relaxed. I wasn't going to learn any more from Berger. Even though I had no solid evidence to tie him to Ben's death and Julie's disappearance, I strongly suspected that he was involved.

Berger slid his chair back and stood up. "Now Mr. DeLucca. I have work to do. Our meeting is at an end. I hope you are satisfied."

I got up, walked to the door, turned and said, "This case has aroused my curiosity. I suspect that there is a lot more to learn before we can call it closed. Arrivederci, Mr. Berger."

I had started out the door when he said, "Oh, Mr. DeLucca, I almost forgot. I had a talk this morning with my friend, the chairman of the Opera Board and he said he'd never heard of you. That's odd, isn't it?"

I left the office with the uneasy feeling that Berger was holding most of the aces, but the game wasn't over yet. There were still a few more cards left to deal. I looked at my watch. The meeting with Berger had taken less than a half hour. I decided to go up to the paint bridge, maybe it was coffee time. As I stepped out onto the paint floor, Bruno came around the corner with a pot of coffee in one hand and a pie server in the other. There were cups and an apple pie on the table. "Vince! Good to see you. You're just in time!" He turned to the paint bridge and yelled, "Ey,Jer! Coffee!"

Big Jer and Doyle came off the bridge and sat down at the table.

Doyle sliced the server into the pie and said, "Julian Bagely told me you had a talk with him last Sunday. Did the old guy tell you anything you didn't already know?"

"Yes, as a matter of fact, he did."

Bruno poured the coffee. "What have you found out about Ben's death so far?"

"All my findings strongly indicate there's more to this than we see on the surface. I have no concrete evidence as yet, but I believe the German director, Paul Berger is right in the middle of it."

Doyle lowered his cup to the table. "I knew it! The lousy krauts did a job on Ben. What are we going to do about it?"

"What's this 'we' shit'?" asked Bruno.

Doyle glared at him. "Hell! We can't let these bastards get away with it."

"Hold on, Doyle," said Jer. "I'm sure Vince here has a plan and until he needs our help, we'll sit it out. Big Jer looked over at me. "You do have a plan, don't you, Vince?"

I thought about my 'plan' and realized I didn't have one. The three men looked at me so expectantly, I had to come with one. "Well, I figured to let Joe Bender in on all of the information that I've gathered, then maybe the police can reopen the case. This situation might call for a government agency like the F.B.I. or maybe the War Crimes Commission."

"War crimes!" exclaimed Doyle. "You mean we're dealing with war criminals? Jesus! If that's the case, we've got to make a move. They've been trying to hunt those guys down for the last nine years."

"Damn it, Doyle," said Jer. "Vince just told you he has no concrete evidence yet. You can't go around accusing people of committing war crimes without evidence."

I wanted to tell these guys the whole story, but I elected to hold back most of it until I was definitely sure that what I suspected was true. I stood up, thanked them for the coffee, went over to the elevator a few feet away and pressed the button.

While I waited for it to arrive, Big Jer said, "Listen, Vince. If you need our help, we'll be ready to assist you any time."

Bruno laughed. "Yeah, Doyle still has his trench coat and hat. He'll give you a helping hand. That is, if his wife will let him."

When the elevator arrived, I nodded to them and stepped inside. Doyle gave me a salute as the doors closed.

My next move was to call Joe Bender and set up a time for a meeting. We met at New Joe's for lunch. I told him all that I knew to date, even the fact that I had been followed and my apartment entered and searched. He couldn't believe it. He sat there amazed, like a kid listening to a fairy tale. We both agreed to hold off bringing in the authorities at the present time. I was to keep digging for positive proof. So far, all I had was circumstantial evidence that wouldn't hold up in court. After lunch, I said goodbye to Joe Bender and told him that I would be in touch.

SEVEN

It was a quarter after two when I pulled out of New Joe's parking lot and headed up toward Vanness Avenue. I hadn't been to my office for some time, so I thought I'd better check my mail and see if there were any phone messages.

It was a gray afternoon. A light rain continued to fall as I drove up Grove Street hunting for a parking space close to my office. About fifty yards from my office building, I saw it, the same gray sedan that had been following me. I slowed down and took a good look. It was a beat up 1950 Ford with Texas plates. The car was empty. I spotted a space across the street, made a U-turn and pulled in next to the curb. As I crossed the street I looked up and noticed that the window blinds of my office were closed. I never close the blinds. Somebody had been in my office. I took the stairs two at a time and approached the office door. I turned the knob and found the door unlocked. Stepping to the side, I slowly pushed open the door with my foot. The strong aroma of cigarette smoke flowed through the open door. Someone was in my office.

I hugged the side of the door jam and figured I'd rush in and surprise the intruder as soon as my heart stopped pounding. Then I heard the voice. A sharp abrupt cutting voice with a strange accent. "Come in, DeLucca. I've been waiting for you."

I stepped through the doorway and sitting at my desk was a small man wearing a black raincoat. His ferret-like face was clean shaven. His half-closed eyes were like slits above his bony cheek bones. A cigarette dangled from his twisted mouth.

I moved forward. "Who the hell are you? What are you doing in my office?"

The ashes from his cigarette fell on my desktop as he spoke. "One question at a time, DeLucca. My name is Wolf Kotchman."

I became angry and moved closer to the desk. "Do you own that gray Ford with Texas plates parked out front?"

"Yes, I do."

"Then you're the son of a bitch who's been following me. Did you break into my apartment?"

"Yes, I did."

I reached over with my left hand and pulled him to his feet by the front of his raincoat. "All right, you little asshole. We're going to take a ride."

His right hand came up fast. He was holding a small automatic pistol. I recognized it as a Beretta. He spoke through the cigarette in his mouth, "I don't think so, DeLucca. Sit down. We must talk."

I looked into his strange eyes and released my grip on his raincoat. "You're tough as hell with that little pop gun, aren't you?" My adrenalin was flowing. I stepped back from the desk. "OK, you said we must talk, so start talking. I want to know why you were following me and what you were looking for in my apartment."

He sat down in the chair leveling the gun at my mid-section. "I will answer your questions, if you will answer mine." He crushed the cigarette out in my ashtray. "You see, I had to find out who you were and who you were working for. Now, I realize that we are working for the same cause."

"What do you mean, the same cause? How do you know what I'm working on?"

Believe me, DeLucca. I know. What I want you to do is fill me in on the few pieces of information I don't have."

"Now, why would I do a thing like that? Who the hell are you, anyway?"

He laid the beretta down on the desk and lit up another cigarette. I noticed that his hands were gnarled and deformed. Inhaling deeply, he let the smoke drift from his mouth as he spoke. "For seven years I have worked with the Hagana."

"The what?"

"It's sort of an Israeli secret service dedicated to seeking out German war criminals and bringing them to justice, Israeli justice. In other words, DeLucca, I am a Nazi hunter working for the Israeli government. Obviously, you have blundered upon an underground network of Nazis funneling ex-SS men to San Francisco under new identities. There are hundreds of them in this country and three times as many in Argentina, living under assumed names. They include businessmen, factory workers, politicians and even government officials. They are organized and protect their own. They cover their tracks so well that it takes years to discover their whereabouts. Many of the most wanted Nazis have been caught and executed or sent to prison, but a few have managed to evade us. The number one name on our list today is Carl Hessler. He was second-in-command at Belzec, a death camp in Poland. He is responsible for hundreds of deaths and maimings. Your investigation at the opera house has brought him to the surface. He is presently working at the San Francisco opera as a director under the assumed name of Paul Berger." He leaned back in the chair as ashes fell onto his raincoat. "So, you see, DeLucca, we are on the same side. Now, I want to know what you have uncovered during your investigation."

"All right, I guess you're for real, but if we're on the same side, you can put away that beretta."

He picked up the gun and slipped it into his side pocket. "Very well. Now, what do you know?"

I didn't like the little man. He was much too pushy, and I had the feeling that he could get me killed. As far as my investigation was concerned, I had done my job. Ben did not kill himself, but only five people knew that for sure: Wolf Kotchman, Paul Berger and his two goons, and me. I figured I'd play along and see what happened. I began to tell the story from the beginning.

"I was called in to investigate the death of Ben Koslo at the opera house. All of my inquiries led me to believe he was murdered by someone at the opera. Julie, his wife, had disappeared and I found out from Ben's folks she was in Belzec during the war."

Kotchman nodded and said, "This I already know. Tell me something I don't know."

The little bastard was making me angry again. "I talked to Julian Bagely, the man who found the body. He told me he had heard sounds coming from the orchestra room and footsteps going down the passageway way under the stage just before he found the body. I went to Ben's house up on Terra Ceda and found that Julie's clothes and other belongings had been searched. The bathroom door had been broken into and a message written with lipstick on the mirror had been wiped off."

Kotchman leaned back with a sneer on his face. "I know all of that. I went over the house thoroughly."

The smart ass. I wondered if he knew what the message said. "Well then, tell me. Were you able to read the message on the mirror?"

"No. I couldn't make out all of it, but just enough to confirm my suspicions."

I smiled. "It wouldn't take a genius to figure out the word help."

"If you had taken the time to study it, Delucca, you would have seen the obvious. The word was not help. The first three letters were H E S, the rest became clear by the length of the lipstick smear. It was the name Hessler."

"How the hell would I know that?"

"You wouldn't. Now, if you will continue."

"Christ! You seem to know it all. There's not much more I can tell you except that I found the address of a butcher shop and also your name and number, which I found out later was also Shoiket's butcher shop."

"I am aware of that. Abe Shoiket is a friend of mine and my Hagana contact here in San Francisco. He called me just after Julie told him that she had seen Carl Hessler on the stage of the opera house. There were only two people that could identify Hessler. Shoiket and Julie Koslo. Now there might be only one."

"Are you saying that Hessler killed Julie?"

"He and his accomplices. They would have to kill her and anyone else who knows or suspects that they are Nazis."

"You mean anyone who suspects them is in danger of losing their life?"

Kotchman didn't answer. He seemed to be in deep thought. He lit another cigarette, then looked up. "What happened this morning at the opera when you met with Berger?"

"Christ! Is there nothing you don't know? How did you find out I had a meeting with Berger?"

"It was easy. I talked to the stage doorman and gave him an Italian name, then I told him I was working with you. He volunteered the information. Now, about the meeting."

"There were two others at the meeting with Berger, a Fritz Kranke and an Otto Kurtz. Berger did all the talking. The other two kept silent and sat on a bench. I asked Berger about a strange incident that happened on stage during a rehearsal. He knew nothing about it. He was arrogant and very sure of himself, until I mentioned Belzec."

Kotchman's eyes popped open. "You asked him about Belzec?"

"Yeah, in a roundabout way. Ben had mentioned Belzec to Berger on stage the night he was killed. Berger gave me a long song and dance about the nasty remarks they had to endure in this country because they were German. He asked me to ease off and let it rest. That's all that was said at the meeting. Then I went to lunch with Joe Bender, the business agent of the stagehands' union."

"I know. How is the lasagna at New Joe's?" He tried to smile, but didn't quite make it.

"OK, since we're working together and we're both up to date on each other's activities, will you please get your ass out of my chair and let me sit down."

He stood up, straightened his raincoat. "I'm up to date on your movements, but it would take you two thousand years to completely understand my activities." As I sat down behind my desk, Kotchman leaned on the desktop. "You said there were two others at the meeting, a Fritz Kranke and Otto Kurtz."

"That's right. Two of the meanest looking devils I've ever seen. They were supposed to be Berger's assistants."

Kotchman reached into his inside pocket, withdrew an envelope, opened it, and handed me three photos. "Do you recognize any of these people?"

The first photo I recognized immediately. It was of a huge man with short hair, a big head and small eyes. Even the German uniform he wore looked too small for his giant body.

I handed the picture back to Kotchman. "This one is Otto Kurtz. No doubt about it."

He looked at the photo. "Yes. He is Gunther Mueller. He was Hessler's bodyguard at Belzec. For several years he dropped out of existence, now he has surfaced and is still doing Hessler's dirty work. This man once boasted that he had killed over a hundred Jews with his bare hands to save bullets for the SS. What about the other two?"

The next one looked familiar, but I couldn't be sure. The hair was different, but the nose was the same. Then I saw the ears; the same large ears that stood out from the head.

I handed the photo to Kotchman. "This one is Fritz Kranke. I'm sure of it. Same nose and I couldn't mistake the ears."

Kotchman studied the picture. "He also worked at Belzec. His real name is Joseph Heitman. He was an informer for the SS. He also is responsible for many deaths. Now, the third and last one. Do you recognize him?"

It was a German officer dressed in an SS uniform. His cap was low on his head. He was tall and rather thin, with a smile on his face. I could see no resemblance at all to Paul Berger. I continued to study the face, then I said, "I don't recognize him."

Kotchman's eyes narrowed. "Are you absolutely sure? This is a photo of Carl Hessler. Look again. There must be something there that you remember. Take into consideration that this photo was taken over ten years ago. People change. Look again."

I handed him the photo. "No. This is not Paul Berger."

Kotchman became impatient. "What did Berger look like?"

"He is heavy set, almost fat. His head is round and his hair long. He wears glasses and has a mustache."

"All right, look at it again." Kotchman handed the photo back to me. "Remember how he looked. He was tall, but not fat. He could have put on the weight. He could have let his hair grow long. He could have special glasses and have grown a mustache. All these things can change a man's looks. Was there any other characteristic you might have overlooked?"

"The man never smiled." I looked again, trying to visualize the German officer about forty pounds heavier, with long brown hair, a mustache, and glasses. One thing was missing. I wiped the smile from his face and the photo took on a slight resemblance to Berger. I looked at Kotchman. "It's possible that it's the same man."

"It's the same man all right, no doubt about it. He made a grave mistake bringing his two bodyguards with him. They are so easily identified."

There were a few things I didn't quite understand about Kotchman's connection with Shoiket, the butcher. I figured I might as well get it out in the open. "You said Abe Shoiket is your friend. Where do you know him from?"

"We were in the camps during the war."

"You were in Belzec?"

"No. We were in Treblinka together for a short time, then Abe was moved to Belzec. We didn't hear from each other until the end of the war. We were the lucky ones. At least we were alive. My one and only attempt to escape left me with these." He held out both of his hands. "They broke them with a hammer." He pointed to my right sleeve. "You too have lost something. Was it the war?"

"Yes. It was the war. OK, Wolf. Now, what's our next move? Do we try to pin down this guy Berger, or Hessler?"

"Yes. We must make a positive identification. If what you say is true, Hessler has changed his identity so well that his own mother wouldn't recognize him. Julie recognized him and paid the price. I am sure that Abe Shoiket will give us a positive identification. But there is one other way to identify Hessler. He had an SS death head tattooed on his right shoulder. By now he's probably had it surgically removed, but maybe there is still some sign of the tattoo. I must use your telephone."

He sat on the desk and dialed a number. "Hello, Abe. Shalom. I will be there in half an hour. Have the files ready. I am bringing DeLucca with me. Yes, DeLucca. No. He's a private investigator working with us. Yes, I'm sure. He may be of some help. Shalom."

'He may be of some help...' Christ! So far I was the one who'd done all of the work. It was no easy job making sense out of all the pieces of this puzzle. Now the little Nazi hunter was taking over.

***

As we left my office, I worried about what our next move would be. To apprehend a nest of Nazi war criminals, we needed a hell of a lot more than a one-armed investigator and a little weasel with broken hands and a kosher butcher. I figured that this case was screaming for the help of some higher authority.

It was still raining when I parked the car in front of Abe Shoiket's butcher shop. He was standing at the door as we approached the entrance.

Kotchman shook his hand while Shoiket kept his eyes on me. "Abe, I take it that you have met DeLucca?"

"Yes. We met." He made no effort to be friendly. He opened the door and went in. "Come. I have the files ready." Shoiket pulled the blind and locked the door. We followed him to the door at the far end of the counter. As I passed the chopping block, I looked at the meat cleaver and remembered the fear in his eyes when he had threatened me. If he was the only one left who could identify Hessler, he had good reason to be afraid.

We stood in front of a small door while Shoiket pulled out his keys and unlocked the padlock. We entered the room and Shoiket yanked the pull cord on a hanging overhead light. The room was small. Against the back wall were metal filing cabinets. In the center of the room was a wooden table and four chairs. To my left, the wall was covered with photographs. The swinging overhead light scanned the wall like a search light revealing the photos of German soldiers. Some of them had a black X across their faces. Soon the light stopped swinging, and I could see other photos. Terrible pictures of prisoners. Faces without hope, waiting for death. Scrawled on the wall above the groups of photos were the names of the major death camps in Poland: Treblinka, Auschwitz, Majdanek and Belzec.

Kotchman stepped close to Shoiket, put a hand on his shoulder and said, "My friend Abe has quite a rogues gallery, wouldn't you say? In his files he has a photo of every wanted Nazi. There is no place they can hide. They will not escape their punishment." He turned away from the wall and faced me. "So, DeLucca. Do you understand now why Abe was frightened when you questioned him? How could he know that you were not one of those gangsters come to silence him, just like they silenced Ben and his wife. You asked him about Belzec and that alone would cause him to distrust you. You see, we are the hunters, but sometimes in this game the hunters become the hunted.

I looked over at Shoiket and could see that he was still suspicious. Turning back to Kotchman, I said, "I understand."

I understood all right. I was to be a third player in their dangerous game, and it made me uneasy. I wondered if it was the kind of game I wanted to play. What I didn't understand was the connection between Shoiket the butcher and Julie Koslo. Now was the time to find out. "Wolf, you told me that you and Shoiket were together at Treblinka and then Abe was sent to Belzec. Is that right?"

"That is correct."

I turned to Abe. "Then you first met Julie Koslo in Belzec?"

Abe scowled and said, "I'm not answering any of your questions."

"Tell him, Abe, so we can get on with our business." said Kotchman.

Abe reluctantly answered, "She was there."

"I talked to Ben's folks, and they said that Julie's family was Polish. Were there a lot of Poles in the death camps?"

Abe looked at me as if I had asked a stupid question. "Of course there were. At first we were put all together, but it didn't take long for them to single out the Jews. That's when the killing started."

"Why was Julie's parents killed and she spared?"

"Her parents were executed because they had joined the resistance. Julie was young, blond and pretty. She caught the eye of Hessler. He had other plans for her."

"You mean he used her for his pleasure?"

"Yes."

"Then why did they cut off her fingers?"

"At first she rebelled and made an attempt to escape. That's when Hessler had her maimed and confined her to his quarters under guard. Rumors in the camp was that she was his mistress and was forced into service to stay alive. That's all I know. I never saw or heard from her again until she came into my shop three weeks ago to buy meat. We recognized each other, but very little was said. Then, last Wednesday night she called me and said that she had seen Hessler on the stage of the Opera House. I believed her and immediately made contact with Wolf."

Shoiket had spilled his guts. I thought about Julie in the camp under the protection of Hessler and wondered if it still applied. "Wolf. Is it possible that Hessler would spare her life again?"

"That's unlikely. She is the one witness who can seal his fate. He wouldn't take the chance, especially at this time. Now, if you are satisfied, Delucca, can we continue? We have a lot to do." Kotchman went to the file cabinet, pulled out a drawer and selected a file. "This is everything we have on Hessler up to five years ago." He opened the file. "The man is cunning and very dangerous. Most of his records have been destroyed. There are no known dental charts or fingerprints. In 1947, we were on his trail in Hamburg, but he eluded us. Three witnesses and two of our agents were killed. In 1949, he surfaced in Argentina with his two bodyguards. This time we were very careful and tried not to alert him. We needed to make a positive identification, so we flew two eyewitnesses from Poland to Buenos Aires and put them under protective guard. I don't know how, but the witnesses and three more of our agents were killed. After that, we lost track of Hessler, until now. This time we must not fail."

I couldn't figure out what he was planning. Was he and he alone going to confront Hessler? Did he plan to put an arm-lock around his neck and drag him back to Israel for trial? What about Hessler's two bully boys? Were they just going to sit on a bench in the dark and do nothing? I was worried.

"Wolf, let me get this straight. You obviously have other agents you can call upon for help, right?"

"Wrong. If I have to call for assistance, my Nazi birds will fly the coop again. We must act now!"

I focused on the word 'we'. He kept saying 'we' and I didn't like the sound of it. "But Wolf. Why not call in a government agency? Tell them what you know and let them handle it."

"DeLucca, you still don't understand. The power structure at the War Memorial Opera House has offered these Germans sponsorship. It's similar to diplomatic immunity. They can do no wrong. They have been welcomed as artists and recruited to build the opera's reputation so that it is comparable to that of the great opera companies of Europe. The city officials would laugh in your face if you cried Nazi's at the opera. The city police department would be crucified if they stepped in and caused a scandal. Imagine the police asserting that Nazi's worked in a city owned building. The Mayor would probably leave town. As for the government agencies...you were thinking of The War Crimes Commission in Washington, right? They've been called in before. By the time they untangle their red tape, the war is over, the suspected criminals disappear into thin air and a great deal of difficult and hazardous work goes down the drain. As for the F.B.I., that's another dead end. It was your government and the F.B.I. that arranged to give many of these gangsters sanctuary in South America. If we called them, they would be dragging their bureaucratic red tape all the way from Washington to San Francisco. No, DeLucca! This is going to be done my way, with or without you."

This guy was either crazy, or one of the bravest sons of a bitches I've ever had the displeasure to meet. The way he talked, he wouldn't trust the Boy Scouts of America. He was obviously obsessed. I wondered what he had in mind for a final solution.

"OK, Wolf. You must have devised some clever plan to pull this off. Do you mind letting me in on it?"

"Not at all, DeLucca. Sit down and I'll tell you." The three of us sat down. Kotchman nervously tapped his fingers on the table. "I do have the beginning of a plan. We are going to kidnap Hessler and his two bodyguards."

My lower jaw dropped. I looked over at Shoiket. He remained expressionless. Kotchman continued. "Not all at once of course. First we take Gunther Mueller, then Heitman and finally, Hessler."

I couldn't believe what I had heard. "We are going to kidnap Hessler and his boys?"

"That is correct."

"How?"

"I believe that with your help, we can work out a plan of attack."

He continued to use that word we. "Supposing we get lucky and do happen to kidnap one of the bastards. What then?"

"I will arrange for a secure place to hold them until we are ready for their transport."

"Transport? Don't you need U.S. sanction and extradition papers?"

"No! Not necessarily. But even if I wanted to go through all of that, the legal implications would tie us up in knots and the criminals would eventually get off. No, DeLucca. My way is fast and sure."

"You spoke of transport. How the hell are you going to get them from here all the way to Israel?"

Kotchman looked over at Abe Shoiket, then back at me. "That part has already been taken care of."

I waited for him to explain. He lit a cigarette, shook out the match and dropped it on the floor, "Now, back to our present problem. I believe we..."

I butted in. "Hold on a minute, Wolf. I asked you a question."

"It would be better for you, DeLucca, if you knew nothing about that part of the operation. Just take my word for it. The arrangements have been made."

"I'm afraid that won't do. I never go into an operation without knowing what I'm getting into. The last one cost me my arm and from what I've been hearing from you Nazi hunters, a guy could lose more than his arm in this operation. Either you let me in on the whole thing, or you and the butcher can handle it by yourselves." I felt like getting the hell out of there and having a few drinks. Kotchman and Shoiket had started to bug me.

Kotchman lowered his head. "All right, DeLucca. You've got a point." He looked up. "Am I correct in assuming that you have agreed to help us?"

"I'm willing to help within limits, but like I said, I don't like mysteries when my life is on the line."

"Then we have an understanding. Abe will tell you all of the details. He was instrumental in the planning and through his brother, we are able to obtain the services of the people necessary to complete the final part of our plan." He gestured to Shoiket. "Go on, Abe. You tell him."

The butcher cleared his throat and moved his chair closer to the table. "My brother Jacob owns an oil refinery and has a distributorship in Toronto. He has connections in Galveston Texas. On the twenty-second of September at 6:00 AM, a Greek tanker, the Erasmus, will leave the port of Galveston and sail non-stop to Athens, then two days later it will leave Athens and go to the port of Haifa in Israel. We do not deal with the authorities until we reach our final destination. That's all." He leaned back and looked at me with contempt, as if I had wasted his precious time with these explanations.

"You said the tanker leaves on the twenty-second of September? That only leaves nine days."

Kotchman peered at me through a plume of white smoke. "That is correct. It is enough time for what we have to do."

I found it hard to believe that I would even consider joining this mad duo. Kotchman chain lit another cigarette and stood up. "Now we must give serious thought to the abduction and the transport to Galveston. DeLucca, I want you to find out where Hessler lives. Study the grounds and the house and tell me if you think it's possible to take him from his quarters. Abe and I will make the necessary arrangements for holding them once they are in our custody. We will meet here tomorrow at 9:00 AM to discuss our findings and make further plans."

I stood up and waited for Abe to open the door. Wolf stamped out his cigarette and said, "Are we in agreement?"

I nodded and asked, "Have you given any thought to how you are going to get the prisoners to Galveston?"

"Yes, I have, DeLucca. The Germans will be transported in a cattle car."

The meeting was over and I was relieved to get out of that cramped, stifling room. It was 7:30 when I dropped Wolf off at his car. He reminded me of our meeting tomorrow at 9:00 and quickly drove off. I had just enough time to go home, clean up and get ready for the only pleasant thing I'd had to look forward to for a long time, my dinner date with Maria.

EIGHT

I arrived at Bonito's at a quarter after nine pm I never liked being late, but I'd had a little trouble deciding if I should wear my one gray suit, or slacks and a sport coat. I'd decided on the sport coat. There were a few people at the bar, but Maria wasn't one of them.

Julio, the bartender, approached me with a smile. "Hey, Vince. I just got a call from my ex-wife and she asked for you. I didn't know you knew Maria."

"Yeah, I just met her yesterday."

"That's good, Vince. You can't go wrong. Maria is tops."

"OK, Julio. Now that you approve, can I have a Martini?"

"You got it, Vince."

Now I knew where Maria had gotten her 'you got it' lingo. I was trying not to think about Kotchman, Shoiket the butcher, and the Germans, but I couldn't erase them from my mind. Later on tonight, I had a job to do. I wondered where Kotchman got the money to finance his Nazi hunting operation. He probably received support from the Israeli government or Abe's brother in Toronto.

"There you go, Vince. Cold and dry."

"Thanks, Julio. By the way, what did Maria say when she called?"

"Said she'd be late." He walked away then turned and said, "Aren't they always?"

Gloria, the hostess set up a small table at the rear of the dining room. I ordered another Martini and looked at my watch. It was a quarter to ten. Where the hell was she? Then I heard her voice. "Hello, DeLucca." I turned on the stool. She smiled. "I tried to be on time, but I couldn't. I'm sorry you had to wait."

"No need to be sorry, Maria. I'm glad you're here. Let me help you with your raincoat."

She was wearing a red dress, the color of Sangria. A black belt encircled her slender waist, and two iridescent pearls dangled from her ears.

"Would you like a drink?"

"Yes. An Irish coffee."

I motioned to Julio. He came over and said, "Maria! Good to see you. It's been a while, you look great."

"Thanks, Julio. How have you been?"

"Doing fine. I've been working here now for three years, and I like it. What'll you have?"

"Bring her an Irish coffee and I'll have another Martini."

"You got it, Vince."

I turned to Maria. "Is this the first time you've seen Julio since the divorce?"

"No. I used to see him often after the divorce, but this is the first time I've seen him in almost two years." She leaned back and looked at me. "Well, DeLucca. I'm famished. When do we eat?"

We took our drinks to the table and ordered dinner. Maria selected the fish, and I ordered a Porterhouse steak. During the salad course, we indulged in light conversation. There was no mention of the opera, or the case I was working on. I figured she was waiting for me to bring it up then she would ask questions.

I reached over and lit her cigarette. She kept her eyes on mine and said, "DeLucca. I've been wanting to ask you a question."

"OK. What is it?"

"How do you manage a steak?"

"Manage it?"

"Yes. How do you cut it with only one hand? I would be willing to cut it for you, if you like."

She wasn't put off by my lack of one arm. I liked that. Maybe she could get used to it. I smiled and said, "Thank you. I appreciate that, but I usually have the chef cut it up for me."

"There must be a lot of everyday things that you find difficult to manage with one arm."

"That's true, but I don't have any trouble doing all of the important things."

She changed the subject. "Did you have the meeting with Berger today?"

"Yes, I did. You were right about him and his two assistants. They're a weird trio."

"Yesterday you said that I was going to work with you on this case. Well, I'm ready for my next assignment."

I knew she would be a big help, but I didn't want her involved because of the danger.

"Did I say that?"

"You sure did."

"Look, Maria, you've already helped me quite a bit by giving me the information about the German staff in the office. You saved me a lot of time and trouble."

"I can do more than that, DeLucca. I expect to be called upon."

"Believe me, Maria. You will be."

After dinner, we had cognac and coffee. It was the first time I had felt completely relaxed in a long while. Maria also seemed content and at ease. It looked to me like we were going to get along just fine.

I glanced at the time. It was a quarter after twelve. I wanted to check out Hessler's house tonight so I could report my findings tomorrow, but I hadn't taken the time to find the address yet. Possibly there would be a number listed under Paul Berger, but then again, he would probably have an unlisted number.

Maria reached across the table and touched my hand. "All right, DeLucca! What's going on? You're miles away from me."

"Oh, I'm sorry. I was just thinking about something."

"Thinking about our case?"

She was persistent and difficult to deny. "Yes. About our case. You said you were ready for your next assignment?"

"Name it, Detective DeLucca."

"All right. Tonight, I am going to put Paul Berger's house under surveillance. Do you know where he lives?"

"Yes, I do. The opera company rented a big house for him. It's out by the beach at the end of Geary Street."

"Can you give me the address?"

"I can do better than that, DeLucca. I'll drive you right to it."

"I can't ask you to do that. Just give me the address and I'll find it."

"No. I don't think you could find it at night. It's hidden from the main street and anyway, this sounds exciting. I want to go along."

It was against my better judgment, but I said, "OK. Only, we do it my way."

She smiled at me. "You're the boss, DeLucca. Let's go."

***

We took Maria's car and in twenty minutes we were at the end of Geary Street enveloped in a thick fog. She turned right. I couldn't even see the street. I was lucky that she'd come along. I never would have found the place.

"Maria. How can you see where you're going? Have you been here before?"

"Yes. I made the arrangements to rent this house for Berger. I came here two times; once, to meet the real estate people and again when I had to deliver some musical scores to Berger. It's quite a large house. This is it. There on the left."

All I could see was a high gray wall that surrounded the grounds. Maria stopped the car in front of a pair of iron gates. Through the gates, I made out a large two-story house barely visible in the fog. The house was dark.

"Maria, would you pull up on the right about fifty yards and turn off your lights. I want to get out and take a closer look."

I asked her to stay in the car, walked across the street and stood next to the wall. It was about eight or nine feet high and constructed of stone blocks. A dim streetlight illuminated the driveway that led to the gate. I walked along the wall to the gate. Pressed against the wall, I slowly craned my neck around the corner to get a better view of the house.

A slight breeze rustled the leaves on a tree in front of the streetlight. Shadows danced on the bars of the gate. Suddenly, out of the darkness, two growling black Dobermans appeared and heaved their bodies against the bars of the gate. I quickly stepped back. They were definitely not friendly. I was afraid their loud barking would wake up the neighborhood and turned back to walk to the car. The dogs continued to bark. I was about thirty yards from the car when the headlights of a car turned the corner coming my way. I flattened myself against the wall in the shadows as the car passed by me and turned into the driveway. It was a dark Buick sedan with two occupants. A big man got out and walked to the gate. The dogs were still barking. He muttered something in German and the dogs became quiet. I recognized the big man. It was Otto Kurtz, who I knew now was really Gunther Mueller. I stayed next to the stone wall and crept closer to my car. Mueller unlocked the chain and pushed the gates open. About thirty feet from my car, I looked back and saw the two Dobermans race out through the gate heading straight for me. I ran across the street with the dogs close on my heels. Maria had started the engine and opened the door on the passenger side. I bounded into the seat and slammed the door shut. The Dobermans jumped against the window glass. We drove off.

I was weak in the knees, and it felt like my heart was going to pound right through my chest. Maria looked over at me. "Are you all right?"

"Yeah. I'm just out of condition. That's all. You were right on the ball when you started the car and got us the hell out of there. Thanks."

"Don't mention it, DeLucca. That's what partners are for."

I noticed then that I had closed part of my coat in the door. I opened the door and pulled the coat free. " Maria! Take a look at this." I held up the bottom hem of the right side of my coat. It was shredded like it had been clawed by a big cat. "It's a sure thing those Dobermans don't like Italians."

Maria puckered up her lips and uttered a low whistle. "Looks like they've got security, with a capital S."

We turned off of the side street on to Geary and started down towards town. I looked around and my heart began to pound again. Two headlights had made the same turn and were closing fast.

There was a reason why they lived behind a wall and had vicious guard dogs. They were afraid of something. Their fear made them dangerous and now the thing that I dreaded most was about to happen. I had wanted to keep Maria out of this, but now she had to help. I threw caution to the wind and let her. How could I tell her that these guys played for keeps?

"Maria! I think we've got some trouble."

"I see them, DeLucca. What shall we do?"

"How brave are you?"

"Brave enough."

"OK. Follow my instructions and we'll try to lose them."

Maria sounded nervous. "What do you want me to do? They're gaining on us."

"Pick up speed. Don't let them to get too close."

Maria stepped on the accelerator. We were doing sixty down Geary Street. "My God, DeLucca! We're going to have an accident!"

I turned around to look. They had fallen back. "You're doing fine. Keep going."

We came off a rise and started down a hill. We were getting closer to the downtown area. "We can't keep up this speed, DeLucca! We're going to...My God! Look!

In front of us was a red stop light with two cars waiting for it to change. There was no oncoming traffic. I looked behind. The Buick sedan was coming on strong. "Swerve to the left, Maria! Go through the light."

"You can't be serious!" By the time she said serious, we were through the light and back on the right side of the road.

The Buick followed us and was right on our tail. I could tell Maria was frightened. Her knuckles were white as she gripped the wheel. I hoped that she wouldn't panic at our next move. We were two blocks away from Grant Avenue when the Buick jolted our rear bumper. They meant business.

"Speed up, Maria! At the next corner, take a hard left."

"A left, at this speed? I'll have to put on the brakes to make the turn."

"OK but wait until you're almost at the cross street." She started the left turn and touched the brakes. The rear end skidded sideways as we turned into the street. "Now! Step on it. Go to California Street and take a right."

As we sped up the street, I looked back at the Buick. It didn't make the turn. "We've got a good lead on them now. You're doing fine, just maintain your speed and get ready to take a hard right on to California." While she made the turn, the Buick had backed up and continued to follow us, picking up speed.

We started down California Street, one of the steepest streets in San Francisco. I leaned forward and gave Maria her final instructions. "Just before we get to Grant Avenue, there's a small alley to the right that goes up to the entrance of the Lamps of China. We've got to turn up that alley before they round the corner on to California. Can you do it?"

"Mother of God, DeLucca! What have you gotten me into? I'll try."

We were doing sixty-five down California Street with a ninety-degree turn coming up. "Get ready! There it is. Put on the brakes and make a hard right."

We skidded twenty yards. She spun the wheel hard right, then stepped on the gas. The alley was dark, narrow, and very steep. She skidded to a stop at the top, six inches in front of a metal loading door. I told her to douse the lights and looked through the rear window. The Buick went on past the alley to Grant Avenue.

I turned back in the seat, took a deep breath. "You did it, Maria. We lost them."

Her hands were frozen on the steering wheel. She stared ahead at the loading door. "DeLucca, how about buying a girl a drink?"

It was a quarter to two. We could still make last call at the Lamps and I figured it best that we stay put for a while, in case the Buick was still out there looking around. I got out of the car, went around and opened the door on the driver's side. Maria was still gripping the wheel. I put my hand on her arm. "Maria, it's all over, and I must say, that was the finest bit of driving that I've ever seen. Come on, let's have that drink. You deserve it."

We walked through the double orange doors, turned right, and sat down at an empty bar. The bartender looked alarmed. "Vince! Are you drunk or something? Was that you speeding up the alley?"

"Hello, Lee. No, it wasn't me." I pointed to Maria. "It was her."

"You must be some wild lady. What will you have?"

"Cognac and coffee for two," I said."

After drinking half of our cognac, we both calmed down a bit. Maria leaned close to me and whispered, "DeLucca. There must be something I don't know. Why were they chasing us? And what were they going to do if they caught us?"

"They just wanted to know who was poking around their place. They probably wanted to throw a scare into us. That's all."

"I don't think that's all, DeLucca. I saw the driver of the Buick. It was Fritz Kranke. Assistant opera directors don't go on wild chases at 2:00 in the morning after someone who happened to walk by their front gate." She sipped the cognac and licked her lips. "There's got to be a lot more to it than that. You're into something big. Something dangerous too. Aren't you, DeLucca?"

I lowered my head, swirled the cognac in my glass and thought about my first meeting with Joe Bender. It was supposed to have been just a simple routine case. I raised my head and looked at Maria. "Yes. I'm afraid you're right. There is a lot more to it and it's damned dangerous. I'm sorry I involved you. I almost got you killed tonight."

"Am I complaining, DeLucca? I did help you a bit, didn't I?"

"Help me? Christ! You saved my life. If it wasn't for you, I would have been dog food back there."

"Well, if that's the case, why don't you let me in on the rest of it?"

"All right. I'll give it to you in a nutshell. Berger and his two play-mates are not who they seem to be. The team of Berger, Kurtz and Kranke, are really Hessler, Mueller and Heitman. All three are wanted Nazi war criminals. They have already killed many times to protect their identity. I have agreed to work with two Israeli agents to put these bastards away for good. So, you see why I didn't want you to know about them. They silenced Ben Koslo and his wife, Julie and will stop at nothing to keep their true identities unknown."

"Jesus, DeLucca! This is fantastic. I thought you were working for the union."

"I was, or, I am, but the more I found out, the more complicated it got. Then I met Wolf Kotchman, the Israeli. He has a wild notion that he wants to kidnap all three and take them back to Israel for trial."

"Kidnap them? How in the world are you going to do that?"

"It'll take some figuring, especially now that the time is so short."

"Why is the time short? Can't you call the police, or the F.B.I.?"

"That was my first thought, too, but Kotchman gave me a lot of good reasons why we shouldn't. He insists that it be done his way. He's made arrangements for a ship going from Galveston Texas to the port of Haifa in Israel on the twenty-second of this month. That's the whole story, Maria. Please keep this between the two of us."

"The two of us? I like that. So, I am your partner after all. But there's only one problem, DeLucca."

"What's that?"

"It seems to me that this fellow, Kotchman, could get you killed. That's one hell of a way to break up a partnership like ours."

At 2:15, we left the Lamps and headed for my apartment. I kept a sharp eye out for the Buick. Maria pulled up in front of my apartment building and kept the engine running. She leaned over and gave me a short soft kiss on the lips and said, "It's been fun, DeLucca. Let's do it again sometime." It sounded as if she'd had it with me and my case, so I opened the door and was about to get out, when she touched my arm and said with deep concern, "DeLucca, take care of yourself, will you?" I got out and closed the door. She smiled then drove away.

Back in my apartment, I was troubled by the same question that Maria had asked. Why did they chase after us and what would they have done if they had caught us? I couldn't believe that they would try to murder us on the street. They didn't know who we were. It didn't make any sense that they would take such a chance to pursue an unknown car. Wolf said that sometimes the hunter became the hunted. Did they think that the occupants of the car were Wolf Kotchman and Abe Shoiket? Could they have taken down the license number? If so, Maria could be in grave danger. I didn't know her telephone number, or where she lived so I grabbed the telephone book and started to look up Maria Martinelli. There were a lot of Martinelli's. Finally, I found her the right one and called. I let it ring for a long time, but there was no answer. Maybe she hadn't had enough time to arrive at her home. I decided I was overreacting and should wait to call her in the morning,

At 7:00 AM I rolled out of bed, reached for the phone, dialed Maria's number, and waited. A sleepy voice answered, "It better be good at this hour."

"Maria, it's Vince."

"DeLucca, do you know what time it is? Give a girl a break."

"I tried calling you after you left, around three this morning and there was no answer. I got worried. Are you all right?"

"That's sweet of you. I'm fine. Now will you let me go back to sleep?"

"OK, but what about tonight?"

"What about it? Have you something planned, like a balloon ride over the bay, or climbing to the top of the Golden Gate Bridge? Go back to bed, DeLucca, and let me get my beauty sleep."

"I have your next assignment ready for you, partner."

"Next assignment? What is it?"

"Meet me at Bonito's tonight at eight and I'll tell you then." I could tell she was yawning as she said, "You're nuts, DeLucca." Then she hung up.

NINE

At ten to nine, Abe Shoiket led me to the back of his butcher shop. Wolf Kotchman had already filled the small room with smoke.

He looked up and said, "Sit down, DeLucca." He stared at me with half-closed eyes. "Now, let's get down to business." He blew smoke across the table into my face and spoke as if he were interrogating a prisoner. "What can you tell me about Hessler's house?"

"I can tell you we'll pay hell trying to get them out of there."

"I'll decide that. Now give me the details."

"There's a nine-foot wall surrounding the house. On the grounds, there are two of the meanest Doberman guard dogs I've ever seen. The driveway leads to a locked iron gate. It's a two-story house set back from the wall about thirty yards."

Kotchman cupped his chin in one of his gnarled hands. "That complicates matters. Did you see anyone on the grounds?"

"I did. First, the damn dogs chased me to the car, then Hessler's two bodyguards damned near killed us in a wild chase down Geary Street. We finally lost them in Chinatown."

Kotchman's eyes narrowed. "You said we. Was someone with you?"

"Yes. A girl who worked in the opera office. Maria Martinelli is her name. She's been a great help to me on this case."

"Does this girl, Maria, know everything?"

"Yes. I told her."

"Telling her what we are involved in was a bad move. You may have put her life in danger. This is disturbing news. The fact that they chased after you means they have been alerted. Hessler probably feels that he is in a good position. Rather than run for it, he has elected to stay and fight. From now on, DeLucca, I would start carrying a gun."

"Hell! I haven't carried a gun since the war."

Kotchman lit another cigarette and stood up. "I'm afraid that's exactly what this is, a war, and just as dangerous as being at the front."

"You think it can get that rough?"

"What do you think, DeLucca? By now, you must have some idea who we are dealing with."

Abe unfolded a map of the city on top of the table. Kotchman leaned over the map, dropping his ashes on it. "What we need is a safe, secure building, someplace that is not in a populated area. I believe we have found such a place." He pointed to the Embarcadero on the map. "This is the spot. Pier 29. At the present time, the pier is not being used. It is condemned and repairs will commence in two weeks. There is a locked gate that opens onto the pier and a storage locker at the far end. It is metal and has a steel roll down door that can be locked. I persuaded the watchman to let us use it for five days with no questions asked."

It seemed like a good location, but I had my doubts about the five days, "Aren't you cutting it a little close, with only five days?"

Kotchman scowled at me. "It is all the time we have. The ship leaves Galveston the morning of the twenty-second. It will take two days to ship our cargo overland to Galveston. That means we must move them no later than the night of the nineteenth. From today to the nineteenth is five days. Enough time to gather our Nazi birds and cage them."

I liked his choice of words like 'Nazi birds' and 'cage'. He acted as if we were going to capture three finches and put them into a bird cage. I had a feeling in my gut that this part of the operation wasn't going to be easy. I was curious about the rest of the plan. "That takes care of one part, Wolf. What about the other two parts?"

He spit the moist cigarette out of his mouth and growled, "I'm coming to that, DeLucca." He tapped his finger on a section of the map close to the pier area. "This is the Southern Pacific rail yard. At 5:00 AM on the morning of the twentieth, an East bound freight will leave for Dallas. After a short layover to drop off cars, it will continue on to Galveston and arrive at midnight on the twenty-first. That will give us time to get to the docks and board the ship." He looked over at me and sneered, "You see, DeLucca, we have done our work. It's all falling into place."

"Yeah? Well, how do you get your birds on the train?"

"That's all taken care of. What is it you Americans say? Greasing the palm? It's the same all over the world. A little cash placed in the right hands, and you can accomplish almost anything. The train yard master was very obliging. He reserved a nice box car with accommodations for three."

The arrogant little bastard was sharp. Sitting there so smug and sure of himself, with the big fat butcher looking on, worshiping his every word. "OK, Wolf. It looks like you've taken care of everything but the most difficult part of the game. Who do you pay off to accomplish the great feat of kidnaping Hessler and his boys?"

Kotchman gritted his teeth and reached into his pocket for his cigarettes. "Yes. That does present a small problem. If what you say is true, it is apparent that we cannot take them easily from their house. That leaves only one option open to us. We must catch them where they work, at the opera house."

I couldn't believe it. He called it a small problem to kidnap a prominent director and his two assistants from the opera house in broad daylight. "Wolf! You must have had other situations like this before. How did you handle them?"

He crushed the empty cigarette package and threw it on the floor, then nervously searched through his pockets. "Yes. We have had a few like this before, but the circumstances were quite different." He walked to the wall and pointed to a photo of a German officer with a black X across his face. "Claus Borman. A former SS Colonel. He was found in Boston, the owner of a clothing goods store. We followed him on the subway and forced him at gun point to remain until the end of the line where a car was waiting to take him away. He never suspected that we were on his trail. He was not armed and gave us no trouble." He pointed to another photo. "This one was a completely different situation. Helmut Stoltz. One of the butchers at Auschwitz. He had been alerted and decided to run. We caught him at the Los Angeles International Airport just as he was purchasing a one-way ticket to Seattle. Rather than being taken, he decided to fight. Two security guards were killed, and three innocent bystanders were wounded before he was shot dead while running for a taxi. We don't want a repeat of that incident. Hessler is worried. He will do everything he can to get us off his back. These three are extremely dangerous, so we must come up with a brilliant plan." He gave up searching through his pockets. "DeLucca, do you have a cigarette?"

I handed him one of mine. He lit up and inhaled deeply, then said, "There is too much at stake to fail now. I would like to hear some suggestions."

I had a few ideas, but they were something just short of murder. Probably someone would get hurt and it could be me. Kotchman's birds weren't going to stand still while we put straightjackets on them.

Kotchman looked over at Abe. "What do you say, Abe?"

"I say we should take them while they are asleep in the house. The gate can be opened, and we can quiet the dogs with a tranquilizer gun. We would have all three at once."

"That would be a bold move, Abe," said Kotchman. "How do we know they don't have more guards watching the house at night and what about alarms? I'm sure Hessler would have the house equipped with an alarm system. If we had more time to find out the unknown factors, it would be a fair plan, but time is short. We must make the right decision today and act upon it immediately." He turned to me. "What about you, DeLucca?"

I had a wild plan that was just as crazy as Abe's, but I figured I might as well spit it out. "By tomorrow afternoon, I could have a schedule of all the night rehearsals at the opera, also I believe I can find out what hours Hessler will be working on stage. If we could create an excuse to detain him after a rehearsal, his two bodyguards are sure to stay with him. After all of the singers, chorus, orchestra, and the stage technicians leave the theatre, we could lock all of the exits so Hessler couldn't get out. We would have them confined to the backstage area."

"Preposterous! How do you propose to do all that, DeLucca?"

"I have friends who work backstage. I'm sure they would help us if I asked."

Kotchman pulled the chair out from the table and sat down. "Do you know what you would be asking of your friends? Why would they endanger themselves by helping us?"

"Because most of them have already fought the Germans, or the Japanese. They're veterans, just like me. Also, Ben Koslo and his wife were their friends. They'll do whatever it takes."

"Very commendable, DeLucca, but as soon as Hessler discovers that he is trapped, he would turn his capos loose and make a fight of it. We could never take them alive. It would end up a bloody gun battle backstage and we just might come out second best. No, DeLucca. It's far too risky. We must think of another way."

I don't know where I came up with these ideas, but since we were speculating on a fantasy, I laid out another plan to Kotchman. "All right. How about this one? If we could capture Hessler first, then send a message to his two comrades that he wanted them to meet him at pier 29. That way, there would be no one around and all three of them would be at the same location."

Kotchman stood up and started pacing the floor. "That one might deserve some consideration. So far we have three plans. Plan number one requires more information about the house and there are too many unknown factors to deal with in the time we have left. Plan number two would put an end to our problem, one way or the other, but it is much too daring and I'm not sure I like the odds. Plan three is sound, but it still has a lot of loose ends. I believe we will be better off if we single them out, one by one. All three at once may prove fatal to all of us."

All of these plans we were kicking around sounded pretty far-fetched. I liked statements like, 'we could take them in their sleep, or 'we could never take them alive,' and then there was, 'take them, one by one.' Not once had anyone mentioned *how* we were going to take them.

"Wolf, it seems to me that the element of risk is high if we try to subdue them by force. I have another idea that might eliminate violence and possible harm to others. It would require some time to set it up, but we would have all three at once, without anyone getting hurt."

"Go on, DeLucca. I'm listening."

"What we need is some tear gas canisters. Hopefully, late after a rehearsal, we somehow get all three of them in the elevator. We stop the elevator in-between floors and from the overhead trap door, we drop the tear gas into the elevator car. After a minute or two, we turn on the power and the elevator continues on to the stage floor. We open the doors, carry them out, put them in a car and drive to pier 29."

Kotchman was interested. "Do you think somehow you can make all the arrangements concerning the elevator?"

"I'm sure that I can."

"DeLucca, let me have another cigarette." He lit up and blew smoke at the ceiling. "I like this plan. Abe, what do we have in the arsenal? Do you have tear gas?"

Shoiket answered immediately, "Yes. I have the old type, but it is very effective. Without a mask, it would render anyone helpless in a matter of seconds."

"Would they be unconscious?"

"In most cases, yes."

"DeLucca. How soon can you know if we can use the elevator to capture our birds?"

"I should be able to find out this afternoon and maybe I can get the rehearsal schedule for the next four days."

I detected a slight gleam in Kotchman's eyes. "It's all falling into place. We shall meet this evening at six to finalize plan number four."

TEN

On my way downtown, I thought of the things I had to do before six pm. First, I would call Maria and ask her if she could find out the rehearsal schedule for the next four days, then I would talk to the scenic crew. There was no way Kotchman could expect to be successful without some inside help. I remembered Big Jer saying that he and his crew would be willing to help.

I arrived at the opera house at 11:30 and walked in through the stage door. Al waved to me as I went to the telephone booth to call Maria. She answered after the second ring. "Maria, this is Vince."

"Good morning, DeLucca. Now this is a more reasonable hour to call a girl. Where are you?"

"I'm at the opera house and I've got to ask you to do something for me."

"Oh no. You want me to drive you somewhere?"

"No. Not that. I was wondering if you had picked up all of your belongings in the office?"

"No. I haven't. I've been trying to build up my courage to go back there. Why?"

"I need a detailed schedule of all the rehearsals for the next four days. Also, I could use information about Berger's, I mean Hessler's personal routine after the rehearsals are over. Can you do that for me?"

"Is this my next assignment?"

"Yes."

"It doesn't sound so difficult. All right, DeLucca. I'll be there as soon as I can."

"I'll be up on the paint bridge. You know where that is?"

"Sure. I know where it is. I'll see what I can dig up and meet you there in about an hour."

"Thanks, Maria."

I stepped out of the phone booth just as Al was breaking for lunch. "Al, I'd like to talk to you. Have you got a minute?"

"Sure thing, Vince. Come on up to the paint bridge for lunch. We can talk there, or is it private?"

"No. I'd like to talk to the scenic crew also."

Al pressed the elevator call button. "Does it have anything to do with the case?"

"Yeah, it does Al, and I need your help."

As the elevator stopped at the stage level, I could hear men's voices inside the car. The doors opened and standing before me were Hessler and his bodyguards. He immediately recognized me. "Well, if it isn't Mister DeLucca, the investigator. I would have thought by now, that you had concluded your investigation."

I felt like calling him Hessler, but that would stir up a swarm of German hornets too early in the game. "I'm just about to wrap it up, Mister Berger. The meeting that we had helped me more than you know."

He brushed by me as he stepped out of the elevator and headed for the stage door followed by his bodyguards.

I looked at Al and smiled. "What do you think, Al? Nice bunch of guys, aren't they."

We stepped into the elevator, Al pressed the button and said, "They won't be winning no popularity contest, that's for sure."

As we started up, I glanced at the ceiling, confirming that there was a small trap door in the center of the overhead.

Sitting around the table were Big Jer, Bruno Guffanti, Phil Cohen and Tommy Doyle.

Big Jer smiled. "Pull up a chair, Vince. You're just in time for apple pie and coffee."

Doyle asked, "How's the case coming along, Vince?"

"It's nearing an end, but I need your help to wrap it up."

"I told you that we would be willing to help, Vince," said Jer. "What do you want us to do?"

"First, let me tell you what we're up against, then you can decide if you want to be involved. I would appreciate it if what I'm about to tell you, stayed right here at this table." I had an attentive audience. All five leaned forward waiting for me to speak. "The director, Berger, and his two assistants, Kurtz and Kranke are really wanted Nazi war criminals."

Bruno choked on his coffee, "Nazi war criminals!"

Big Jer leaned over the table. There was concern in his voice. "I know we all joke about the Germans here at the opera, but war criminals? Are you sure?"

"I'm sure. All three have been positively identified. There's no doubt about it. Their names are Hessler, Mueller and Heitman."

"God damn!" exclaimed Doyle. "I knew it all along. When do we hang their asses?"

"Will you shut up, Doyle," said Bruno. "Let the man finish."

"They murdered Ben and I believe they might have killed his wife also. She knew Hessler during the war at Belzec, a death camp in Poland. I am working with two Israeli agents, who want to take all three back to Israel for trial."

I was about to continue when Bruno looked overhead and held up his hand. He whispered, "Someone's up on 2F, close to the rail."

Big Jer turned to Doyle and said in a low voice, "Check it out, Doyle."

Doyle quickly entered the elevator. As we heard the elevator going up, we also heard footsteps moving quickly away from the rail on the floor above.

"Someone's up there all right," said Phil.

Al sliced himself a piece of pie. "Hell, it could be anyone. Probably one of the electricians."

Two minutes later, the elevator came down and Doyle stepped out.

"Who was it?" asked Jer.

"I don't know. When I got up there, I could hear someone going up the steel ladder to the fan room. I heard the door close. By the time I got there, whoever it was, was long gone. If it was one of the krauts, he sure wore some strong aftershave. The whole floor stinks."

"I don't think it was them," I said. All three came out of the elevator just as I was coming up, and the elevator hasn't moved after I got here." I remembered the perfume that Hessler's secretary wore and wondered if she could be spying for her boss. "Could it have been a woman's perfume? Possibly Hessler's secretary?" Why didn't he check the smell out himself?

"It could have been," said Phil. "Or maybe Al's right and it was just one of the electricians checking out the cables on the border lights."

"I doubt that, Phil," said Bruno. "If he was going to check out his border lights, he would do it from this level, not go up to 2F. Shit!

This is the first time we ever paid attention to anyone on 2F. This war criminal thing has got us all jumpy."

Big Jer poured himself a cup of coffee and looked over at me. "Might as well continue, Vince. No one's up there now. You were saying that you and two Israeli agents are working together, and they want to ship the krauts back to Israel for trial."

"Yes, that's right. All the arrangements have been made to transport the prisoners, but the tough part is to capture them and hold them."

"You're working with two Israeli agents?" asked Phil.

"The hell with all the questions, Phil," said Doyle impatiently. "Go on, Vince. Let's get to the meat."

"OK. I've discussed several ways to go about this with the Israeli agents and we came up with a plan that I think will work."

Phil leaned forward. "What are the names of the Israeli agents, Vince?"

"Jesus Christ!" bellowed Bruno. "What the hell difference does it make. Let Vince finish."

"I just wanted to know. That's all."

"You think they might be some of your long-lost cousins, Philsy?" joked Doyle.

I directed my answer to Phil. "Their names are Kotchman and Shoiket."

Phil sat back in his chair and smiled. "Those are good Jewish names."

"Look, Phil!" said Bruno. "We're all very glad that you approve. Now, will you let the man finish?"

Big Jer leaned forward. "Go on, Vince. You were talking about a plan."

"That's right. I figured it like this. After rehearsal, Hessler and his bodyguards get into the elevator and go up to their office. My intention is to stop the elevator between floors and drop tear gas into the car from the trap door overhead. Then the elevator would continue down to the stage level. The three of them could be taken out without a struggle. Do you think it can be accomplished?"

"Sure it can," said Jer. "That is, if we can get them in the elevator. Bruno, call Irv Louche and ask him to come up here. Tell him we want to talk to him about something." Bruno went to the house phone to call, while Jer gave me the low-down on Irv Louch. "Irv is the maintenance man for all the elevators in the building. He'll have to be told what's going on, and you're going to need him to turn the power on and off. Also he will brief you on the elevator."

"OK. That's fine with me. Do you think he will help?"

"I'm sure he will."

"OK. Then after the elevator goes to the stage floor, we open the doors and carry Hessler and his boys out to a car and take them to pier 29."

"Why pier 29?" asked Bruno. "Are you going to put them on a ship?"

"Kotchman has provided a secure place to hold them at the pier until we move them to a freight train that's heading for Galveston. Then a Greek tanker will take them the rest of the way, to the port of Haifa in Israel."

Big Jer moved his chair away from the table and stretched his legs. "Damn, Vince! It looks like you dealt yourself into one hell of a game."

"I know. This thing has sort of ballooned out of hand. Believe me, it's dangerous. I wanted all of you to know the details before you committed yourselves to help me."

Phil Cohen banged his coffee cup down on the table. "I'm with you, Vince."

Al Ferrigno followed suit. "You're gonna need me at the stage door."

Bruno reached for his cup and set it next to the other two cups. "I wouldn't miss this. You can count on me."

Doyle slammed his cup against the trio of cups. "I'm with you all the way, Vince. I've got the same feeling in my gut that I had when we hit the beach at Iwo."

The four looked over at Big Jer. He slowly reached for his cup, took a sip, then set it down next to the cluster of cups. He looked at me and said, "Well, Vince. It looks like you've got yourself a crack assault team."

I could tell that all five had at one time been in a theatre of war. This episode with the German war criminals had reignited the deep feelings that went with it: fear, anxiety, excitement, and pride. I wondered if Wolf Kotchman would appreciate the help he was going to receive from this bunch of Americans.

The elevator doors opened and out stepped a large man dressed in blue overalls and wearing a soiled Stetson with the brim turned up. He grinned and said in a loud voice. "Don't tell me the bridge cables slipped again and you want me to raise the bridge up three feet?"

Big Jer stood up. "No. The bridge is OK. Irv, meet Vince DeLucca. He's got a story to tell you. Better sit down and have a cup of coffee. It's quite a tale."

After I related the whole plan to Irv, he looked at the rest of the guys and asked, "Is he serious?"

"I'm afraid so," said Jer. "What about it, Irv? Will you help?"

"Sure, I'll help. Just let me know when."

"Vince here will give you that information."

"I'm waiting for Maria to show up with the schedule so we can pick the right night," I said. "As it is now, we plan to pull it off after a rehearsal, probably within the next four days. I'll know the exact night and hour definitely by this afternoon."

Irv threw his large frame back in his chair. "OK. As far as I can see, there's no problem on my end. The main power switch for the elevator is in the basement. I'll be able to turn it off and on anytime you want, but I'll need to set up a signal light that can be operated from the stage door."

"I can handle that," volunteered Al. "I'll be standing by the stage door the whole time."

Irv tipped his hat back. "OK. Now whoever is going to ride on top of the elevator car, needs to know a few things."

Doyle's eyes flashed with excitement. "That job was made for me."

"Hold it a minute, Doyle," I said. "I can't ask you to do that. One of the Israeli agents can handle that job."

"Hell! It's no different than pulling the pin on a hand grenade. Believe me, Vince. I can handle it, with pleasure."

Irv looked over at me and I nodded.

"All right, Doyle," said Irv. "You have to use a stepladder to climb up to the trap door, then you crawl up on top of the car and stand right over the trap. When the elevator is moving, you must stay clear of the cables."

"That's simple enough," Doyle said with confidence. "Where do I get the tear gas bomb? And are you sure we don't need more than one?"

"Christ, Doyle!" said Bruno. "You're not going to blow them up. You're just going to gas them."

I knew then that what we were going to do would take a lot more planning and possibly a dry run. It could turn into a nightmare if everything wasn't well timed. "Doyle, I'll bring the tear gas the night we do the job. You'll have plenty of time to go over your moves before the real thing. The way it looks right now, Irv will operate the elevator switch, Al will be at the stage door and stand by the signal light, Doyle will be on top of the car with the tear gas, and Bruno, Phil, Jer, and I will be at the stage entrance waiting for the elevator. Kotchman and Shoiket will be waiting in a car to drive them to the pier."

Irv opened the elevator door, turned, and said, "You let me know what night and I'll be ready. But there is one thing I must insist on. If this thing backfires and there's trouble, don't involve me. I'm a city employee and if they knew the elevator was tampered with and I was responsible, I'd lose my job. You understand?"

I nodded, "Yes, I understand, Irv. No matter what happens, your name will not be mentioned." As the elevator departed with Irv, I turned to the others. "What about the rest of you guys. Aren't you worried about your jobs?"

"Hell no!" said Jer, speaking for the rest of the crew. "We're all out of here in three more weeks. We've got nothing to lose. Besides, it's about time somebody did something to straighten things out around here. We're made for the job. As for Irv, he's all right. He'll do his part."

He paused, thinking.

"Listen Vince, I've got an idea. You mentioned driving these guys to the pier. What kind of car are they going to use?"

"I guess it will be Kotchman's sedan."

"How are they going fit?" Big Jer looked over at Bruno. "What about the truck?"

"That's right." beamed Bruno. "We could use the truck. It even has a lift gate."

"Yeah, and we could get the big clothing hamper from wardrobe and put them in that," added Doyle.

Jer slapped Doyle on the back. "Good idea. It will make moving them a hell of a lot easier. That big bastard must weigh close to three hundred pounds. What do you think, Vince?"

"Sounds good to me."

"I've got to be getting back to the door," said Al. He got up and pushed the elevator button. "I just thought of something that should be done after you move the Germans out of the elevator. I'll open the stage doors and set up a fan to blow all of the gas out of the building. We wouldn't want anyone to know that we used tear gas in the building."

"That's a good idea." said Jer. "OK boys, it's time. Let's go back to work. Vince will tell us when he's ready."

"What night do you think it'll be, Vince?" asked Doyle.

"I'll know today. I'm supposed to meet Maria here with the rehearsal schedule in a few minutes."

Bruno cleared the table while Phil and Doyle walked out onto the paint bridge. Phil put a hand on Doyle's shoulder. "Looks like you got the leading role in this campaign. Ever use tear gas before?"

Doyle grinned. "Piece of cake, Philsy."

ELEVEN

At quarter after one, Maria stepped off the elevator. Big Jer pulled out a chair and she sat down, crossing her legs, smiled and said, "Here's your information DeLucca." She opened a folder, took out a printed sheet of paper and started to read. "Tonight, the fourteenth, there is a short rehearsal, with piano, from six to eight. Thursday, the fifteenth, there is a dress with orchestra. It usually lets out at 11:00 or 11:30. Friday, the sixteenth, is the final dress and Saturday, the eighteenth is opening night." She lit up a cigarette and waited.

"Maria, this is just what we needed. What do you think, Jer. Which one of these nights would be best?"

He leaned over to look at the schedule. "Well, I think tonight would be too soon and it's an early rehearsal. Friday, the final dress is always a big affair. Lots of guests and people hang around for hours after the rehearsal. But Thursday, the fifteenth, probably would be our best bet. Everyone clears out of the theatre as soon as they can."

I thought it over and said, "All right, tomorrow night is the night. The sooner the better, since we might have had an inquisitive visitor up on 2f. Maria, did you happen to find out what Hessler does after the rehearsals are over?"

"Every rehearsal that I have been to, he's done the same thing. While the orchestra is leaving the pit, he goes backstage and confers with the lighting designer and talks to some of the singers. Then, he and his two bull dogs take the elevator up to his office and close the door. What they do up there, I can only guess. Probably have a schnapps while they sit around and praise each other."

"How long do they stay in the office?"

"Not long. I know because I used to stay and type up all of the rehearsal notes. Maybe, ten minutes or so. Then they take the elevator to the stage and leave the building. On occasion, Berger sends Fritz out to pick up the car and drive it around to the stage door."

"Is this his standard procedure after every one of his rehearsals?"

"As far as I know, DeLucca."

"OK, then it's settled. We go tomorrow night. Do you think we can all meet here about an hour before the rehearsal ends? It's important that we go over the plans in detail."

"Sure," said Big Jer. "I'll tell all of the guys and have them ready for a final briefing at 10:30 tomorrow night."

Maria looked on as we talked. I knew she wanted to ask a lot of questions, but she held off. As we came out of the elevator, Al winked and said in a whisper, "Vince, tell me when and I'll be ready."

"We're on for tomorrow night, Al," I said as we walked out the stage door to the street.

Maria was bursting with curiosity. "DeLucca! What is going on? What is happening tomorrow night?"

"After the rehearsal we're going to try to take Hessler and his boys out of the theatre without too much fuss."

"Take them out? How do you intend to do that?"

I didn't have the energy to explain it all to Maria, so I suggested, "Why don't you come with me to meet Kotchman tonight, then you'll know everything there is to know about tomorrow night."

"I would like to go, if you don't think I'll be in the way."

"In the way? Hell no. You're my partner, aren't you? We'll have some lunch, then we'll go to the meeting. What do you say?"

"You're the boss, DeLucca. I'm with you."

I enjoyed being with Maria. Even though she had a lot of doubts about this whole operation, she seemed genuinely concerned about my safety and made no bones about it. If she only knew the kind of danger we were all in, then she'd really want out. I had already gotten in too deep. There was no turning back for me, but I really wanted to keep her out of it from here on.

It was going to be hard for me to explain my feelings to Maria, but I had to make her understand.

"Maria. I can't back out now, especially after I asked those boys at the opera to help me. I can't do anything else but see it through. Maybe you better not come with me to meet Kotchman. I think the less you know about this, the better off you'll be. I know you're concerned about me and that goes both ways. You're very special to me and I want to keep you safe."

"That's sweet of you Delucca, but you're not getting rid of me that easy. I'm starving. When do we eat?"

The afternoon passed quickly. We had Campari's and crab at Fisherman's Wharf. Then we walked along the wharf breathing in all of the sights. Before I knew it, the sun was setting, and it was nearing the time for the meeting with Kotchman. Maria said she would drive me back to my car afterwards, so I left the Volkswagen parked in the lot at the Wharf.

When we arrived at the butcher shop. Shoiket unlocked the door and let us in. He gave Maria a strange look, then led us to the back room.

Kotchman sat at the table smoking a cigarette. He looked up at Maria. "So, DeLucca. Now you have three arms, instead of one. This must be Maria."

The wiseass didn't deserve a formal introduction, but I made the effort anyway. "This is the Nazi hunter I told you about. None other than Wolf Kotchman, and this..." I pointed to the butcher. "is his right-hand man, Abe Shoiket. Gentlemen, meet my partner, Maria Martinelli."

Kotchman stared at me with his penetrating eyes, removed the cigarette from his mouth and said in a cutting tone, "We have work to do. I assume you have something to report." The little bastard always kept the upper hand.

"Yes, I do." I thought I'd let him sweat a bit before I gave him the information.

He became impatient. "Well! I'm waiting. What did you find out?"

I pulled out two chairs from the table and Maria and I sat down. I leaned back and waited another ten seconds before I spoke. "Maria was able to get the rehearsal schedule for the next four days. We figured tomorrow night would be the best time to hijack the Germans."

Kotchman abruptly crushed his cigarette out in the ashtray. "You said we. Are you forgetting I am in charge of this operation, and I will make all of the final decisions?"

"I am aware of that, Wolf. Do you want me to continue or not?"

"Very well. Proceed."

"All right. Now, the elevator maintenance man is willing to help us, providing he's kept anonymous because he doesn't want to jeopardize his civil service job. The scenic crew will be ready to help us in any way they can. Maria tells me that Hessler and his bodyguards usually go up to the office after the rehearsals, then in about ten minutes, they take the elevator down to the stage level and leave the building. The plan is to stop the elevator between floors and drop tear gas into the car from the over-head trap door. After a minute or two, the elevator will continue on to the stage. That's where we put them into a hamper and roll them out to the truck. Then, it's on to the pier."

"What truck, DeLucca?"

"The guys at the opera will let us use their truck. It has a lift gate, so it will be easy to put the men inside. That's about all there is to it."

"Not quite, DeLucca. What makes you think that a group of amateurs could successfully carry out such an operation?"

He was starting to make me angry. "They're not amateurs. With time running out and your reluctance to call in professional help, I would have thought you would be thankful for all the assistance you could get. Those guys could be putting their lives on the line. Stop bitching about the help and let's get the show on the road."

"Very colorful, DeLucca. Obviously something you picked up at the opera, but this is not a show. It is the real thing, and I must be sure of every detail before I will agree to follow this plan." He faced Maria. "I'd like to see the rehearsal schedule." She looked at me, I nodded, and she opened the folder and handed it to him. He studied it as he lit another cigarette. "I can see why you thought tomorrow night would be best. It appears that it is the only night, other than the final dress. Was there a particular reason for selecting tomorrow instead of Friday?" He addressed his question to Maria.

"Yes. The final dress rehearsals are long drawn-out affairs. A lot of people gather backstage, and they always stay late, but the first dress is usually a closed rehearsal."

"What does that mean?"

"It means there are no invited guests. It lets out early and the theatre empties out fast."

Kotchman continued to question Maria. "Do you know for a fact that Hessler always goes up to his office after the rehearsals?"

"That's been the case every time I've been there."

"How do we know there won't be any other people in the elevator?"

"There is only one secretary left in the office and she stays late typing up the notes and changes for the next day."

Kotchman seemed satisfied with the answer. He turned to me. "How is the elevator stopped in between floors?"

"A switch will be set up at the stage door to connect with a signal light in the basement. When the elevator starts to come down, the doorman will flip the switch to let the maintenance man waiting in the basement know it's time to turn the power off to stop the elevator between floors. After the tear gas is dropped, we wait a minute or two, then signal again for the power to be turned back on to let the elevator drop to the stage level."

I could tell that Kotchman was trying to find a flaw in the plan. "How does the doorman know when to signal for the power shut off?"

The elevator call-buttons light up when the elevator is in use. When the down button lights up, we'll know they're coming down."

"That's not good enough, DeLucca. We might know the elevator is coming down, but do we know who is in it? No! We must have someone call from the office the moment Hessler and his bodyguards enter the elevator."

I had to admit that Kotchman had a point. We couldn't take the chance that someone other than Hessler might be in the elevator when the tear gas was dropped. "For once we agree, Wolf. Let's see, how do we go about this?"

Maria was quick to find a solution. "I could do it. After the rehearsal, I'll say that I have to pick up some of my things from the office. I'll wait until I see them leave their office and start for the elevator, then I'll call the stage door. It could be done in a matter of seconds."

Kotchman leaned forward and said, "Now, we're getting somewhere. Next, the tear gas. Abe will handle that part of the operation."

"Wait a minute, Wolf. I checked out the over-head trap in the elevator and Abe could never fit through that opening. I've already got a man for that job. I figured you and Abe would be waiting in the truck to take them away."

"Who is this man that you have selected?"

"His name is Doyle. He's volunteered to ride on top of the car and drop the gas."

"Very well. I suppose we will have to use this man Doyle and hope for the best." He crushed out the stub of his cigarette and reached for another. Abe struck a match and lit it. "Now, after the tear gas is dropped inside the car and the elevator stops at the stage, then what?"

"Then we lift the bodies into the clothes hamper and roll it out to the truck."

"You are overlooking a few important details, DeLucca. Abe, how many gas masks do we have?"

"We have four."

"Good. One for the man on top of the car and two for the men at the elevator and one for the doorman. How did you think you would be able to go into that elevator without masks, DeLucca? Another thing, Abe. We may need chloroform. We have no idea what effect the tear gas will have on each German. They may have to be rendered unconscious before loading them into the hamper. We will also need three pairs of handcuffs."

Abe nodded. "We have the handcuffs."

Kotchman stood up and started to pace the floor. "If it is to be tomorrow night, I must insist that we have a briefing at the opera house. Possibly a run through. Without it, this could be a disaster. Do we agree on that point?"

"No question about that, Wolf. I took the liberty to call all of the team to meet at 10:30 tomorrow night up on the paint bridge. We can assign duties and run through the whole operation. Does that meet with your approval?"

"It does. After we load the Nazis into the truck, Abe will drive it to the pier. One man will be with him, and I will take a man with me in my car. Once we have them locked up securely, the two extra men will drive the truck back to the opera. Hessler and his comrades will be under constant guard, until it's time to move them to the freight yards. Are there any questions?"

I wondered where I was to fit into the last phase of the operation. "What did you have planned for me, Wolf?"

"After the lock-up on the pier, your job is finished, DeLucca. I can handle the rest of it."

"What you're saying is that you and Abe are going to guard the prisoners for three days by yourself, without any relief?"

"That is correct. Either Abe or myself will be with them until we get them to Haifa. This time, they will not escape Israeli justice."

"OK. But guarding those three bastards day and night doesn't sound like an easy job."

"I'll worry about that, DeLucca. So, at 10:30 tomorrow night, we meet at the stage door, and you will take me up to talk to the volunteers. I want to meet this man, Doyle. His job must be executed with the utmost timing. Tomorrow morning, Abe and I will go to the pier and prepare the locker for our guests." He walked toward the door, turned, and said, "Until tomorrow night."

Maria and I walked out of the shop to her car. She gave me a hard look and said, "I think you're all mad. And that Kotchman, he gives me the creeps."

"He is a little weird, but I've got an idea he knows what he's doing. Anyway, after tomorrow night, it'll all be over. I want to thank you for all the help you've given me. It made my job a lot easier."

"I have to admit, DeLucca, so far it's been exciting. I hope it all turns out well."

As we drove down to the wharf where my car was parked, I thought about the events leading up to tomorrow night. If it all went as planned, it really would be over, but I had a funny feeling in my gut. I had that feeling before. At Anzio.

We arrived at the wharf, and I got out as Maria pulled her car up behind mine and turned off the engine. We both spoke at the same time then paused.

"I'm sorry. You go ahead." I said.

"No. you were saying?"

"I was going to say that I know a place just two blocks from here that serves the greatest raviolis. It's called the San Remo Cafe. how about keeping an old private eye company?"

I'd love to, DeLucca, but only on one condition."

"What's that?"

"That you let me buy dinner."

"Not on your life. When Detective DeLucca invites a girl out to dinner, he pays."

"Well, then at least let me buy you an after-dinner drink."

"You're on. Let's go. I'm starved."

TWELVE

The San Remo was a typical Italian restaurant with red-and-white checkered tablecloths and half-burned candles stuck to the bottom of saucers. We sat down at a table next to a window overlooking the fishing boats tied up to the dock. I ordered the raviolis and a bottle of Chianti. The flickering candle put a sparkle in Maria's eyes as she looked at me across the table.

"DeLucca. What happens when this case is over?"

"What do you mean?"

"Will I ever see you again?"

"I'm counting on it, Maria. Our relationship doesn't end with this case. I would hire you in a minute if I had a good business, but things haven't been going so well for me. This is the first job I've had in three months, and it'll just barely pay my rent." I thought of Joe Bender and the fact that I hadn't called to let him know what was going on. I knew I had earned my money.

After dinner, Maria insisted on buying me that after-dinner drink. We sat for a long time, each of us trying to read the other's mind. The waitress brought the check. I pulled out my wallet, opened it on the table and to my surprise saw that I had only fourteen dollars. The bill was twenty-eight dollars. After all my big talk about paying for the dinner, I found myself in an embarrassing position.

"Maria. This is really ridiculous, but I don't seem to have enough money to pay the check. I hate to ask, but..."

She took the check and smiled, "Where does it say that a girl can't buy dinner for her fella."

I touched her arm. "Thank you, Maria." Strange, but somehow I felt that I didn't have to make any explanations. It was a comfortable feeling. "Maria, would you like to come over to my place for a cognac, or coffee? We could talk over a few things about tomorrow night. I'm worried about you being up there in the office with Hessler and his two goons. I wish there was another way."

"Don't be silly. I'll be fine. I'll be in another office watching the elevator and they won't even see me. As soon as I see them standing at the elevator doors, I'll call down to the stage door. You are worried about me, aren't you?"

"Yes. I have been ever since that night we were chased down to Chinatown."

"You worry too much. Come on, let's go and have that cognac."

It was 11:00 p.m. when we arrived at my apartment. I parked my car in the stall, while Maria parked hers on the street. I met her at the gate, and we walked up the stairs hand-in-hand. I checked for the toothpick before opening the door. It was still there. We entered the apartment, and I turned on some lights and asked her to sit down while I poured two cognacs. We sat in comfortable silence, sipping our drinks and looking at one another.

Maria broke the silence. "DeLucca. How's your love life?"

"Not so good. How's yours?"

"Nothing to rave about, but maybe…" she paused. "I've been wondering how you wash your back with only one arm?"

"It isn't easy, but I manage."

"I could wash your back for you."

"You could?"

"Yes."

"When?"

"Now, if you like." She stood up. "Do you have a bathtub or a shower?"

"It's a bath with a shower."

"OK. I'll run your water, and you get ready for the best back scrub you've ever had."

She went into the bathroom and turned on the water taps. I sat there for a minute, thinking about Maria washing my back in the tub. Most women were turned off by the missing arm. The skin drawn tight over a stump above the elbow usually discouraged any lovemaking, but Maria was different. I had the feeling that she liked me just as I was. There was no doubt that she aroused me, so I figured I'd take advantage of the good feeling. I went into the bedroom, took off my clothes, and put on my bathrobe.

When I entered the bathroom, she was standing in front of the tub. She smiled and said, "Your bath is ready, sir."

I opened the bathrobe, let it drop to the floor and stepped into the hot water.

"Sit down, DeLucca. I can't wash your back while you're standing."

I lowered myself into the water and leaned forward while she knelt beside the tub and soaked my back with a washcloth. I closed my eyes and tried to relax, as she gently moved the cloth over the surface of my back. She stopped and laid the washcloth over my shoulder. I opened my eyes. She was disrobing. "I'll get my dress all wet doing it this way," she said as she stripped. I wanted to look at her body but kept my eyes straight ahead. I felt her legs touch me as she stepped into the tub. "Do you mind, DeLucca?"

I slid forward so she could sit down close behind me. She soaped the washcloth and began to wash my neck, then she reached under my arm and washed my chest. After a rinsing, her small delicate fingers caressed my arm and shoulders. I felt her shapely body against my back. She leaned forward and kissed my neck. Her arms wrapped around me and held me tight as she continued to kiss me. I lowered myself in the water, turned on my side and reached for her head with my left arm. She gently leaned into my embrace, as her slightly parted lips met mine. I remembered the first kiss she had given me in the car. I had wanted much more, and now her soft lips were mine. She held my head and continued to slowly move her lips over my face, finally covering my mouth with a warm lingering kiss. She started to move her hands over my body. I breathed in the sweet scent of her, as I gently bit the base of her neck. The only sound I heard was the dripping faucet and her breathing. Then she stopped breathing.

Raising her head, she said, "DeLucca! Did you hear that?"

I listened. "No. I didn't hear anything. What was it?"

"I don't know. It sounded like someone was in the apartment."

"Don't worry. It's probably coming from next door." I moved in for another bite then froze hearing a noise coming from the living room.

Chapter ?

I quickly stepped out of the tub, put on my bathrobe, and whispered to Maria, "You were right. There's definitely someone in the apartment. Don't move or make a sound."

Maria was frightened. "DeLucca, be careful."

I opened the bathroom door a crack and noticed all the lights were off. I knew that we had turned on two lights when we came in. My heart started to pound as I moved through the dark hallway into the living room. I made it to the desk, opened the drawer, and slowly removed my .38 revolver. Then I reached for the switch on the desk lamp.

Suddenly, a crushing blow struck me on the back of the neck. I was stunned and fell to the floor, but held on to my revolver. I heard Maria cry out, "DeLucca! What's wrong? Are you all right?"

As I tried to raise myself off the floor, I heard the swish of a knife blade and felt a sharp pain in my right shoulder. Maria ran into the room and turned on the lights as a dark form disappeared through the open front door. I regained my feet and moved toward the doorway, gun in hand. My assailant was gone.

I turned to Maria, "Did you see who it was?"

"No. I didn't. My God, DeLucca! What did he do to you? Look at your shoulder."

I looked at my right shoulder. Blood was soaking through my bathrobe. Maria ran to the bathroom as I inspected the wound. He had cut me good. A deep slash curved across the top of my shoulder. I knew he had been aiming for my neck, but as I was getting up, he struck and missed the mark by a few inches.

Maria quickly wrapped a towel tightly around the wound and brought me my clothes. "There's an emergency clinic about a mile from here." She helped me with my shoes and grabbed her purse. "We better get moving. You're losing a lot of blood."

THIRTEEN

I t took twenty-two stitches to close the wound. A tight bandage was taped over my shoulder. The doctor joked that I was fortunate that I didn't need a sling for the arm, because I didn't have an arm. Under other circumstances, I would have smiled, but I kept thinking that had the knife slash been a little higher, I wouldn't have needed anything.

Maria walked me to the car. I leaned back in the seat as she drove me home. We both knew who had tried to kill me. Maria was angry because I refused to call the police, but I had my reasons. The doctor at the emergency room had doubted my story about slipping in the shower and cutting my shoulder on the broken glass door. I figured if we could get by the next two days, it would all be over.

When we returned to the apartment, it was three in the morning. I sat down in my chair, while Maria made some coffee. My shoulder started to ache, so I took a codeine pill and wondered if the German assassin was confident that he had killed me. If he wasn't, he'd probably be back. I stood up painfully, went to the desk, and got my gun, then I checked to make sure the door was locked.

The telephone rang as Maria walked in with the coffee. We looked at each other with alarm. "Don't answer it, DeLucca." I knew what she was driving at. It could be them calling to confirm the kill. If I answered, they would know they had failed to put me out of the game.

"Maria, you answer the phone and if they ask for me, tell them I can't be reached."

"But, DeLucca. Don't you think...?"

"Please, Maria. Do it."

On the seventh ring, Maria answered the phone. "Yes?" After a moment she held her hand over the receiver and whispered, "It's Wolf Kotchman. He wants to talk to you...says it's urgent."

I took the phone. "Hello, Wolf. What's the emergency?"

"They're on to us. Somehow they know we are planning something. Shoiket's shop and apartment have been burned to the ground. All the files have been destroyed and Abe barely escaped with his life. It was no accident."

"I guess they've been busy tonight, Wolf. They tried to kill me right here in the apartment a few hours ago. I just came back from the hospital."

"How badly are you hurt?"

"I'll live...a knife slash on the shoulder. Don't worry, Wolf. I'll be there tonight."

"I'm very sorry about this, DeLucca, but remember what I said about the hunters becoming the hunted. The sharks are on the prowl, so watch out. They know we are planning something and there is only one possibility, Delucca. There's a leak at the opera. Use every precaution. They are capable of anything. I will see you tonight at 10:30." He hung up.

I lowered the phone and tried to fathom what Kotchman had said. "A leak at the opera?" It wasn't possible, unless the unknown person on 2F had heard just enough to tip off his or her friends.

I went to the couch and sat down. Maria cuddled up beside me, and put her head on my chest. "DeLucca, I'm frightened."

I wanted to tell her that I was frightened too, but instead, I hugged her close and tried to console her. "Don't worry. Everything will be all right." Just before I fell asleep, I could see the dawn light filtering through the drapes.

Strange dreams and the pain in my shoulder jolted me awake. I was lying alone on the couch now with a blanket over me and it was 9:30 in the morning. I had slept about five hours. I carefully raised myself to a sitting position and lit up a cigarette. I wondered where Maria was. A note on the coffee table that said she had gone home to clean up and change. She would pick me up at 7:30 for dinner, told me to rest and that there was fresh coffee on the stove. A P.S. at the bottom read, "Those Germans sure know how to foul up a good thing."

I was exhausted and my shoulder was throbbing. I needed more sleep. After a cup of coffee and another cigarette, I went into the bedroom, undressed, set the alarm for 6:00P.M. and plopped myself on the bed. In a matter of seconds, I was out.

It was a fitful sleep, filled with the kind of dreams where you never win. The alarm went off and I woke in a dark room. After a quick shower and a shave, I went to the closet and selected my outfit for the night's work: a pair of black slacks, a black turtleneck sweater with the right sleeve cut off, and a gray sport coat. I grabbed my leather shoulder holster hanging in the closet, strapped it on and put the .38 in it, but found the pain in my right shoulder made it impossible to wear. I took it off and tried tucking the gun in my belt. That also felt very uncomfortable. I set the gun down on the coffee table, just as the phone rang.

I immediately picked it up and without thinking, said. "DeLucca." No one answered. I waited but there was still no response, only a loud click. Whoever it was had hung up. I had done the very thing I hadn't wanted to do. I'd let Hessler and his bunch confirm that I was not dead.

The phone rang again. I picked it up and yelled, "All right, you bastards, come on and get me. This time I'll be ready for you."

"DeLucca? Is that you? What's wrong?"

"Maria?"

"Yes, what happened? Are you all right?"

"Yeah. I'm just a little jumpy, that's all. I just had a call and whoever was on the line wouldn't talk. I'm going to get out of here. Maybe you better meet me at Bonito's at seven."

"I'll be there, and DeLucca...be careful, will you?"

I felt I had a right to be overly cautious, after all, they tried to kill me once and what was to prevent them from doing it again? I turned off the lights and left by the fire escape exit stairs which led to the back of the parking garage. Halfway down, I realized I had forgotten my gun. I decided to forget it and started my short walk to Bonito's.

One Martini later, Maria arrived. She approached the table smiling. "DeLucca, you look nice. You must have gotten some sleep, but should you be drinking?"

"A couple of Martini's are a hell of a lot better pain killer than those pills the doctor gave me. Sit down, beautiful, and we'll have some dinner."

"You think I'm beautiful?

"I sure do."

"A girl likes to hear that now and again." She slipped into her chair and reached for my hand. "DeLucca, I'll be so glad when this is over."

The dinner was a quiet affair. We both ate very little. What we were about to attempt tonight weighed heavily on both of our minds. I wondered how the boys at the opera were holding up. Kotchman and Shoiket were old hands at this kind of thing, but for the rest of us all this was like something out of a James Bond novel. I kept looking at my watch. Time was going too slowly, and I'd had my fill of coffee.

Our conversation lapsed into silence and Maria gazed at me sadly. I glanced again at the time and said, "Well, I guess we might as well get this over with. Where did you park your car?"

"In the parking lot. Is it time to go?"

"Yeah, by the time we drive to the opera house it'll be about 10:30. Shall we?"

FOURTEEN

We pulled up to the stage door a little after ten. Maria parked the car, then we went into the building. Al greeted us at the door and said that all of the guys were up on 1F. He would wait for Kotchman and bring him up when he arrived.

As we stepped out on 1F, I could hear music echoing up from the stage below. All of the guys were sitting around the table. Big Jer stood up, gave Maria his chair, and said, "We're all set, Vince. The rehearsal has got about another hour to go."

I looked into the faces of the eager volunteers. "I might as well tell you what happened last night. The Germans are getting restless. They burned out Shoiket's shop and apartment. They also attacked me at my apartment. Damn near put me out of business. They're nervous and dangerous. They must have been tipped off, possibly by whoever was up on 2F yesterday. I don't know how much they heard, but it was enough to make Hessler realize that they'd been identified."

"We're still going through with it, though, aren't we, Vince?" asked Doyle with nervous anticipation.

"I suppose. It's up to Kotchman."

"It would be a shame to back out now," said Bruno. "We've got the truck ready and the clothes hamper is sitting next to the stage door."

"The signal light is set up," added Irv. "We're ready."

"Hey, Vince, when does this guy Kotchman get here?" asked Doyle.

"He should be here any time now. He wants to double-check again on the operation and possibly have us stage a rehearsal of our own." We could hear the elevator start down as it was called to the stage floor, then a few seconds later, it started up again. We all waited in silence. The elevator doors opened and out stepped Wolf Kotchman with Abe Shoiket who was carrying a bag slung over his shoulder. They were followed by Al, the doorman.

Al looked perturbed, "Say, Vince. I thought this guy's name was Fagoni. I didn't know he was the Israeli."

Kotchman stood in front of the table looking down at the group. The scowl on his face remained, as he said in a sharp rasping voice, "So, DeLucca. These are your volunteers. I expect that you've told them exactly what we're up against."

I stepped up next to Kotchman and said with confidence, "We're ready to do the job. Let me introduce you."

"Never mind the introductions. Time is short." He looked at his watch. "Exactly when will the rehearsal be over?"

Big Jer said, "In about forty minutes."

"All right, let's make those forty minutes count." Wolf's small piercing eyes scanned the group sitting at the table. "First, I want to know who the elevator engineer is."

Irv raised his hand. "I am."

"What is your name?"

"Irv."

"Very well, Irv. I am told that the main power source for the elevator is in the basement. Is that correct?"

"Yes."

"Have you set up a signal light to the stage door and have you checked to see that it works?"

Irv looked over at me with an expression of dismay, then answered Kotchman. " It's set up and it works."

Kotchman turned to Al. "I assume you are the stage doorman. What is your name?"

"Al Ferrigno."

"You will be standing by the stage door the entire time and will relay the signal to Irv on the main power. You will wear a gas mask. Any questions?"

"No questions. I know what to do."

"Remember, Al, there can be no delay with the signal. DeLucca will give you a warning to stand by, then he will give you a go. It must be timed perfectly." He turned toward me. "DeLucca, you will be at the stage door and time your signal so that the elevator stops in between floors, then you will wait thirty seconds before signaling for the power to be turned on. Is that clear?"

"It's clear enough, Wolf. Go on."

Kotchman lit a cigarette and threw the match on the floor. His eyes turned to Maria. "You will be in the office, close to the elevator, and call to the stage door when Hessler and his men are about to descend to the stage level. Are there any problems that might arise?"

Her eyes sparkled as she said, "No problems that I can foresee."

"Good. Now, where is this fellow, Doyle?"

Doyle stood up. "That's me, captain."

Kotchman studied Doyle, then stomped his cigarette out on the floor next to the discarded match and said, "Your part in this operation is very important. Have you ever used tear gas before?"

"No, I haven't, but it can't be much different than handling grenades."

Kotchman turned to Shoiket. "Open the bag and give me a tear gas bomb." Shoiket handed him one and Kotchman immediately threw it to Doyle.

Though surprised, Doyle caught and inspected it. "Jesus! I've never seen anything like this. When did they use these? In World War One?"

Kotchman took the canister from Doyle and handed it back to Shoiket. "It's old, but will do the job. Abe, show him how to use it." Once Abe finished demonstrating how to activate the canister, Kotchman spoke again. "Good. Now, let us go over your part, Doyle. You will wear a gas mask and travel on top of the elevator car. After the car is on the office level, you will wait until it starts to go down. When it stops between floors, you open the trap door, drop the gas canister into the car, close the door then wait until the elevator starts up again and continues down to the stage floor. Is that clear?"

"No problem, Captain. It'll come off like clockwork."

I could tell that Kotchman had his doubts about Doyle as well as the rest of us. Big Jer sat back and calmly took it all in. He seemed amused by Kotchman and his friend Shoiket.

Kotchman lit another cigarette and continued on with the plan. "DeLucca. I have made a few changes. I want Abe to be with you at the stage door. He will have the handcuffs and the chloroform if its needed. There are only four gas masks. One for Doyle, Al, Abe and...we'll need one more man." He looked over at Big Jer. "You, you will wear a gas mask and help transfer the cargo from the elevator to the truck. Then I will need two of you to assist in unloading the truck." He looked at Phil. "What is your name?"

"Phil Cohen."

"Shalom." Kotchman turned to Bruno. "And you?"

"Bruno Guffanti."

"Good. Both of you will come with me to the pier to unload." He looked at his watch. "We have just enough time left now for Doyle to climb up on top of the elevator car to familiarize himself with the surroundings. Make sure everyone is ready at his post in plenty of time. We can't have delays. Are we all agreed?"

No one spoke as Shoiket laid his bag on the table and pulled out four gas masks and three pairs of handcuffs. Doyle carried a ladder into the elevator, put on his gas mask, climbed up through the trap, and positioned himself over the door, staying clear of the cables. Jer and Al tried on their masks and adjusted the straps to fit. It seemed everyone was ready. Now it was just a waiting game until the rehearsal ended.

Kotchman sat back in silence, smoking a cigarette. Occasionally, he looked at his watch, then looked over at me with a frown as if I had something to do with time passing too slowly.

Al stood up. "Well, I guess I'd better get down to the stage door." Irv joined him in the elevator.

Kotchman snapped, "Al, you forgot your gas mask! And remember to call us as soon as you see Hessler going up to the office in the elevator." Abe threw Al his mask just before the elevator doors closed.

Tension was high. Phil shuffled a deck of cards and asked, "Want to play some blackjack while we're waiting?"

"Hell no!" barked Bruno. "Cards? At a time like this?"

Phil shrugged and Doyle fumbled with his gas mask. "Christ! When the hell is this damn rehearsal going to be over?"

Big Jer glanced at his watch. "Another ten minutes at least. Calm down, Doyle."

"I am calm. It's just that these German operas never seem to end."

The music finally swelled to the last act crescendo. Kotchman stood up, sensing the finale was near. "We wait here until Al calls from the stage door."

The orchestra thundered as the curtain came down. We could tell by the activity on stage that the stage crew were starting to leave the theatre. We waited impatiently for another fifteen minutes.

Doyle paced nervously. "Jesus! Why doesn't Al call? Maybe the krauts aren't going to take the elevator this time."

At that very moment the red elevator call button lit up and the house phone rang. Bruno answered, listened a few seconds, hung up, and returned to the table excited. "That was Al. He said that Hessler and his bodyguards are waiting for the elevator right now and the backstage area is just about empty."

I looked at Maria. "You were right. All three of them are going up to the office. Looks like we lucked out."

Kotchman ground out his cigarette on the floor and stared at the light on the call button. "It's time we go to our posts. As soon as the light goes off, call the elevator up here, and Doyle will position himself on top of the car. Maria, go to the office now and stand by to alert us. After Doyle is ready, the rest of us will take the stairs down to the stage. Bruno, you and Phil get the truck ready. Park it in front of the stage door. Remember, DeLucca, the timing for everything must be exactly right. We only have one chance and if it's not properly timed, we will fail."

Maria reached for my hand and whispered, "Be careful, DeLucca."

FIFTEEN

We followed the plan and after Doyle was situated on top of the elevator car, we all left the paint bridge by way of the stairs, and took up our positions. Kotchman, Bruno and Phil waited in the driveway in front of the stage door. The back doors of the truck were open with the lift gate down. Al remained in his booth at the stage entrance, while Big Jer, Shoiket and I waited by the elevator.

Jer touched my shoulder. "Vince, I sure hope Doyle is holding out okay on top of the elevator. It's been a long wait."

"Yeah, it's been a while, but they should be coming down soon."

At that moment, the stage door house phone rang. Al quickly picked it up and listened. Three seconds later he hung up and leaned out of his booth. "Vince! That was Maria. She said the secretary finished her typing and is coming down now. Hessler and his boys are still in the office."

I said to Big Jer and Shoiket, "Let's get out of sight. The secretary is coming down." We moved just inside the door that led to the stage and waited.

Shoiket was worried. "I hope this fellow Doyle doesn't drop the gas on the secretary."

"He won't," Jer assured him. "He knows he's got to wait until the elevator stops in between floors."

I pushed the door open a crack and watched the elevator. The down light went on and seconds later the doors opened and the secretary appeared. She said goodnight to Al and went out the stage door leaving the scent of her strong perfume behind.

We waited another agonizing fifteen minutes. Then the stage phone rang and Al received the message. "Vince! Maria says they're ready to come down, but only two of them. Hessler and the big one."

I relayed the message to Jer. "Damn it! Only two of them are coming down. You and Shoiket, put on your gas masks and bring the clothes hamper up next to the doors."

The elevator went up to the office level and stopped between floors. Moments later, it started again on its way down. I held up my hand and three seconds later, I dropped it. Al flipped the switch on the signal light and the elevator abruptly stopped, trapped between floors. A moment later we heard the tear gas canister hit the floor of the car. I checked my watch, waited another thirty seconds then signaled Al. He flipped the switch again and the elevator continued descending to the stage level where we were waiting. White smoke and gas fumes poured out from under the doors. Protected by his mask, Big Jer pulled open the elevator doors. Face down on the floor Hessler was coughing and trying to cover his face with his coat. Gunther Mueller was holding his eyes with his left hand and butting his large head against the side of the car. In his right hand, he held a German luger. Big Jer rushed forward and handcuffed Hessler's hands behind him, while Shoiket and Al went for the gun wielding Mueller. Al grabbed Mueller's right hand holding the gum and aimed it up in the air as

Shoiket wrapped a chloroformed towel over Mueller's face. Even with the tear gas and the chloroform, the big man still had plenty of fight left in him. Shoiket kept an arm locked around Mueller's neck while Al hung on to Mueller's gun wielding right arm with both hands.

Al yelled, "Jer! I can't hold him!"

Jer moved in fast and tried to dislodge the gun from Mueller's grip. The German seemed to have the strength of three men as he fought bitterly before the chloroform did its job and managed to fire the luger twice. The bullets slammed into the overhead of the car before the big man weakened, dropped his gun and fell to the floor with a thud.

Shoiket handcuffed him as Bruno and Phil came running in. Phil was alarmed, "We heard the gunshots. What happened?"

"Where's Doyle?" asked Bruno.

The gas had started to clear, so big Jer and Al pulled off their gas masks and looked up at the ceiling of the car. There were two splintered bullet holes to the left of the trap door.

"The big bastard got off two shots into the ceiling." said Jer." Bring the ladder."

Bruno placed the ladder below the trap door, and I started to climb up, but then the trap door opened. Doyle pulled off his gas mask and grinned down at us. "Christ! Vince, you didn't tell me the krauts had guns. They damn near hit me."

"Jesus!" said Phil. "Wait until Irv sees his elevator."

"Never mind Irv`s elevator." said Jer. "Are you all right, Doyle?"

"Yeah, they missed me." He climbed down the ladder. "There were only two of them in the elevator. What happened to the other kraut?"

The missing kraut was a problem. I figured he either took the stairs to get the car or was still up in the office. Then I realized Maria should have been back down here from the office by now.

I ran to the stairs and took them two at a time. Two flights up I was on the office level. As soon as I stepped out onto the floor, I knew something was wrong. Hessler's outer office door was open but no one was there. I started down the hallway. From the office across from the elevator, I heard Maria cry out. "No! Stay back."

A snarling voice said, "I'm going to cut you in pieces, you Italian whore."

I rushed into the office and saw Maria and Heitman circling around a desk. Heitman held a gleaming knife in his hand. Automatically, I reached for the .38 in my belt then remembered I had left it at home. I grabbed a chair to crash it down on his back, when Heitman heard me and turned. His mouth curled up into that strange grin of his. He crouched and moved toward me waving the long blade back and forth. I figured that same knife had slashed my shoulder last night. Now, he was going to try to get another piece of me. I held up the oak chair in my left hand, shielding myself as I backed away from Heitman's knife.

Maria stood behind the desk, looking on in horror. Heitman had a crazed look on his face. He slowly inched his way closer, waiting for his chance to slice me up. Maria grabbed the phone on the desk and started to dial. Heitman quickly turned back facing Maria. I swung the chair and hit him on the left shoulder. The chair slipped out of my grip, but Heitman fell sideways against the desk, momentarily stunned. I rushed in, hoping to deliver a knockout blow, but he whirled around. His right hand moved like lightning and the blade ripped my coat, slicing through my sweater. A thin ribbon of blood appeared against my white T-shirt, just above my belt. The sight of my blood caused him to move in fast. I caught his right wrist as he brought it down with a stabbing thrust. He pushed the blade close to my face, pounding my body with his left fist. I had no defense and took the punishment. I knew that no matter what, I had to hang on to his knife hand. Maria came up on his right and struck him on the side of the head with the telephone. He stopped hitting me long enough to slam his left fist into Maria, knocking her to the floor. He turned his attention back to me and grabbed the back of my neck with his left hand as he tried to force the blade into my throat. I knew I couldn't overpower him. I mustered up the last of my strength to twist aside and butted my head into his as hard as I could, hitting the bridge of his nose. I heard the cartilage and bones breaking and his face turned red with blood. He let up enough that I had room to bring my knee up into his groin. He bent over in pain, but still held onto the knife. I kicked him in the shin bone, then kicked his legs out from under him. He fell backwards onto the floor and I stomped on his knife hand to make him release the blade then I kicked it against the wall.

Gasping for air, I stumbled back against the desk trying to support myself. Maria got up off the floor and came to my side. Heitman recovered quickly. He stood up, holding his bloodied nose, and bolted for the door. I didn't have the strength to stop him. Big Jer met him head on and put an arm lock around his neck, while Abe Shoiket handcuffed his hands behind him then roughly led him away.

Big Jer looked at me. "Well, we got all three, Vince. Jesus! What happened in here?"

I sat down on the desk and looked at my ripped coat and sweater. "The guy cut me. I don't think it's that bad."

Maria pulled up the bottom of my sweater. "Let's take a look, DeLucca."

I'd been lucky. The tip of the blade had sliced through my clothes and cut my stomach, no more than an eighth of an inch deep.

"You better see about that cut," said Jer.

Maria pulled on my arm. "I'll drive you over to the emergency clinic."

"No! It's not that bad and I don't feel like trying to explain how it happened. Two nights in a row at the hospital with a wild story would be too much and it might jeopardize the operation."

"What you need is a long rest." said Jer. "It's all over now. The two Israelis are on their way to the pier. Bruno and Phil went with them to help them lock up the krauts. Al is blowing the gas out of the building with a fan, and we'll clean everything up here, so why don't you go home. It's been a successful operation."

Maria held my arm as we started for the door. When we got to the stage door, there were slight traces of the gas. Irv was inspecting the bullet holes inside the elevator. "How did it go, Vince?"

"Just fine, Irv. Sorry about the holes."

"No problem. I'll have them covered up by tomorrow."

Al handed me a brown briefcase. "The big kraut dropped this in the elevator along with his gun. I thought the Israelis would want to look it over."

"Thanks, Al. There might be some papers in there that they would be interested in." I turned to Big Jer. "I want to thank you and all the guys. You did a first-rate job. Without your help it couldn't have been done."

I took Maria's hand. "Let's go home, Maria. I've had it."

On the way home, I leaned back in the seat and closed my eyes. The right side of my body throbbed with pain. My coat and sweater were ripped up and blood had run down onto my pants. I had seen better days.

Maria turned onto Vanness Avenue and headed for North Beach. She glanced over at me. "Oh, DeLucca, you're a mess. I still think we should go to the hospital."

"No. I'll be all right. I just need a little rest. In a couple of days, I'll be as good as new. You know, that's the closest I've come to death since the war. It took the two of us to get out of that scrape alive. I'm proud of you. Are you sure you're all right?"

"Yes, I'm fine, but I don't think I've ever been so frightened. I'm sorry you had to take all that punishment."

"It might have been different if I still had two arms. What do you think the opera people will do when Hessler and his bunch don't show up for the final dress and the Saturday night performance?"

"I really don't know. Nothing like this has ever happened before that I know of. They'll probably call his home, then I suppose they will report them missing to the police. Do you think the police will suspect foul play?"

"Hell. I don't know. That depends."

"On what, DeLucca?"

Well, on a lot of things. First of all, we don't know just how many Nazi sympathizers there are in high places at the opera."

"You can't be serious. Nazi sympathizers at the opera?"

"I don't know, but it's very possible. Maybe this briefcase will provide the answer."

"What are you going to do with it?"

"When I get home, I'll check out the contents. If there's anything important, I'll get it to Kotchman."

"You're not saying that you have to go down to the pier and deliver it?"

"I guess so, unless he contacts me. I don't have any other way of getting in touch with him."

"DeLucca, I know you're not telling me everything. You expect more trouble, don't you? Is this bad dream ever going to end?"

I touched her knee. "Don't worry, Maria. The bad dream is over. Everything will be OK." I looked down at the briefcase and wondered if it really was over.

As soon as we entered the apartment, Maria helped me off with my coat and sweater. Then she inspected the wound on my stomach. "You were lucky, DeLucca. A little deeper and it would have been very bad."

After dressing my wound, she made a pot of coffee, while I sat down in my chair and closed my eyes. This whole thing had taken its toll on me. I was physically and mentally exhausted but not ready to sleep yet with so many questions still unanswered. Kotchman said that I had blundered onto a network of Nazi war criminals. Could there be more of them? Was it possible that people holding high positions in the opera organization would support and protect Nazi war criminals? Who had been listening to our conversation up on 2F? Could there be someone else in Hessler's group, or was I just suffering from a case of nerves? No, I told myself, it couldn't be possible that someone on the board of the War Memorial Trustees would have an alliance with the Nazis.

Maria stood in front of me with two cups of coffee. "Well, DeLucca, are you going to open the briefcase?"

I took one of the cups and took a bracing sip. "Yeah, I might as well get to it." I reached for the case, set it on my lap, flipped the latches and opened it. Inside was a German luger lying on top of stacks of musical scores. The gun smelled of burnt gun powder. I put it on the coffee table and took out the sheets of music. Under the sheet music was a folder containing the opera rehearsal and performance schedule. So far, I saw nothing of interest. On the bottom of the case was a full clip of ammunition for the luger, three monogrammed handkerchiefs with the letters P.B., a black shoe brush and a bottle of aspirin. I ran my hand around the inside of the case but felt nothing else.

"That's it, Maria. Nothing very important. No need for me to go to the pier now. What I really need is sleep."

She leaned down and kissed me. "And sleep, you shall have. I'll call you this evening to see how you're doing."

"Wait! Where are you going?"

"DeLucca, I've got a home to go to and a lot of things to do. My laundry, for instance, and a million other things that I have neglected since joining your combat team." She went to the door, turned to smile at me and said, "Get some sleep, DeLucca. I'll be talking to you soon." I could hear her high heels clicking down the hallway as she headed for the stairs.

Sixteen

I went to the bedroom and plopped myself down on the bed, but sleep wouldn't come. I looked up at the ceiling and thought about the events of the last week. I'd had more than my share of trouble, but I figured that the good had outweighed the bad. I had met Maria. I had survived the attacks by the Germans, lucky to be alive. I had uncovered a bunch of Nazi war criminals, and I'd met a group of great guys at the opera. The one question still bothering me was what happened to Julie Koslo. If she had been killed, why wasn't her body recovered? The briefcase was a disappointment. I'd expected to find secret documents, but the Germans were pros and had managed to elude capture since the war. I supposed they wouldn't be carrying secret documents around in a briefcase. They probably had them locked up in a safe at the rented house. Then there was Kotchman. Why was he so insistent on not informing the authorities? Did he know some reason why the authorities couldn't be trusted to apprehend and prosecute these war criminals, or did he want all the credit for the Israelis?

Once again I closed my eyes, but my mind would not succumb to my tired body. I finally rolled off the bed, went into the living room and opened the drapes to a gray San Francisco dawn.

After a cup of coffee and a pain pill, I started to put the sheet music and the rest of the contents back into the briefcase, all except for the luger. I put that and the clip of ammo in my desk drawer next to my .38. The black shoe brush had fallen on the floor and as I stooped to pick it up, I noticed that the top of it had moved slightly. I pushed on it and the top slid open, revealing a small compartment. Inside, was a small brown address book that fit snugly into the compartment. I took it out and opened it. The pages were filled with German writing. I flipped through it and came upon something I could read: a list of names grouped by cities and states. The places included San Francisco, Chicago, Florida, Wyoming and New Mexico. There was one page dedicated to cities in South America, Mexico, and Canada. It was like taking a page out of a telephone book for any city in the United States. I wondered if the names represented supporters of the Nazis. Or were these war criminals living under assumed names? Either way, this list had to be investigated.

I slid the top closed on the shoe brush, put it back in the case, then closed the case lid, and laid it on the coffee table. As I held the address book in my hand, I began to realize that whoever was in possession of this book was in grave danger. I wanted to hand the ball off to Kotchman as soon as possible. Another thought occurred to me. That I should make a copy of these names and hide it. I had no idea what Kotchman would do with the book, but if anything happened to him or it, at least I would have a copy. I went to the writing desk and started to write down all of the names and addresses from the small book. There must have been over seventy-five names and, in my tired condition, it took me some time. When I finished, I folded the paper several times and tried to think of a safe place to hide it. In the kitchen, I had a bag of coffee beans. I took a cooking pot and poured half of the beans into it, then I placed the folded paper into the middle of the bag and refilled it with the beans from the pot. I resealed the top of the bag and put it in the cabinet under the sink.

I laid my gray pants and coat and a clean shirt on the bed, put the address book in my bathrobe pocket, and went into the bathroom to take a shower and shave. As I stood under the stream of hot water, I remembered the interrupted bath that Maria and I had been enjoying together. She'd said the Germans really knew how to foul things up and she was right. I came out of the shower, toweled off, and started to shave. It was 8:00 in the morning by the time I started to dress.

As I walked out into the living room, I felt a cold draft and saw the front door was wide open. I checked for the briefcase on the coffee table. It was gone. That answered one of my questions. Others were involved. The little brown address book was a time bomb, and I was carrying it. I knew it wouldn't take long for them to discover the book was no longer in the shoe brush. I slipped on my coat, went to the desk, took out the .38 and put it in my belt. I took out the luger and the clip too and dropped them into my coat pocket. This time I would be well prepared.

Sixteen

I hurried down the back stairs of my apartment building to the parking garage and drove toward Pier 29 at the Embarcadero.

On the way, I had the feeling that I was being followed, but I couldn't tell for sure. The traffic was heavy, and I kept an eye out for a black Buick sedan. I passed Pier 29 and kept on going. Making sure no one was on my tail, I made a U-turn, doubled back, and parked in front of Pier 31. I sat in the car and suspiciously surveyed the passing cars. I hadn't thought of how I would make contact with Kotchman. He said there was a locked gate and at the end of the pier a storehouse. I had no way to call him, but I had to get through that gate. I started the engine and drove forward until I was beside Pier 29. I saw the gate to the left of the pier entrance. It was about eight feet high and locked with a chain and padlock. I could see the pier stretching out into the fog and at the end of it thee small storehouse where Kotchman was holding his prisoners. I reached into my inside coat pocket and felt the address book. I also felt the rapid beating of my heart. I had to do something soon. Directly across the street was a coffee shop, so I made a U-turn, parked the car in front of it and went inside. I had to think this thing out. The damn book made me a target and I needed to get rid of it. From the coffee shop, I could see the gate across the street. I waited and watched then saw someone on the pier walking toward the gate. It was Abe Shoiket. I ran out of the coffee shop and crossed the street as Shoiket was unlocking the gate.

He looked up and saw me as I stepped up to the gate. "What are you doing here?"

"I've got to see Kotchman, right away."

"Why? Your job is finished. We can handle the rest of it."

"I'm sure you can, but I've come across some information that he must know about."

Shoiket undid the chain and opened the gate. "What information? We know all we have to know. You put us in danger coming here."

I was just about to blow my stack when he said, "Come in. Tap four times on the metal door. Wolf will let you in. I will be back as soon as I go get food for the pigs." He let me through then went out the gate, closed it, and locked it.

I started down the pier toward the end thinking Kotchman had found a perfect place to hide his prisoners. There was no one around but the sea gulls. From somewhere off in the bay I could hear the bellow of the fog horns. I could see now why the pier had been condemned. Some of the deck planks were missing and I could see through the gaps where the dark water lapping against the pitched pilings below. The safety rail was collapsing in places and one could easily have fallen into the murky water below.

As I approached the store house, I saw a small door to the right of a dented metal roll curtain. I tapped on it four times.

Kotchman's voice inside growled, "Did you forget something, Abe?"

I answered, "It's DeLucca! I've got to see you. It's important."

The lock on the door clicked and the nozzle of a beretta along with Kotchman's angry face appeared in the open crack. "It's not good, DeLucca. You coming here. What's so important that you have to see me?"

He kept the door narrowly ajar and stared at me through the opening. His eyes were bloodshot, and his face looked more gaunt than usual.

"Open the door and let me in and I'll tell you what's so important."

The hinges creaked as he let me step inside. He quickly closed the door and locked it again before he faced me and snarled, "Are you sure you weren't followed?"

"I was careful. No one followed me."

I looked around the inside of the store house. The four walls were in shadow. A single light bulb hung from a cord attached to the corrugated steel ceiling. Large coils of cable and turnbuckles were stacked on the plank deck against the walls. Below the light bulb was a small table with two chairs. The floor was littered with cigarette butts and the room had the strong odor of creosote.

"Jesus! What a place. Where do you have the Germans stashed?"

"They are nicely tucked away in the back." He pointed to a small, barred door at the rear of the room. "Now, what is so important that you had to come down here to see me?"

I reached into my inside coat pocket. "I found this address book hidden in the top of a shoe brush. It was in the briefcase the big one dropped in the elevator. Most of it is in German, except for the names and addresses of people living here in the U.S." I handed the book to Kotchman. "Do you read German?"

He opened the book. "Certainly, I read German." He carefully pondered the first page, then turned it over and continued to read each of the following pages.

"What does it say, Wolf?"

"One moment, let me finish." His face took on a look of disbelief as he continued to turn the pages. Finally, he looked up and said, "The list, DeLucca. You have found the list."

"How important is it?" I asked.

"Important! This book contains the names of all the remaining war criminals and also the sympathizers that help support them. If they knew we had it, our lives would be worth nothing. They would hound us to our graves." He leaned close to me and whispered, "Who else knows about this list?"

"I don't know, Wolf. I put the book in the pocket of my bathrobe. After I took a shower, I came out and someone had broken into my apartment and taken the briefcase."

Kotchman stared vacantly at the floor. "Then they know you have the book. Who knew that you had the briefcase?"

"Only the boys that helped us. Al gave it to me, and I guess the rest of them knew I had it. That's all."

Kotchman rubbed his chin. "Aren't you forgetting someone?"

"Who?"

"The girl, Maria."

"You can't be serious, Wolf. Are you suggesting that Maria tipped off the krauts?"

Kotchman stood up. "Someone did. It's obvious there is a leak at the opera house. They know you have the book, and you led them right to me. We've got trouble, DeLucca."

"Listen, Wolf. I'm sure I wasn't followed here. By the time whoever took the briefcase found out the book was gone, I was already on my way here to the pier. They couldn't have followed me."

"I would like to believe that, DeLucca. If it's true, they have no idea where we are, but as soon as you surface, they'll be on you like a swarm of angry bees. We don't know exactly how many allies Hessler has, but we do know they will sacrifice their lives for the list." He sat down at the table and fingered the pages of the book. "I must get this list to my people in Miami immediately. It's incredible. Every name and contact in the U.S., Canada, Mexico and South America." He looked up at me and said, "I'm afraid you will have to stay under cover until this affair is over. It is too dangerous for you to go home. By now, they must be frantically searching for you. There is a strong possibility that they are also looking for your girlfriend, Maria, too. If they find either of you, they will make you tell them where I am holding their comrades. You must contact Maria and tell her to find some place to hide. She knows too much. Once I expose the list to my people and I have Hessler on the freight heading for Galveston, only then, can any of us relax."

I sat down and tried to understand the implications of my involvement with the damn list. Kotchman kept talking about "they." If *they* find you. If *they* knew you had the list. *They...* who the hell are *'they'*?

"Wolf, take a look at the list and see how many names are under San Francisco?"

Kotchman turned the pages. "Here it is. Three names: Woodmond S. Chambers, an architect. He lives in North Point, Roger P. Cullen, in Hillsdale, he's an attorney, and Morton W. Townsend, a banker who lives in Saint Francis Woods."

"I've heard that name before. Wolf, I think that Townsend guy is on the Board of Trustees at the opera. I remember seeing the name on the letterhead of some papers Maria took from the office."

"There you have it, DeLucca. Nazis. Right here in your own territory. People with influence and power. Don't you remember, I told you that you had stumbled on a network of Nazis?"

"Yeah, but if I remember correctly, the word you used was blundered."

I started to worry about Maria. If what Kotchman said was true, she could be in danger. I'd have to call her, but what would I say? That she had to hide from a bunch of Nazis who wanted to torture her into revealing the whereabouts of a brown book? Hell, she didn't even know about the book. But she did know where Kotchman was holding the Germans. I was sorry that I had involved her so deeply in the operation, but she had insisted on knowing all about it. I needed to talk to her, and soon.

Kotchman and I both jumped as we heard four taps on the metal roll curtain. Kotchman stood up. "That's Abe with the food." He picked up his gun and went to the door. "Abe?"

"Yes. It's me."

Kotchman unlocked the door and opened it. Shoiket came in carrying a large shopping bag and set it on the table.

Kotchman re-locked the door and said, "Abe, DeLucca has brought us the list. He found it in the German's briefcase. We now have the upper hand."

Shoiket didn't seem impressed. He looked at me and said, "That's all the more reason for DeLucca to move his car from across the street."

Kotchman's eyes narrowed. "What? You parked your car right across from this pier? If they see it, you've given away our hiding place."

I had the feeling now that I should have given the damn book to the F.B.I. seeing as I was still a target with or without the book. Maria was my first and only concern now so I stood up and started for the door.

"Before you go, DeLucca, I want you to see my captives." Kotchman pointed to the shed door. "Open it up, Abe."

Shoiket went to the door, unbarred it, pushed it open and stepped aside. I followed Kotchman as he moved into the small room, about eight by ten. The walls were of corrugated tin, bolted to steel I-beam framing. On the floor, a chalk line was marked in a semi-circle in front of three army mattresses. Sitting on the floor were Hessler, Heitman and Gunther Mueller. Their right hands were handcuffed to a chain that was wrapped securely around an I-beam on the wall. This enabled them to stand up and move around with one hand left free to reach just within the chalk line on the floor. They looked like three Buddhas in dark suits sitting cross legged on their mattress thrones.

Hessler raised his head defiantly. The big one, Gunther Mueller, looked as if he were going to growl and snap like a mad dog. Heitman sat quietly as though dejected. His face was covered with dried blood from the broken nose I'd given him.

Kotchman extended his hand toward the three Buddhas and said, "You see, DeLucca. Give them a taste of their own medicine and they are lambs waiting for the slaughter, just like the Jews in the camps. At least, we give them a place to sleep with food and water."

Shoiket stepped into the room, glared at Hessler and said, "It's too good for these pigs. If I had my way, it would be different. They would suffer like we did."

Kotchman put a hand on Abe's shoulder. "We must feed them just enough to keep them alive. It wouldn't do to bring back three corpses for trial. Don't worry, my friend. They will receive their punishment in due time."

We started to walk from the room. The chains rattled as Hessler stood up. He clenched his fist and yelled in a piercing voice. "You will pay for this! Just like Koslo, all of you have signed your own death warrant!" Shoiket moved forward quickly and knocked Hessler down. Gunther Mueller made a grab for Shoiket's legs and got soundly kicked in the head. The giant man shook his bald head, raised himself up off the floor and charged Shoiket. Abe stepped back behind the chalk circle beyond the reach of the chain just in time. The room shook as Gunther ran to the end of his chain and was jolted to an abrupt stop. We left the room and Abe barred the door.

Kotchman sat down at the table, looked up at me and said, "It won't be long before we will have three wild beasts and soon they will be tearing at one another. There is nothing like captivity to equalize the general and the private." Kotchman lit up a cigarette and laid his gun on the table. "Hessler still insists that he is not Hessler, but we know he is."

I thought I'd ask a stupid question. "Are you certain, Wolf?"

"We have no doubts at all. Abe has identified him. He would never forget that face and do you remember me telling you about the SS death head tattooed on Hessler's right shoulder? Well, when we first brought him here, we stripped off his shirt and on his right shoulder was a scar, like a burn, showing where the tattoo had been removed." He sat back in the chair and flicked his ashes on the floor. "DeLucca, go now. I wouldn't go back to the apartment, if I were you. That's one place they're sure to be waiting for you." He extended his gnarled hand and said, "Shalom, my friend. Take care of yourself."

Shoiket opened the door and I followed him down the pier to the gate. He unlocked the chain and let me out onto the street. I felt like I was being turned loose in a pool full of hungry sharks. I walked across the street, got into my car and drove off, heading for the freeway that would take me south on the Bayshore. At South City, I turned off and found a telephone booth. Maria was upset when she answered. "DeLucca! Where have you been? I called and called. Were you asleep?"

"No, I wasn't asleep. Listen to me, Maria, and do exactly what I tell you."

"What's wrong?"

"Just listen. Pack a small bag and drive south to Colma. Meet me at Malloy's Bar. It's right across from the cemetery. Can you find it?"

"Yes, but..."

"Please do as I ask, Maria. I'll tell you everything when I see you in about a half an hour."

"You're the boss, but..."

"Just do it, Maria."

SEVENTEEN

A mile from Malloy's, I had the feeling again that I was being followed. A green panel truck had been on my tail for the last two miles. I turned up a side street and pulled to the curb. The panel truck went on by. I turned back onto the freeway and headed for Malloy's.

There were two customers sitting at the bar. I sat down and ordered a double Martini. Halfway through the drink, my hand stopped shaking. I wondered how they learned I had the briefcase. No one but the scenic crew, Irv and Al knew that I had it. There'd been no one else in the building when Maria and I left. Who had entered my apartment and taken the briefcase? Whoever took it also knew that Hessler and his boys had been taken prisoner. Could it be that someone unknown to all of us had been watching the abduction? Maybe they were on the street outside of the stage door. It wouldn't be too hard to put two and two together if they saw the clothes hamper being put into the truck. And what about Heitman? He'd been handcuffed and led into the back of the truck. That could have been the tip off, but then why wasn't the truck followed to the pier? Or was it followed?

The second double did the trick to help me relax. Things didn't seem so severe anymore, and I felt braver, fearless. Maria arrived at 4:20, saw me at the bar and joined me. "DeLucca! What's this all about? Are you okay?'

I smiled and took her hand. "I'm fine. It's you I'm worrying about."

I ordered her an Irish coffee, then I told her everything I knew—all about finding the brown book, taking it to Kotchman, my suspicion of an informer, and the danger we were in.

She sipped her coffee, looked up at me, smiled and said, "So what else is new, DeLucca? Ever since I met you, it's been a whirlwind of danger and intrigue. Is it always this way with you?"

"No, in fact, since the war, I've led a very dull life. I had no idea this thing would develop into a cloak and dagger operation. We're going to have to lie low for a few days."

She toyed with her straw. "Do we lie low together?"

"Preferably together, yes."

"Do you have any idea where, DeLucca? I brought my overnight bag with me."

"I have a friend who owns a weekend cabin on the beach at Princeton. It's just a little south of Rockaway Beach. I'm sure he'll let me use it for a couple of days. I'll call him."

"Have you used this cabin for a secret rendezvous before?"

I slid off the stool. "No. this is a first." She smiled as I went to the telephone.

Jack Calwell owed me a couple favors and agreed to let me use the cabin. The key was under a flat rock to the left of the door.

Maria turned as I approached the bar. "Is it all right?"

"It is. I think it would be best if we took both cars. Think of it as a vacation for two in a nice little villa overlooking the blue Pacific. We'll stay put there until Sunday and enjoy ourselves. By Monday, it will all be over but the shouting."

As we left Malloy's, Maria looked worried. I could tell she didn't believe me when I said it would all be over that soon.

Highway 1 South always had its share of fog in the evening, but this night, the fog was as thick as I'd ever seen it. Maria kept following close behind. My wipers were working overtime but I still couldn't see the white line down the middle of the road. Good, I thought. Nobody could follow us on a night like this. My eyes were tired, and the Martinis had made me drowsy. I realized that I hadn't slept for two days. No wonder I couldn't keep my eyes open. I didn't have any idea where I was so when ahead on the right, a dim orange neon light for a coffee shop appeared out of the fog, I pulled off the road and parked. Maria drove up next to me, clinging to the steering wheel.

She rolled down her window, as I stepped over to her car. "Jesus, DeLucca! Where the hell are you taking me?"

"Not sure. Want some coffee?" She opened her door, grabbed my arm and we headed for the orange light.

The coffee shop was empty. We had a cup and asked the owner where we were. It turned out we were only four miles from Princeton. As we left the coffee shop, the proprietor said good luck. I knew we would need it to find the small dirt road that turned off the main highway toward the beach. By inching along and some miracle, I found the road and forged on ahead. When we stopped, I could hear the surf close by but couldn't see the water. I stepped out into the fog and could see a cabin. Maria joined me.

"Is this the villa overlooking the blue Pacific?"

I had to smile. "It's not exactly the Ritz, is it?"

After finding the key under the rock, we went in and turned on the lights. A compact kitchen adjoined a combination bedroom and living room with a bathroom at the rear.

Maria threw her bag on the bed, turned and looked at me. "You look tired, DeLucca. You haven't slept since I last saw you, have you?"

"No. I'm bushed and my damn shoulder is giving me hell."

"Did you bring your pain pills with you?"

"No. I didn't think I'd need them. Let's see if Jack keeps any booze in the place."

In the kitchen cabinet, I found a half-full bottle of scotch. I grabbed two glasses and went into the bedroom. Maria had pulled back the covers on the bed and started to unpack her bag.

"How about a drink? I found some scotch in the kitchen."

"Why not, DeLucca? What the hell."

I poured, handed one of the glasses to Maria and sat down on the bed. Maria sat next to me, sipped her drink and laughed.

"What's so funny?" I asked.

"A month ago, if someone had told me I'd be sitting on a bed in a cabin on the beach, drinking straight scotch with a one-armed detective after being chased all over San Francisco by Nazi war criminals, I'd say they were nuts." She laughed again. "But here I am." She reached over and ran her fingers through my hair. "Tell me, DeLucca. What makes you so irresistible?"

I finished my scotch, threw the glass on the bed, leaned back and laughed. "I guess it must be my dynamic personality."

She leaned back on the bed laughing. I turned and kissed her. She returned the kiss tenderly and continued to stroke my hair. "You need rest, DeLucca. Let's go to bed. You undress and crawl in and I'll be with you in a minute."

She rose from the bed, picked up her bag and went into the bathroom. I took off my clothes, slipped in between two cold sheets and lay back staring at the ceiling. The sound of the surf soon lulled me into a trance. My eyelids were like lead. I started to float off into a deep sleep. The last thing I remember hearing was the bathroom door opening, the light switch being turned off and my own heavy breathing.

"Good morning, DeLucca."

I smelled salt sea air and heard the sound of heavy surf. I opened my eyes and sitting beside me, wearing a shorty nightgown was Maria. She leaned forward and stroked my temple. "DeLucca, you were fantastic last night."

"I was?"

She kissed me. "Yes, you were."

"I don't remember. What did I do?"

"Nothing. You did absolutely nothing. Poor darling. You were so tired."

I reached over and drew her close to me. "Well. I guess we'll have to do something about that, won't we?"

She wrapped her arms around my neck and murmured my name in between kisses. Her warm body melted into mine as we clung to one another. The steady pulse of the waves beat to the slow rhythmic motion of our bodies.

She raised her head from my chest and asked, "Does it hurt?"

"Does what hurt?"

"Your shoulder, silly."

I bit the nape of her neck and whispered in her ear. "Not a bit."

The scent of her perfume mingled with the sea air, and the surf became louder and louder.

That Saturday tuned out to be the best day I'd ever had. Maria and I walked barefoot along the beach. We picked up a bottle of chilled

Chablis from the local market and sat on the end of the pier eating boiled shrimp dipped in a spicy sauce. The pleasant hours seemed to fly by too fast. We sat in the sand holding hands and watched the sun make its final descent toward the sea. There was no mention of the opera, Kotchman, or the Nazi menace that lurked just outside our Shangri-La.

At dark we walked back to the cabin and prepared to go to dinner at a secluded seafood restaurant out on Rockaway Point. I ordered my usual two Martinis. Maria sipped white wine and we both enjoyed the fresh sea bass. At 10:00 we were still sitting at the table drinking cognac and coffee.

Maria was first to mention the forbidden subject. "Well, DeLucca. It looks like we're missing opening night at the opera."

"That's right, tonight is the opening. I wonder how they got along without their German director."

"I imagine it was a success. Most opening nights are."

"Tell me, Maria. Have you ever been to an opening at the opera?"

Maria sipped her cognac. "Yes. I used to go to all of them."

"I didn't know you were so fond of opera. What is it like?"

She looked off into space, as if recalling a memorable night. "Oh, you wouldn't like it, DeLucca."

"Go on, tell me. Maybe I would."

"Well, it's like Cinderella going to the ball. All glitter and show. Standing ovations and curtain calls. Throngs of people dressed in their finest. Women with their jewels and fancy gowns. The men in tuxedos. Bright lights and champagne parties after the performance. That's about it, DeLucca."

"You're right. I wouldn't like it. Sounds like a big event."

Maria reached over and took my hand. "This is a big event. I enjoyed today more than you know. I wish it would never end." She got up. "I must go to the little girls' room."

All good things must finally come to an end. I couldn't help thinking about Kotchman. Tomorrow by this time, he would be on his way to the train yards with his three prisoners. I wondered how the two of them were going to handle such dangerous men in close quarters. Possibly I should have stayed to help, but he'd insisted that I go. I remembered his words. "Shalom, my friend." There was a finality to his words that disturbed me.

Maria returned, refreshed and smiling. I paid the check, then we walked out to the car and drove back to the cabin on the beach.

All of the fresh sea air and the exercise had made me feel good. My shoulder was starting to heal and I was no longer aggravated by constant pain. I lay back on the bed and waited for Maria to join me. My mind wandered, but as always came back to Kotchman. I wondered what kind of life a man like that would have. No love or family and very few friends. Just a constant dedication to his only cause: seeking out the war criminals and bringing them to justice. What happens to a man like that when there are no war criminals left? Or maybe he figures there'll always be more Nazis to hunt.

Maria slipped in next to me and turned off the bed lamp. "What are you thinking about, DeLucca?"

"Oh, nothing much."

"You were in deep thought. Come on, tell me."

"Well, if you must know. I was thinking about the first time we met. You must have thought I was a real nut. A one-armed guy peeking around the corner of the doorway, giving your lovely legs the once over."

"You were looking at my legs?"

"Yes, I was."

She crept closer to me. "I didn't know you were a leg man."

"Oh yes. I'm a leg man and a breast man and a neck man and a..."

She closed my mouth with a kiss. "DeLucca. You talk too much."

On Sunday morning I woke up alone in bed. The sun was streaming in through the kitchen window, and I smelled bacon cooking. I rolled out of bed and checked the time. It was 9:00 a.m. Through the windows of the living room, I could see Maria out on the sun deck standing over a table while pouring two cups of coffee. I slipped on my pants and joined her.

"Breakfast is served. Come and get it."

The table was set with two plates of bacon and eggs, coffee and toast. "When did you do all of this?"

"While you were still asleep, I drove to the store and picked up a few things. Didn't you think I could cook?"

"No. I mean, yes. What I mean is, I'm surprised. This is great."

"Sit down, DeLucca, and eat. Don't get used to this kind of treatment because I'm really a lousy cook."

After breakfast, I sat back, lit up a cigarette and looked at the rolling ocean in front of us. "This is the life, Maria." She handed me the Sunday Examiner. I filed through it, found the sports page and handed the rest of the paper back to her.

"Just like a man. Give him the sports section and that's all he's interested in. Aren't you even a little bit curious about the opera's opening night?"

"Nope."

She found the theatrical section to scan through it. "I like to see what the rich women wear. Sometimes they—."

I looked up. "Sometimes they what?" Her eyes were wide and her face tense. "What's wrong?"

"DeLucca, look!"

She handed me the paper. There were a lot of pictures of the opening night crowd. "So what?"

"Look at the picture on the bottom right."

I glanced down and was shocked. It was Hessler standing in the center of a group of costumed singers. I read the blurb: 'Paul Berger, renowned German director takes curtain calls to a standing ovation after the opening night performance of Wagner's Flying Dutchman.' I looked back at the picture. He was dressed up like a stuffed turkey and had a smile on his fat face. It was definitely him, Carl Hessler. I looked up, trying to understand. "Maria! What the hell do you make of this? I saw him locked up in chains at the pier Friday afternoon. How could he...unless, somehow he escaped. If that's the case, there might be something about it in the paper." I grabbed the front page and there it was. "Double slaying at the Embarcadero, execution style."

That headline meant one thing to me. Kotchman and Shoiket had both been killed. I started to read the article.

"DeLucca, what is it?"

"Listen to this. 'Saturday at 8:50 a.m. two male bodies were recovered from the bay. One of the men had been brutally murdered, execution style. He was found floating face down, approximately two hundred yards off the end of Pier 29. His hands were handcuffed behind him and he had a bullet hole in his right temple. The body was identified as Abraham Shoiket, the proprietor of a butcher shop in the Twin Peaks area. The second body was found under the pier by workers, shot in the chest by a small caliber firearm. The second body has yet to be identified. The coroner reports that both deaths occurred around noon on Friday. Police Chief George Arnold refused to speculate on whether the two deaths were related. An investigation is in progress.'" I crumpled up the paper and threw it on the floor. "I'll

172

be a son of a bitch! So much for justice. The God damned Nazis killed Shoiket and Kotchman and now they're walking around scot-free. I'd sure like to bust those bastards, but I don't know how to do it."

Maria touched my arm. "Now is the time to go to the police, DeLucca. Let them handle it."

"Maybe you're right. I suppose I could shed a little light on their investigation. I can identify Kotchman's body, and I know who murdered him and Shoiket. I'd have to tell the whole story from the beginning. Do you think they would believe me? Hessler will have an alibi and I have no concrete evidence except my fantastic story about Kotchman hunting Nazis. The fact is, I have no proof to substantiate any of this. Christ! I might be the one thrown in jail because of my accusations. I've got to think this thing out."

"Please, DeLucca. Hand it over to the police. They will believe you. They must."

I leaned back in the chair, lit a cigarette and thought about the copy of the list hidden in my apartment. I seriously wondered if I could be next on the German hit list. I made a decision. "Maria, pack your bag. Our short vacation is over. We're going back to town."

The trip back to the city gave me a chance to sort things out by myself. I suggested to Maria that she drive home, and I would go to the apartment, get cleaned up and go to the police. She wanted to go with me, but I told her I'd rather go alone. She kissed me goodbye and said she would call me tonight.

I knew Maria was right about me telling the police, but I didn't think she fully understood all of the problems involved. She said the police would believe me. I had my doubts. With no evidence or witnesses to back me up, it would be my word against the Germans, but now with Kotchman and Shoiket both dead I had a duty to tell what I knew, no matter the consequences, but my heart wasn't in it. I pulled into the parking garage at the apartment. The cabin on the beach and Maria were long gone and I found myself back in the war zone.

I started up the stairs to my apartment. Unlocking the door, I intended to walk straight to the bar. I needed a drink, but as I entered the living room, I stopped in my tracks. The place looked like a wrecking crew had worked it over. Somehow I wasn't too surprised. The desk drawers were upended on the floor. Papers and books were scattered throughout the room. The bookshelves were tipped over, the couch was turned on its side, and the lining underneath ripped out. I went to the kitchen and found it in the same state as the living room. I looked under the cabinet on the sink. To my relief and amazement; the coffee beans in the bag were untouched. My hiding place for the list had survived the search. I removed the coffee beans, took out the folded piece of paper and put it in my pocket. I figured I might as well have that drink now. Then I heard a sound coming from the bathroom. I never could have imagined that the sound of a flushing toilet could bring cold chills up my spine, but there it was. My toilet was flushing. Someone was still here.

I became furious at the idea that some bastard would break into my home, ransack it like Attila the Hun, and then take a leak in my bathroom. His pissing was really pissing me off.. I figured I'd get this son of a bitch. Reaching for my .38, I remembered I left it in the car, but my right-hand coat pocket was still heavy with the luger and ammo clip. I managed to get it out of my pocket but couldn't cock it with only one arm. I sat down on the kitchen chair and put the gun between my knees, pulled back the hammer and let it slam forward. Now I was ready.

I tiptoed down the hallway to the bathroom door and stood to the side with the luger ready. I heard water running in the sink, then it stopped, and I waited. As the doorknob turned and the bathroom door opened. I gritted my teeth, then I got the shock of my life. Standing in front of me was Wolf Kotchman. I was speechless.

"About time you got home, DeLucca. Got a cigarette?"

"What the hell, Wolf! I thought you were dead."

"I see you read the paper. Please, lower the gun. I'm not the enemy."

Kotchman looked worn and haggard. His bony fingers and thumb of his right hand were sticking out of a plaster cast that covered most of his forearm. "You look like hell, Wolf. I think we could both use a drink."

I set aside the gun, then tipped the couch back to an upright position, poured two cognacs, handed one to Wolf, and sat down. I had a lot of questions to ask. "How long have you been here, Wolf?"

"After Hessler escaped, I came here thinking you still might be in town." He sat next to me and took a gulp of cognac. "This is how I found your apartment at 6:00 p.m. Friday night. I didn't have any place to stay, so I moved in for the next two nights. They must have broken in here after you left for the pier on Friday afternoon. They were looking for the book obviously."

"The book...do you still have it?"

"No. They have it."

"Tell me what happened. How did Hessler escape and what happened to your arm?"

"My arm is broken, DeLucca, but I was lucky, or I would have ended up like poor Abe." Kotchman's hand trembled as he lit a cigarette. "They knew, DeLucca. They knew where we were the whole time. Someone must have followed the truck to the pier Thursday night, or maybe they followed you, I don't know, but they knew everything. They had outside help and I underestimated their cunning."

"When I read about the murders at the pier and the two bodies, I figured one of them was you."

"It would have been but for a stroke of good fortune. After you left the pier Friday afternoon, I told Abe to feed the prisoners and leave the door to the shed open. I sat at the table studying the names on the list. I knew I must pass the list on to the proper people as soon as possible. After a short time, I looked up and noticed that the shed door was closed. I called to Abe, but there was no answer. I heard the movement of chains and whispering coming from the shed. I picked up my gun, went to the door and called again. Still there was no answer. I knew then that my prisoners had forced a compromise. I kicked open the door and there were Hessler and Heitman standing in front of me. Hessler had Abe's gun in his hand. Beside him was Gunther Mueller. He had wrapped his chains around Abe's neck and was strangling him. I had no choice but to try and shoot Hessler, but before I could, someone I didn't see from behind the door knocked the gun out of my hand with an iron pipe."

"Where the hell did the fourth person come from?"

Kotchman chain lit another cigarette. "I knew immediately. It was no mystery. Under the mattresses there is a trap door in the floor and a wooden ladder that leads down to the water. I should have been more cautious and sealed it. Evidently, Hessler's allies came by boat."

"Are you saying they escaped in a boat under the pier?"

"That is correct. Mueller dropped Abe to the floor unconscious. While Hessler had his gun on me, Mueller took the keys from Abe, unlocked the handcuffs attached to the chains and handcuffed Abe's hands behind him, then Mueller went into the other room and took the book I had left on the table. The fourth man opened the trap door and climbed down the ladder to a waiting boat. Hessler continued to watch m, as Mueller pulled down a rope attached to a pulley on the ceiling and tied it around Abe and lowered him down to the boat, then Mueller followed down the ladder. Hessler handed the gun to Heitman and followed Mueller through the trap door. As his head reached floor level, he looked up at Heitman and told him to kill me, then dump my body in the bay and meet him at the house after. Hessler continued on down the ladder and I heard the outboard motor start and the boat move off from the pier."

Kotchman paused, reached for another cigarette and lit it.

I grew impatient. "What happened next, Wolf?"

He took a deep drag on the cigarette and continued with his story. "Heitman held the gun on me. My beretta was on the floor, only a short distance away. I took a chance and dove for it. Heitman pulled the trigger, but he had forgotten to put a shell into the chamber. He panicked and while he was frantically working at the automatic, I fired a shot and hit him in the chest. He staggered back and fell down the trap into the water. I suspected that they had killed Abe, but I wasn't sure until I read the morning paper. He was a good man, but careless. He let his hatred overrule his caution. Now I am back where I started. Only now, I know what I'm up against."

"What you're up against? You're still going to try and capture Hessler?"

"I've made a commitment, DeLucca. I can't quit now."

"But how? It seems hopeless. Why not come with me to the police and tell the story. They'll hold Hessler and investigate the whole thing."

"It's too late."

"What do you mean, it's too late?"

"Hessler is gone."

"How do you know?"

"Never mind how I know. After the opening night performance, he and Mueller cleaned out their office and moved out of their house by the beach."

"When did you find out all of this? You must have been asking a lot of questions at the opera."

"I found out late last night, but this morning I came across an interesting piece of information concerning Hessler. He booked a flight to Chicago which leaves the San Francisco Airport at 4:20 this evening. The reservation is for three. Paul Berger, Otto Kurtz and a woman, Miss Rosalinda Chapman."

"A woman? That's strange. I wonder how the woman fits into this. Could it be his secretary?"

"I doubt it, but it's possible. Now for the plan."

"What plan? Hessler has disappeared and you think he's booked a flight to Chicago. You lost your man Shoiket, the only witness, and you have no documents to prove your claims. What the hell can you do now, highjack the plane? Let's face it, Wolf. You need outside help. Why don't we leave it with the authorities and see if they will do something. Frankly, I've run out of steam."

Kotchman ground out his cigarette in the ash tray and stood up. His next words were harsh. "It's what I expected to hear, but I hoped I was wrong. Here you are, a battle-hardened veteran, who lost an arm to the Germans. You've been chased, stabbed, threatened and had your home violated but when the going gets rough, you're like all Americans. You run out of steam."

He had touched a nerve which was exactly what he'd wanted to do. "Hold it a goddamn minute, Wolf. Ever since you came into my life, you have depended on the assistance of Americans. Those guys risked their lives to help you. You're the one who let the krauts escape, not the Americans. And I'll set you straight on another thing. Americans don't run out of steam when things get rough. That's when they really get going and don't you forget it." I surprised myself by becoming so angry. Once again I was playing right into his hands.

Kotchman's face broke into a smile and he said amiably, "Now that's better, DeLucca. Once more, we understand one another. So, let's put our heads together and find a way. Don't forget the ship leaves Galveston at 6:00 a.m., Thursday the twenty-second, and I intend to be on it with Hessler."

I leaned back, took a swig of cognac and shook my head. "You're impossible, Wolf."

"I know. Impossible people do impossible things. Nothing can be gained without risk, and believe me, DeLucca, everything is possible."

"All right, Wolf. Let's look at the information we have. The only thing we know is that Hessler has booked a flight to Chicago and it leaves in..." I looked at my watch. "...forty minutes. First, we should call and see if the reservations are confirmed, and then... I don't know what the hell you're going to do but at least we'll know where he is."

Kotchman lit a cigarette and paced the room. "It's possible this flight to Chicago is only a pretense to throw us off of his trail. If that's the case, he's somewhere in the city hiding until he thinks it's safe to travel. Call the airline, DeLucca. It's a start. Maybe they'll have the address and phone number where he is staying."

I called United Airlines. Flight 542 was scheduled to leave at 4:20, destination Chicago. The flight reservations had been confirmed for passengers, Paul Berger, Otto Kurtz and Rosalinda Chapman. The telephone number given was the office number of the S.F. Opera.

Kotchman continued to pace the floor, smoking cigarettes, while I took a shower, shaved and made a pot of coffee. At 4:45, I called United again and asked if the passengers in question had boarded the plane. They checked and reported that flight 542 was airborne and these particular passengers had not boarded. Wolf rubbed his chin. "So, our birds didn't fly. I was right. They're still in the city, but where? Any ideas, DeLucca?"

"Yeah, we could check all of the airlines' passenger lists for all of the flights from yesterday through Wednesday of next week."

"How could we do that?"

"That's what I mean. It's hopeless, unless..."

"Unless what?"

"I don't know who you talked to at the opera, but it might be a good idea to call Al, the doorman. Maybe he's heard something about Hessler."

I dialed the stage door as Kotchman looked on with anticipation. "Hello, Al. This is DeLucca."

"Hey Vince! I was wondering about you. What the hell's going on? I know those three krauts left here Thursday night in handcuffs, but on Saturday night, I see Berger in his tuxedo and the big bald-headed ape walking in as big as life. Then I read about the murders down at the pier. Jesus! What's going on?"

"Al, things got a little fouled up. I can't explain it now, but the reason I called is I know you hear a lot of personal conversations between the artists and the directors. Did you happen to hear anything about Berger leaving here or where he's going?"

"No, I didn't, Vince. All I know is after the performance, Berger went up to the office and stayed there for about an hour. Then he left the building, him and the big one, carrying three suitcases. I asked his secretary where he was going, and she said he had pressing engagements and had to take a flight out as soon as possible. She didn't know where he was going and he didn't leave a forwarding address. That's all I know, Vince."

"Al, is Berger's secretary named Rosalinda?"

"No. Her name is Hilda something. I can't pronounce it. Why?"

"Oh, the name came up and I thought it might be his secretary."

"Listen, Vince. I'm sorry the bastard got away. Maybe you'll tell me about it sometime. Oh, by the way, did that little Jewish guy get killed? I read there were two bodies, but only one was identified."

I looked over at Kotchman. "No. That little Jewish guy is still alive and kicking. Al, is anyone up in the office right now?"

"No. Everyone's gone home. They won't be back until morning."

"Would it be possible for Kotchman and I to come over and look around Berger's office? Maybe he left behind a clue that might help us find out where he is."

"Sure, Vince. I'll let you in, but I don't think you'll find anything up there. It's been cleaned out."

"We'll be there in twenty minutes. Thanks, Al." I hung up, looked at Kotchman and said, "It's a shot in the dark, but worth a try."

EIGHTEEN

At 7:00 p.m., we parked in front of the stage door. It was a cold Sunday night, and the street was deserted.

Al smiled as he let us into the empty opera house. "Hello, Vince. I'll get the elevator for you. I've got some coffee here when you get through. Good luck."

All the rooms were dark. Kotchman followed me to Berger's office where I searched for the light switch and turned it on. Al was right, the office had been cleaned out. The desktops were wiped off and the drawers were empty. Even the wastepaper baskets were empty. I checked the metal file cabinet. All the file drawers were empty except the one on the bottom. It had a thick padlock on it. The cabinet was made of heavy gauge metal and even a crowbar wouldn't break that lock. It would take a pair of bolt cutters, or a hack saw, but I knew Kotchman needed to get into that file drawer.

We went back down to the stage door. Al had three cups of coffee ready for us as we stepped out of the elevator. "Did you guys have any luck up there?"

I sipped the hot coffee. "Not yet, Al, but there's a padlocked file drawer we need to open. Do you know who would have the key?"

"If it's the big green cabinet in Berger's private office, only Berger would have the key."

"In that case, we need some bolt cutters."

"There are cutters in Irv's machine shop, but I'm not supposed to take anything out of there." After some thought, Al said, "Hell, if you want the bolt cutters, I'll get them for you. Can you cut the lock without damaging the cabinet?"

"Yes. I think we can."

"Good, then I'll put another lock on it, return the bold cutters, and no one will know the difference." He smiled. "Except Berger maybe but I don't think we'll be seeing him back around here for a long time."

Kotchman put his cup down, lit a cigarette and spoke for the first time. "Al. Where do the janitors empty the wastepaper baskets from the offices?"

"It all goes down to the trash bin in the basement."

"Has the trash been picked up yet?" asked Kotchman.

"No, they don't come 'til Tuesday."

"Then the papers would still be in the trash bin."

"Yeah. Those offices were cleaned last so they should be right on top of the heap."

"Good. DeLucca, I think we should have a look."

I remembered the basement and trash room from when Julian Bagely had given me the tour. We went down and I turned on the light. A big gray trash bin stood against the wall. I looked inside and saw Al was right: the top was filled with office papers. Kotchman scooped up a hand full and started to inspect them. I did the same. We were looking for anything related to Berger's activities. We carefully sorted out all of the papers, but none so far had anything of importance written on them. Suddenly, Kotchman singled out a small piece of paper, scrutinized it and said, "DeLucca. What do you make of this?" He handed me a sheet of crumpled note paper. Scribbled on it were the words, "Ace Airways. San Jose."

"This could be something, Wolf. Maybe a small airline. I've never heard of it. I'll call San Jose information and see if it's listed."

When we got back to the stage door, Al had the bolt cutters for us. As soon as we entered the office, I dialed San Jose information. Ace Airways was listed as a small private charter line, owned and operated by Ace Conlin.

"DeLucca, let's give Ace a call."

"It's after seven. They might not be open." I said as I was dialing "

After five rings, a woman's loud shrill voice answered. "Ace Airways. We fly day or night. We fly anywhere, if the price is right. This is Rosy. What can I do for you?"

I grimaced and moved the receiver away from my ear. "I'm trying to locate a business associate of mine. His name is Paul Berger. I heard him mention Ace Airways and I wondered if he engaged your services."

"Hold your horses, honey, while I check." I could hear her popping gum as she turned pages. "Oh yeah, you are in luck tonight. We have a Mister Paul Berger and two others flying out of here at six on the nose tomorrow night."

"Can you tell me their destination?"

"Sure I can, but that information is supposed to be confidential."

"I understand, but it's very important and I'd really appreciate your help."

"Yeah? Well, seeing as your being a business associate, I guess it's all right. It says here, Santa Fe, New Mexico." She giggled, "I won't tell anyone, if you don't."

"Thank you for your help."

"You're welcome, I'm sure. Bye."

I lowered the receiver and faced Kotchman. "Well, we know where they're going. Hessler and two others are flying out of San Jose, Tuesday night at 6:00 pm headed for Santa Fe, New Mexico. So, what now, Wolf?"

Kotchman stared off in space. I could almost hear the wheels turning. "So, it's Santa Fe is it? That means Hessler has supporters in Santa Fe. A likely place to hide. I have a few ideas."

"Like what, Wolf?"

"I'll tell you as soon as I work them out. However, I think we should pay a visit to a Mister Ace Conlin in San Jose, but first, let's open that file drawer."

We heard the elevator start in the hallway. Someone had called it to the stage floor. No one but Al should be in the building, so I figured it must be him, but we both startled when the in-house phone rang.

I picked it up. It was Al and his voice was close to panic. "Vince! We got trouble. The big kraut is on his way up. I had to let him in. Berger sent him to pick up some papers. Did you break the lock yet?"

"No."

"Good. You guys better take a sneak."

"Thanks, Al." I put the phone down. "Wolf! Gunther Mueller is on his way up to get some papers Hessler left behind. What the hell do we do?"

Kotchman wrinkled his brow. "It could be our chance to capture him. Do you have your gun with you?"

"Yes, I do." I could hear the elevator coming back up to the office floor. "Wolf! There isn't much time."

"This doesn't fit into my plan. Quick, DeLucca! Turn out the light and get behind the door. We'll have to deal with this now."

I heard the elevator doors open then heavy footsteps coming down the hall. Kotchman crouched behind the desk with his beretta ready. I hugged the wall behind the door and held my breath as Mueller entered the outer office, turned on the lights and walked directly to the file cabinet in the private office. I watched as he reached into his pocket and took out a key. He knelt down, opened the lock, slid the drawer open and removed a brown manila envelope from a cardboard file.

I waited for Kotchman to make his move, but he remained motionless behind the desk. In those few short seconds I had little time to think, but my foremost thought was, what would Maria say if she knew that I was here still playing cat and mouse instead of going to the police.

Mueller put the envelope in his inside pocket, closed the drawer, locked it and stood up. My heart was pounding, as he walked by me to the outside office and the hall. I heard the elevator doors close, then all was quiet.

Kotchman got up from behind the desk. "Quick, DeLucca. Down the stairs. We'll follow him. He'll lead us straight to Hessler."

We ran down the two flights of stairs to the stage door. Al was surprised. "What happened up there?"

"Nothing, Al. Did you see him leave the elevator?"

"No! He didn't come out here. He went down to the basement."

"Let's go, Wolf. He's down in the basement."

We took the stairs to the basement. When we got to the bottom, we stopped to listen. "Do you hear that, Wolf?"

"Yes. It sounds like footsteps on cement."

I remembered the tunnel that joined the two buildings under the courtyard. "This way, Wolf. I know where he's going."

We passed the trash room and came to the elevator. To the right was the cement corridor. The large, dark figure of Mueller was silhouetted against the light bulb at the far end of the passageway. His footsteps echoed through the tunnel.

"DeLucca." Kotchman whispered. "What's at the other end of this tunnel?"

"There's a door that goes into the War Memorial Trustees building. That's probably where Hessler is. Are we going to try to take Mueller now?"

"No. It would be far too dangerous. We'll wait and..."

At that moment, the plaster cast on Kotchman's arm brushed against the water pipes that ran along the walls of the tunnel. The sound reverberated off the side of the passageway. We remained still and watched. Mueller stopped and turned back. We flattened ourselves against the wall in the dark as Mueller walked toward us.

His deep voice resounded through the tunnel. "Who is der?"

I pulled the luger out of my coat pocket. "Shit! He's coming right at us."

Kotchman held his beretta and fingered the trigger. Mueller's footsteps were like the loud ticks of a giant clock measuring precious time that was running out. His giant frame was getting closer, then we heard the automatic click of a handgun. He was armed and unless we ran like rabbits, we were in for a fight.

Mueller was clearly aware that someone was at the end of the corridor watching him. His voice thundered through the passageway. "Come out! Who is der?"

Kotchman whispered, "Stay where you are, DeLucca. I'll handle it." His voice cracked though the tunnel, "Gunther Mueller! Put down your gun. This is Wolf Kotchman."

Mueller wasn't impressed. Three bright flashes came from his gun. The sound was deafening as the bullets ricocheted off of the wall, sending cement fragments flying like shrapnel. There was a sharp sting on my forehead. Kotchman lowered himself to the floor, raised his gun and prepared to fire. I heard the hammer hit the firing pin, but there was no report. He rolled over on his back, trying to reach into his coat pocket, but the cast on his arm hindered his movement. "DeLucca! My clip's empty." Two more bullets from Mueller's gun slammed into the wall as the giant rushed forward, snarling like a mad dog. He was about forty feet from me. I raised the luger and fired. Mueller uttered a guttural cry of pain and stopped.

His gun flashed again. The bullet narrowly missed me as it tore into the water pipes close to my head. I quickly moved away from his line of fire.

Kotchman reloaded his gun and stood up. "I can't see him. Where did he go?"

I whispered to Kotchman, "The only way out of here is the door at the end of the tunnel. Listen! I think I hit him. He's probably up there somewhere." We could hear heavy breathing and the sound of a body dragging along on the floor.

Kotchman walked deeper into the tunnel. "Come on, DeLucca. Let's finish the job."

"We better watch ourselves, Wolf. There might be a lot more fight left in him."

I had no more than finished the sentence, when another barrage from Mueller's gun sent us back against the dark cement walls. When the ringing echo of the gunfire died down, I could hear more movement ahead. It sounded like Mueller was up and walking again, but dragging one leg. He had reached the door at the end of the tunnel.

He shattered the light bulb with his gun barrel and the tunnel was plunged into total darkness.

The door at the end opened for a second, then closed. Kotchman lit his lighter and ran to the door. He tried to open it, but it was securely locked. "We've lost him, DeLucca, but look here." He held the lighter close to the floor. "You hit him all right. He's losing a lot of blood. We're finished here. It's time to leave before the police come. The gunfire is sure to bring them."

"Wolf, I'm all for calling the police and ending this thing once and for all. We'll tell them the truth. They can search the building, find Hessler and Mueller, and hold them for investigation."

"DeLucca! We know the truth, but do you think the local authorities will believe our story? We would be the ones that held for investigation. Face it, the Germans have the upper hand. A respected opera director and his assistant are hunted down in the basement of the opera house. One of them is wounded or killed by someone without authority who says he is working with an Israeli agent tracking down Nazi war criminals. DeLucca, they would laugh right in your face. My plans are clear. Now that I know what Hessler is going to do, I intend to take him back to Israel. This I am going to do. After I'm gone, you can do what you want, go to the police, or the F.B.I., but remember, you are up against a powerful organization that can chew you up and spit you out. Let's finish what we started. We're so close now."

On the way back to the elevator, I began to think that Kotchman might be right. I decided to finish the game, no matter what it took.

As we got into the elevator, Kotchman noticed my head. "You're bleeding. How bad is the injury?"

"It's not serious. I was lucky."

"It was not luck, DeLucca, when you shot Mueller, you saved my life and I won't forget it."

Al was nervous when we came up to the stage entrance. "Jesus, Vince! I heard the shots down there. What the hell happened? I was about to call the police. Jesus! Look at your head."

Kotchman stood at the stage door, waiting impatiently while I tried explaining to Al. "We had a little trouble down there in the basement. Mueller attacked us and damn near got us both. He's wounded but escaped through the door at the end of the tunnel. Believe me, Al, we had no alternative but shoot back. Mueller forced the fight, but if there's an investigation, do what you have to. I'll understand. Thanks for all your help, Al."

I joined Kotchman at the door. Al unlocked it and let us out. On our way to the car, I turned to look back. Al was still standing at the door with a bewildered look on his face. He waved goodbye and I waved back.

On the drive to my apartment, I noticed that Kotchman didn't seem unnerved by the action we had just gone through in the basement. My hand was still shaking, but he sat quietly, as if he were planning his next campaign. He turned to me and spoke with confidence. "So, DeLucca. The Hessler affair is about to come to an end."

"How do you figure that He's flying to Santa Fe. It'll still take some doing to get him."

"Yes, it will, DeLucca, and I've got a plan that can't fail if we work it right."

"There you go with that 'we' stuff again. You're not going to be satisfied until you get me killed."

"Don't worry. This phase of the operation will not be dangerous."

"Yeah, I'll bet. Just shaking hands with you is dangerous."

When we got back to the apartment, Kotchman explained his plan to me and I had to admit, it didn't sound all that dangerous.

"So, early tomorrow morning we drive to San Jose and find out where this Ace Conlin has his charter business. He must have been recommended to Hessler. He's probably noted for his no-questions-asked and fly-you-anywhere-for-a-price policies. Hessler must be paying him big money for that service. Hessler and Mueller would be able to carry anything they wanted on a flight like this, including their guns. The flight from San Jose to Santa Fe is about the same flight time as from San Jose to El Paso, Texas."

"What the hell does El Paso, Texas have to do with it?"

"I was coming to that. We will talk the owner of the charter line into flying his passengers to El Paso instead of Santa Fe. I have strong contacts in El Paso. When the plane lands, my people will pick up Hessler and transport him to Galveston in plenty of time to board the ship." Kotchman sat back with a look of self-satisfaction. "What do you think?"

"What makes you think we can persuade Ace Conlin to fly them to El Paso?"

"We can either bribe him with money, or threaten him with legal action."

"What kind of legal action?"

"We can threaten to ground his operation and pull his license for agreeing to transport a wanted man out of the state, but perhaps if we gain his confidence, he might agree to do it for patriotic reasons alone. That's the way you flag-waving Americans are, and a fellow with a name like Ace Conlin, should be quite patriotic. I believe we can't miss."

"Don't let the name fool you, Wolf. Did you ever think that he might be one of Hessler's men?"

"Yes. That did occur to me, but I seriously doubt it."

"Okay, assuming all goes our way, what happens at El Paso? How do you get Hessler through the airport without him causing trouble?"

"I've already worked that out. About twenty minutes out of El Paso, there is a small private airfield. There's not much traffic, just a few crop dusters and private planes. That will be our landing field. So, after the plane takes off from San Jose, you will drive me to the airport and where I will make arrangements to fly to Galveston. Then, DeLucca, we will part company. I'm very tired. Wake me at six in the morning. Good night."

I watched him walk into my bedroom and close the door. I poured myself a stiff scotch and sat down on the couch mumbling to myself about the man's rudeness. Asking me to be his alarm clock. The nerve.

I had to admit though that Kotchman's plan had merit. If it all worked out the way he said, I would be rid of him for good. I counted the deaths so far centered around Kotchman's effort to capture Hessler and his men. There was Ben Koslo, Abe Shoiket and Julie Koslo. If there was an investigation, the whole story would have to be told. The list would have to be produced and presented as evidence.

The telephone jarred me from my thoughts. It was Maria and she was mad. "DeLucca! Where have you been? I've been calling you. What did the police say? DeLucca! Are you there?"

"Maria, I'm sorry but something new came up in the case. I'll tell you all about it when I see you."

"It sounds like you didn't go to the police. You didn't, did you?"

"No. I couldn't. Not just yet."

"Why?"

"Kotchman is alive."

"Alive! But I thought..."

"I know, but the other body at the pier turned out to be Heitman. Kotchman barely escaped with his life."

"How do you know that? Have you seen Kotchman?"

"Yes. He's here with me now. He's got a plan and we're going to make another attempt to get Hessler."

"Oh, DeLucca, you poor sap. Don't you know he's using you? He doesn't care about you. Haven't you had enough of Kotchman and his plans?"

That was a good question. The truth was, I had had my fill of him, but... "Maria. It will be over Tuesday night, believe me. Then we'll be free of the whole thing."

"I've heard that before, DeLucca. I'm coming over." Her voice turned soft. "I want to see you."

"No, I can't see you right now, Maria. Listen, please. I want you to do me a big favor. Stay right where you are. Write a letter, do your laundry or whatever, but stay put until this is over. I'll call you Tuesday night at eight I promise. I'll tell you everything then. Will you do that for me?" I thought I heard a sob. "Maria, please."

"All right, DeLucca. I love you." She hung up.

I slowly lowered the phone, feeling like two cents, but at least I knew Maria would be safe. I turned out the lights and plopped down on the couch for some much-needed sleep.

The next morning came early. Wolf and I hit the Bayshore Freeway at 6:30 and headed for San Jose. The weather was overcast. I had given some careful thought to Kotchman's plan. It seemed like a painless way to get Hessler to Galveston if Ace Conlin would play ball. That was a big "if" in my book, but Kotchman seemed confident that with the right approach, we'd be successful.

About twenty minutes from San Jose, I learned what he thought was the right approach. "It's very simple, DeLucca. We tell him I work for the Israeli government and you work for the American government and we have one common cause, to bring these Nazis to trial. Is there any patriotic American who would not assist us in such a cause?"

"You want me to pass myself off as a government agent?"

"Why not? You've been doing government work. You have credentials, don't you? A license with your picture on it. It should be convincing enough."

I asked myself how convincing we two would be—a sawed off runt with a cast on his arm and a one-armed man with a P.I. license. The plan was so bizarre that it just might work.

NINETEEN

I t was a quarter after eight when we stopped at a coffee shop and called Ace Airways. The gum-chewing secretary answered the phone again and said that Ace Conlin would be back at 9:00 a.m.. I made an appointment and told her it was official government business, something to do with Aeronautical Safety. I gave my name as J. W. Walsh and asked for directions.

At the far end of Airport Drive, I pulled up next to a red sports car parked in front of a small hangar, facing the runway. Beside the hangar was an office with a sign above the front door that read: "Ace Airways, Ace Conlin Private Charters."

Kotchman lit a cigarette and leaned forward to study the hangar. "DeLucca. When we go in there, let me do the talking. Don't forget, you are a U.S. Government agent assisting the Israeli Government. Are you ready?"

I nodded and we walked up the steps to the office door. Kotchman entered first. Sitting at a desk to the right of the door was the gum-popping secretary. She looked exactly as I had imagined. She had a chubby round face surrounded by short bleached blond hair.

Her jaws worked on the gum as she said brashly, "Good morning, gentlemen. One of you has got to be J. W. Walsh. Right?"

I nodded. She pressed the intercom button and announced, "J. W. Walsh to see you, Ace. Do I send them in, or what?"

The door to the inner office opened, and standing in the doorway with an electric shaver in his hand was Ace Conlin. He was in his late thirties, heavy-set, and wearing a pair of Khaki pants and a soiled white T-shirt. From the looks of him, he seemed to be nursing a hangover. He gave Kotchman and me the once over with bloodshot eyes, then smiled and said, "You guys are with the Safety Commission?" His smile turned to laughter, as he motioned us to enter the office. "Come on in. Have a seat and I'll be right with you." He slipped on a clean white shirt and tucked it into his trousers, then, still chuckling, he looked at us.

It was obvious that he was amused by our claim. Kotchman and I didn't exactly look like representatives of any Safety Commission. I glanced at Kotchman and found it difficult to keep a straight face.

Ace sat down behind his desk. "OK, boys. Which one of you is Walsh?"

I was about to answer when Kotchman took over in his own tactless way. "There is no J. W. Walsh and we are not safety inspectors. We are government agents. My name is Wolf Kotchman. I'm with the Israeli Government and this is Agent DeLucca with the F.B.I."

Ace leaned back in his chair and continued to smile. "I knew this morning was going to be interesting, but this? This is ridiculous. What would you government boys be wanting with me?" He studied Kotchman. "Did you say you worked for the Israeli government?"

Kotchman pulled out his identification and flashed it in front of him. "That is correct. Now, let us proceed with our business."

Ace's smile faded. "OK, you've got me interested. I take it this is one of those covert operations and you want me to fly you to a place that's not on the regular flight pattern. Is that right?"

Kotchman became impatient. "No! That is not why we are here."

"It's not? Well, why the hell else?"

"If you will allow me to continue, I will explain why we are here."

Ace sat back and looked at me as if to say, Who is this pushy little bastard?

Kotchman lit a cigarette. The smoke curled up into his half-closed eyes as he spoke. "I'll come directly to the point. For the past six years I have been hunting Nazi war criminals. Many have been brought to trial, but one clever criminal in particular has successfully eluded me until now. During the past week, I have been able to identify him, and with the help of Agent DeLucca I have tried to capture him, but once again he has escaped. We now know where he is and with your help, we can safely apprehend him and finally bring him back to Israel to answer for his crimes against the Jewish people."

Ace stood up and put his hands on the desk. "Hold it a minute. You're going way too fast for me. You say you hunt Nazis? Christ! I thought you boys had already caught all of the big fish. Just how the hell can I help?"

Kotchman stared into Ace's face. "Mister Conlin, I can give you some figures that will shock you. There are still seven to ten thousand war criminals hiding in this country alone, not to mention the thousands in Canada and South America. We have a long way to go before we can come anywhere near settling the score. Unfortunately, the assistance we receive from many of the foreign governments is far from what we would expect."

Ace returned to his seat and opened a pack of cigarettes. "OK. That's alarming news, but you said you needed my help. What kind of help? I have no knowledge of Nazi war criminals."

"Yes you do, Mister Conlin. You have a charter flight leaving tomorrow night for Santa Fe. Am I right?"

Ace lit his cigarette, blew the match out and said, "You seem to know quite a lot about my business. How did you know?"

"Never mind how we knew. The man that chartered the flight told you his name was Paul Berger. Is that right?"

"That's right. He said that he worked at the San Francisco Opera as a director. You're not telling me that Berger..."

"That's exactly what I'm telling you. Paul Berger's real name is Carl Hessler. He's a former S.S. officer who served during the war at Belzec, a concentration camp in Poland. Berger's associate is Gunther Mueller, another S.S. butcher. These men are very dangerous and are high on the wanted list. Now, I want to know where they are and when are they due to arrive for the flight?"

Ace rubbed his cigarette out in the ashtray. "Jesus! You boys are too much. Nazi war criminals. Christ! You want to know where Berger's staying? He's at the Hilton, right here in town. I had breakfast with him and his strange girlfriend just before I came here. I don't know anything about any Gunther Mueller."

Kotchman moved his fingers impatiently. "Go on. How did Berger contact you?"

"There's not much to tell. He called me two days ago and said he would pay me one thousand dollars to fly him and two other passengers to Santa Fe. Their names were Otto Kurtz and a woman by the name of Rosalinda Chapman. I agreed and we set up a meeting this morning at the Hilton. It was then that he told me, there would only be two passengers on the flight, he and the woman. He wanted me to cut one third off the price, but I flatly refused. He paid me five hundred dollars in advance. I am to receive the balance when we land in Santa Fe, but then he insisted that we fly out a day earlier. We are supposed to leave here at 5:30, today."

"I see." said Kotchman. "Otto Kurtz is really Gunther Mueller but he was wounded in the attempt to apprehend him in San Francisco. The wound might have been serious enough to keep him from leaving with Hessler. Hessler knew we were close, so he wanted to get out as soon as possible."

Ace stood up and looked down at Kotchman. "OK, I leveled with you, so why don't you come clean with me and tell me what you want from me?"

"It's very simple, Mister Conlin. Instead of flying your passengers to Santa Fe, I want you to fly them to a designated air strip just outside of El Paso, Texas. All you have to do is land, then my people will take Hessler and the woman off the plane and you will never see them again. That's all there is to it. Do you have a map? I will show you where the field is located."

Ace eyed Kotchman with suspicion as he opened his desk drawer and removed a book of maps. He selected the proper map and laid it on the desk. Kotchman stood and approached the desk. He put his finger on the map and traced the distance between San Jose and El Paso. "You see, the flight time should be about the same, and at night, there could be no way Hessler would know that he wasn't going to Santa Fe. Twenty five miles to the East of El Paso, there is a small crop dusting field. It's big enough for you to land. I will arrange to have landing lights and also a refueling operation, to get you back home." He pointed to the field on the map, then he looked at Ace. "Is this all clear to you?"

"Sure. It's all clear enough, but you didn't once ask me if I would do it. This whole thing sounds a little fishy to me. You two boys come in here and give me a sob story about the thousands of war criminals still at large. Then you tell me that my paying customer is a Nazi criminal and has to be taken back to Israel for trial. You give me my new flight plan and instructions on how to carry it out. Then you ask me if I understand. If I did what you suggest, I'd not only be out the five hundred, but I just might lose my license for filing a false flight plan. I don't know anything about Israeli agents, but I do know that they don't have any one-armed F.B.I. men in the field." He looked at me. "No offence, fella, but I'm afraid this will take some looking into by the proper authorities."

He smiled as he pulled out a bottle of scotch from the desk drawer. "Here, have a drink before you go. There's glasses on the table."

Kotchman's face contorted in anger. "You refuse to serve this cause for your country and mankind?"

Ace poured himself a scotch. "Under the circumstances, yes. I refuse. I flew fighters off a carrier in the Pacific for three years. I fought my war and as far as mankind is concerned, you can have it. I'm a businessman and I have bills to pay. I would fly Adolph Hitler to Santa Fe, or any other place for a thousand bucks."

At that statement, I stood up and poured myself a drink. Kotchman had come on too strong, but I still thought a deal could be worked out. It was obvious now that it was a matter of money.

I spoke for the first time since we entered the office. "Ace, would you agree to do it as planned for a price?"

Ace took a slug of his scotch, smiled and said, "That I would."

Kotchman looked at me and realized that I had salvaged his operation. He asked in a condescending manner, "Mister Conlin. Would you fly your passengers to El Paso for an additional five hundred dollars?"

Ace finished his drink, set the glass on the desk and said, "Make it an additional thousand, cash, up front, before I take off, you buy lunch, and you've got a deal."

Kotchman responded immediately. "That's out of the question! You were going to fly to Santa Fe for a thousand, why should the flight to El Paso cost more?"

"The extra five hundred is for hazard pay."

"Hazard pay! I told you there would be no danger."

"You told me a lot of things, Mister Kotchman. It's what you didn't tell me that bothers me. I was going to fly a businessman to Santa Fe for a thousand dollars. In good weather, it's a very simple flight to a well-known airfield with the proper facilities for landing and takeoff. Now, you tell me that my passenger is a dangerous criminal and you want me to change my destination to a crop dusting field out in the boonies. I don't know exactly what I'm getting into. There are a lot of unforeseen things that could happen on a flight like this. I could mention quite a few problems that I have to worry about, while you don't endanger yourself at all. It's easy to say my people will take him off the plane when you don't have to be there and how the hell do I know if your people will show up? The more I think about it, my price is too low." Ace poured himself another drink and sat down. "The price stands."

Kotchman made a gesture to the ceiling and reached for his cigarettes.

I thought this would be a good time for me to put in my two cent's worth. "Wolf, this is your chance to bring Hessler back to Israel without any more killing. I think the price is right. Pay the man."

Kotchman blew a plume of smoke in the air and reached for his billfold. He opened it and peeled off ten one-hundred-dollar bills, laid them on the desk and growled. "You strike a hard bargain, but we are in agreement."

Ace's sports car was too small for all three of us, so we piled into my Volkswagen and headed for the airport bar and restaurant. On the way I tried to figure out Ace Conlin. He seemed straightforward enough. There was a bit of larceny in him, and I wondered if he always worked for the highest bidder. Once he was airborne, would he try to shake down Hessler for more money? I dismissed the thought. It would be far too dangerous for him to attempt that with Hessler. I figured I'd take him at his face value. If Kotchman wasn't worried, why should I be worried, but in this kind of business, who could you trust? Maria entered my mind. That's a girl I could trust. If all went well, I would call her tonight after I'd seen Kotchman off for the last time.

We parked in the parking lot and walked to the bar. Ace ordered a scotch on the rocks. I had the same. Kotchman ordered a beer and went off in search of a telephone.

Ace put his forefinger in the glass, twirled the ice cubes, then looked over at me and said, "What was it the little guy called you? Agent DeLucca, wasn't it?"

"Yeah, that' was Kotchman's idea to make more of an impression on you. I'm Vince DeLucca, a private investigator in San Francisco. I happened to run into Kotchman while I was working on what I thought was a routine case at the opera house. As soon as I realized what I was dealing with, I joined forces with him. It's been a rough week and I'll be glad when it's over."

"You know, Vince, when you boys walked into my office, I didn't think you were for real. It struck me kind of funny, you two being safety inspectors, then this guy Kotchman hits me with the Nazi hunting bit. It's got to be on the square. No one could put on an act like that."

"Believe me, Ace, it's no act. That's the way Kotchman is, but he seems to get results."

"If you don't mind my asking, Vince, how did you lose your arm?"

"I got it shot up in the war, at Anzio. The medics tried, but they couldn't save it. Now, I'm sort of used to using just one arm. How about you, Ace? You say you flew fighters in the Pacific?"

"Yeah, looks like we were fighting on different sides of the globe, but against the same enemy. Listen, Vince. Don't think I'm against putting those Nazi bastards away. You probably thought I didn't care what happened to them, as long as I made a buck. Well, that's not true. It's just the way your buddy presented his proposition, sort of expecting me to fall all over myself to do him a service. When I met this guy, Berger, I didn't like him, but it was a paying job. Now I meet the little guy, and I don't like him either. He and the German are a lot alike. I think, if it wasn't for you, I would have told Kotchman to stuff it."

"I know the feeling, but I'm glad you decided to help. After tonight, I'll be able to rest easy."

"Rest easy! Christ, Vince. You know this can't be that easy. Listen, I want you to give me your card or tell me where you can be reached. Just in case something goes wrong tonight, I want someone to fall back on. I hate flying blind."

"Nothing is going to go wrong."

"Maybe not, but 'Murphy's Law,' you know. Do you mind?"

"No. Not at all." I handed him one of my cards.

Ace downed his scotch. "Thanks, Vince. Another drink?"

"Sure. Why not?"

Halfway through our second scotch, Kotchman returned to the bar. There was a strange excitement in his voice. "Well, DeLucca, my plan is taking shape." He turned to Ace. "I have a reception committee ready and waiting to meet your plane. There will be adequate landing lights and, as I said, fuel will be available. All you have to do is land then wait in the cockpit until my people take Hessler from the plane to a car. There should be no problems. DeLucca, after we make sure Hessler is safely on the plane and airborne, you will drive me back here. I have a flight out to Houston at 6:45." He seemed quite pleased with himself. "All right gentlemen, time for lunch."

We took our drinks and moved to a table overlooking the wet tarmac. During lunch, Kotchman had very little to say. He was busy eating a large crab salad and a plate of roast beef. It was the first time that I had seen him eat. He devoured his lunch like a starved animal. After lunch, we ordered coffee, all except Ace, who ordered another drink.

Kotchman scowled and looked at his watch. "It's approximately three hours before flight time. Another drink and you won't see the runway."

Ace raised his glass and peeked at Kotchman through the rim of the glass. "You're paying me to fly an airplane. It does not include altering my social life. Don't worry, your Nazi will be delivered in one piece."

"I assume that you know your business. However, it would be advisable for you to have a clear head. There is too much at stake to blunder now."

Ace looked over at me, smiled and took a swallow.

Kotchman lit another cigarette, leaned forward and said, "Now, Mister Ace Conlin, tell me about the woman."

Ace lowered his glass. "What woman?"

Kotchman snapped, "The woman with Hessler. If I remember correctly, you said that you had breakfast this morning with him and his strange girlfriend. Tell me about her. Why did you think she was strange?"

Ace thought for a minute. "Well, for one thing, she didn't utter a single word. She just sat there with a vacant look on her face. I wouldn't be surprised if she wasn't on something. The German introduced her as Rosalinda Chapman. Yeah, she was strange, all right."

"What did she look like?"

"She was a blonde. Had very little makeup on, wore a light purple suit with a white blouse buttoned up at the neck."

"How old would you say she was?"

"Hell! I couldn't tell. Maybe twenty-five or thirty."

"Is there anything else you can tell us about her?"

"Yeah, something happened that was weird. She was wearing a pair of purple gloves and while Berger and I were discussing terms about the flight, I noticed that she was painfully tugging on her right glove. Finally, she pulled it off and I could see she was missing some fingers. Berger became furious, grabbed the glove and slapped her across the face. Then he told her to put the glove back on. It happened so fast no one in the restaurant seemed to notice. I was going to say something, but then I thought I'd better stay out of it. The girl put the glove back on and remained silent, staring into space during the rest of the meeting. That's what I call strange."

I looked at Kotchman. "There's only one person who fits that description: Julie Koslo."

Kotchman's eyes narrowed as he fingered the rim of his coffee cup. "Yes. Julie Koslo. This is strange indeed. He didn't kill her when they first kidnapped her. He has kept her alive and is taking her with him to Santa Fe. What strange kind of relationship could there be between my only witness and the Nazi butcher?"

Ace put down his drink. "Hold it a minute. Who is this Julie Koslo? Is there something I should know?"

Kotchman was preoccupied, so I explained about Julie Koslo. "This woman was in a German concentration camp during the war. From what Wolf tells me, she is the only one alive who can positively identify Hessler. Evidently, Hessler kept her alive, but for reasons only he knows."

Ace looked down at his empty glass. "You don't suppose he has something planned for her during the flight, do you? Christ! If what you say about this guy is true, he just might want to get rid of me, too. This God damn flight could be my last."

Kotchman quickly looked up. "No! If he has planned anything, it won't be during the flight. I'm sure of that. Whatever he has in mind, it will happen when he gets to Santa Fe." His eyes opened a bit wider and gleamed. "But now, you see, he won't be going to Santa Fe. This is more than I had hoped for. My number one witness is alive and very soon, she will be in my hands."

TWENTY

The sun made a late afternoon attempt to punch through the gray cloud cover. Warm patches of light brushed the distant mountains and reflected off of the wet runway. This could be a good omen. It was 4:15 P.M. I realized that in forty-five minutes, I would be free. The Kotchman affair would be over.

As we drove back to Ace Conlin's hangar, I thought about the list in my pocket. I was going to give it to Kotchman, but he already had his prize: Hessler and a witness. I figured the Israeli government wouldn't mind if I gave the list to the F.B.I. I was through hunting Nazis. Let the proper authorities handle it from here on.

I turned into the driveway in front of the office. Kotchman leaned forward from the back seat and suggested that I park in back out of sight. I parked behind the building and then we went into the office.

Ace looked at the empty reception desk. "Where the hell is my secretary?" He checked her desktop and tore the top sheet from a note pad and read it. After a moment, he looked up. "Your boy Hessler called and said he would be here at 4:30." He checked his watch. "He should be on his way right now."

Kotchman nervously lit a cigarette and asked, "How much prepa-ration is there before you're ready to leave?"

"Hell! I'm ready now. I just have to warm up the engines, get clearance from the tower and I'm on my way."

Kotchman flicked his ashes on the floor. "All right. You better go start warming the engines. I don't want Hessler to come into the office. It's best you leave as soon as he arrives, but before you go, I want to go over the check list. I assume you have enough fuel in the tanks?" Ace looked over at me and smiled as Kotchman continued. "And don't forget, all you have to do is land, then sit in the cockpit and wait. Hessler and the girl will be removed from the plane."

"I won't be able to just sit there," said Ace. "Someone has to go back and open the hatch."

"Very well, as soon as you open the hatch, go back into the cockpit and wait. I expect that you will coordinate the position of the landing field with your maps. It wouldn't do to get lost."

"Christ, Kotchman! Are you sure I can fly the damned plane? Don't worry, I can find the field. Just you make sure that it has lights and that your people are waiting for us." Ace turned to me, gave a quick salute and said, "See you around, Vince." Then he walked out through the doorway.

The window in the outer office looked out onto the driveway; beyond was the hangar and Ace's plane. Kotchman closed the venetian blinds and we waited inside. At a quarter to five, a taxi drove up the driveway and parked in front of the hangar. The driver got out, went to the rear of the cab and opened the trunk. Hessler got out of the back seat and the girl followed him. She was just as Ace had described her, a tall blonde in a light purple suit. Her once pretty face was expressionless. She stood aimlessly by the cab while Hessler grabbed two suitcases and a small flight bag from the trunk. Ace opened the hatch of his plane in the hangar and said something to Hessler. The drone of the plane's engines made it impossible to hear what he said.

As the taxi drove away and Hessler turned toward the plan, the girl started to walk slowly toward the office. Hessler put down the suitcases and yelled at her. She walked faster, then broke into a run.

Kotchman grabbed my arm. "DeLucca! She's heading straight for this office."

"Yeah, I know, and here comes Hessler after her. What the hell do we do?"

"Quick, DeLucca, lock the door. I don't want Hessler to see us."

I rushed to the door and locked it. Through the screen I saw Julie Koslo at close range now. There was terror in her eyes as she pressed her face against the screen and cried, "Help me."

I had to do something. I reached for the latch just as she was yanked backwards away from the door. Hessler had her by the arm. He roughly dragged her to the plane and pushed her up through the hatch. He returned for the suitcases then climbed aboard. The hatch closed and a few minutes later the plane taxied away from the hangar on its way to the runway.

Kotchman lit a cigarette and blew smoke against the venetian blinds. "For a minute there, DeLucca, I thought you were going to let her in."

"I was. She needed our help and we just stood by and let the bastard drag her away."

"Believe me, it's better this way. One neat little package, all wrapped up and ready for delivery." He glanced at his watch. "I've just enough time to catch my flight. Shall we go?"

Twenty-Two

The San Jose Airport was almost empty. It was a wet Monday night and traffic was slow. Kotchman picked up his one-way ticket to Houston and we walked briskly to Gate 16.

His flight was boarding as we passed through the gate check. He quickly headed for the door leading to the flight platform. I wondered if he was even going to say goodbye when he stopped and turned to face me. "Well, DeLucca. This is where we part company. Even with all of our differences, I have come to realize that we make a good team. Shalom."

"Goodbye, Wolf, and good luck."

He smiled and said, "Luck has nothing to do with it." He walked off and disappeared through the open door.

On my way to the airport bar, I noticed a lighter spring in my walk. I felt as if I'd just been relieved of a heavy burden. Kotchman would soon be at thirty thousand feet heading for Houston. I was finally free of him.

I ordered a Martini and as I sat enjoying my drink, I tried to relax and think about my next move. I should have been relieved that I was finally out of it, but something kept drawing me back into the troubled waters. It was the damned list of names that I had copied from the German's brown notebook. It could be possible that Kotchman would retrieve the list from Hessler, but I had my doubts. Hessler would probably destroy the book before he'd surrender it to Kotchman. My copy might be the only one left. If it were known that I had it, I might be in a lot of danger. The sooner I put the list in the hands of the F.B.I., the better my chances.

I had to do something with it and soon. Now that Kotchman was gone, I was on my own and had to protect myself as best I could. I had told Maria that I would call her Tuesday night at eight, but things had wound up faster than I'd figured. There was no reason not to call her now but I knew that when she found out about the shooting at the opera, she would insist that I go immediately to the police. I still had my doubts about trusting the local police.

I reached into my inside coat pocket and took out the list. I studied the three names under San Francisco. All three were prominent men. The one name I recognized was Morton Townsend. He was on the board of trustees at the opera. I wondered how these three fit into the chain of events that had happened in the last week. It was a sure thing that Hessler and his boys had outside help when they escaped from the pier. Also, my apartment had obviously been searched. It seemed to me an organization was working hard to protect the Nazis and also to protect themselves from being exposed. I decided, the hell with the local police, I'd go directly to a federal government agency, tell the whole story, give them the list and be done with it. But first, I needed to call Maria.

I went to the telephone in the corner of the lounge and dialed her number. It only rang one time before Maria answered. "Yes."

"Maria."

"DeLucca! Thank God! I've been worried sick. Have you seen the papers?"

"No, I haven't. What about the papers?"

"My God, DeLucca! The police are looking for you. They want to question you about a shooting at the opera house. What is going on?"

My reaction should have been panic, but down deep I'd known there would be repercussions resulting from my action in the basement of the opera house. I had to get a newspaper.

"DeLucca! Are you there?"

"Yes. I'm here. Listen Maria, my business is finished here and—"

"Where are you?"

"I'm at the San Jose Airport."

"San Jose? What are you doing there?"

"Look, Maria. If what you say is true about the police, I've got to hole up for a while until I know what I'm up against."

"DeLucca! You're not serious. You mean you're not going to the police to straighten this mess out?"

"I will, but not right now. I've got to have time to think. It's all so damn complicated."

"Where will you go?"

"I could go to Santa Cruz, it's not far from here."

"All right, DeLucca. I'll meet you there."

"You'd drive all the way to Santa Cruz?"

"If it's the only way I can find out what's going on, yes, I would."

"You're one in a million, Maria. OK, meet me in the bar at the Dream Inn. It's right on the beach. It'll take you about an hour and a half to get there from where you are. It's seven now. So leet's make it nine o'clock. I'll book us in for the night. We'll have a few drinks, and I know a place where they serve great abalone. How does that sound?"

"You're amazing, DeLucca. The police are looking for you and all you can think of is having a few drinks and some abalone."

"Why not? It could be our last dinner together for a long time."

"Please, don't joke about it. You're in serious trouble. I'll be there as close to nine as I can, and by the way, DeLucca, I missed you."

I went back to the bar, finished the Martini and gave some thought to my dilemma. First, I'd get a newspaper, then head up over the mountain to Santa Cruz. I picked up a San Francisco Examiner from a newsstand and glanced at the front page on my way to the parking lot. I found nothing. I got in the car and searched through the rest of the paper. On page five, I found it.

'Suspect sought for questioning in Opera House gun battle.'

I read the article through. Maria was right. The police were out looking for me. They called me an unemployed private investigator with one arm, and described my 1950 blue Volkswagen. I wouldn't be hard to spot. The article also said that Julian Bagely had heard the gunfire in the basement. He'd hidden in the trash room until it was quiet, then discovered several shell casings and a pool of blood. He immediately called the police. There was no mention of how the police had linked me to the shooting, but I had my own ideas about that.

How the hell was I going to get from here to Santa Cruz? By now, they might have an all-points bulletin out on me. Every cop and his uncle would be looking for a one-armed guy driving a blue Volkswagen. I wouldn't get very far. I decided to rent a car. That way, at least half of my identity would be covered.

TWENTY-ONE

At a quarter to eight, I pulled out of a car rental parking lot in a new Ford and started up over the mountain on Highway 17. Halfway to Santa Cruz, I started to realize how serious my situation really was. What if I had killed Mueller? The police would have to hang the killing on someone, but there'd been no mention of a body. If I had killed him, I would need someone to verify my story, and Kotchman was long gone.

The road leveled off as I came down off of the mountain. I could see the lights of the city sparkling against the background of the dark Monterey Bay. Santa Cruz had always been my favorite hideout. Even before the war, I used to spend time on the beach and up in the mountains among the redwoods. After the war, I made it a habit to get away from the hectic pace of the city and stay a few days at the Dream Inn. I especially liked it in the off-season when the weather was bad. There weren't too many people in the hotel then and the bar was never crowded. The Inn was like my private club on the bay.

I laid down my credit card and checked into a room on the fourth floor. Then I went to the bar to wait for Maria. I sat at the far end and gazed out of the big window overlooking the pier and the beach. The hotel lights lit up the surf line where a man was walking his dog along the beach. He kept throwing a stick into the water and his dog would leap into the foaming surf to retrieve it and run back. I envied the simplicity of the operation. No complications, just a dog bringing back a stick to his master over and over. I wished I were that man, or even the damned dog.

I ordered a cognac and coffee while waiting and wondered if the local police here had been alerted to keep an eye out for me. I dismissed the thought when Maria walked into the lounge. I motioned to her. She smiled and came toward me. While she unbuttoned her topcoat, I ordered an Irish coffee for her, and then the questions began.

I told her everything that had happened to date—going to the opera offices at night, searching through the trash bin and finding the name of the air charter line, the shooting in the basement, and the trip to San Jose. I told her about Ace Conlin, Hessler, Julie Koslo, and finally about putting Kotchman on a plane bound for Houston. I also told her about the list. It all sounded so fantastic that I wondered if she believed me.

She looked into my eyes for a long time, then gently touched my hand. "Oh, DeLucca. What have you got yourself into? Is there no end to this bad dream? Where do we go from here?"

I squeezed her hand and smiled. "Well, for starters, we'll go down to the pier for a good bottle of wine and a gourmet plate of abalone."

We finished our drinks and prepared to leave. As I helped Maria on with her coat, I noticed two men standing on either side of the entrance to the lounge dressed in dark suits. They had their eyes on Maria and me. As we walked toward them, the tall blond one stepped forward, barring our path, while the younger one who looked like he should still be in college walked around to stand at our backs. I figured they must be the police.

The one in front of me displayed his badge and said, "S.F.P.D. Vince DeLucca? Would you and the lady please come with us? We have a car waiting."

I looked over at Maria. "Looks like we'll have to postpone our dinner for another time."

She held my arm and said, "Please believe me, DeLucca. I didn't know the police were here. They must have followed me."

"It's all right, Maria. They would have caught up with me sooner or later."

College boy behind me moved in close and frisked me, then took Maria's purse and inspected the contents.

I looked at Blondie and asked, "Am I under arrest?"

"My orders are to take you both in for questioning. That's all I know. Now, if you will follow me."

"Wait a minute. You're not taking her in. She isn't involved in this."

The man behind us said nervously, "We're wasting time. Get going." He started to push me toward the door.

"Hold it!" I said. "We both have cars here. I've got a rental plus my other car is at the San Jose Airport."

Blondie sneered, "You'll have to take care of that after you're questioned downtown. No more delays. Let's go."

We walked out into the night and headed for an unmarked car, a dark maroon Pontiac sedan parked at the far end of the parking lot.

Maria squeezed my hand. "DeLucca, I've never been picked up by the police before. How long will they hold us?"

"There's no reason to hold you, and if they don't arrest me, they can't hold me either. I'll call a lawyer as soon as I get the chance. It'll be all right. Don't worry."

How many times had I said to Maria, "It'll be all right," but so far nothing had ever seemed to turn out right at all.

When we got to the car, I noticed that it was a new deluxe model, a very expensive car for a couple of young detectives. Blondie opened the rear door and told us to get in. College boy moved into the back seat next to Maria. Blondie got into the driver's seat, started the engine and drove out of the parking lot. When we got to Ocean Avenue, instead of turning right for the freeway, we turned left, heading out of Santa Cruz on Highway 1 in the direction of Half Moon Bay. I saw now that the car was not equipped with a police radio and the more I thought about it, the more I thought these two so-called detectives weren't all that convincing.

I leaned forward and asked Blondie, "How come you're going back on the coast road? Isn't that the long way? I thought you guys didn't want to waste time."

Blondie didn't answer. College boy reached over Maria and pushed me back into my seat.

We hit a straight stretch of road doing about sixty when Blondie said, "I think we're being followed."

College boy turned and looked through the rear window. I glanced back and saw a pair of headlights dancing on the road behind us. Blondie picked up speed and the lights stayed with us.

"What do you think?" asked Blondie.

College boy kept his eyes on the headlights. "I don't know. It could be that they're following us." For twenty minutes, Blondie and his partner refused to answer any of my questions. I could tell Maria was frightened, and she had a right to be. I suspected that our two abductors were not detectives. I should have asked for their identification when I had the chance, but it happened so fast and I had no reason to doubt them at the time.

My suspicions were confirmed when we turned off Highway 1 at San Gregorio and started up a curvy road into the redwoods. I knew exactly where we were, about twelve or fifteen miles from La Honda. Maria looked at me with alarm.

Furious, I leaned forward, put my hand on Blondie's shoulder, and said, "If I were you I would stop the car! Turn around and take us back to Santa Cruz. This is the first time I've ever been taken in by a pair of phony detectives."

College boy reached past Maria and yanked me back. I clenched my left fist and turned on him then saw his hand held an ugly, snub-nosed .38 pointed at my head. Maria gasped in shock.

I lowered my fist and yelled, "You assholes are going to answer to charges for kidnapping. Where the hell are you taking us?"

College boy waved the gun in my face. "Sit back and shut up! You'll see soon enough."

Maria inched closer to me. I realized our situation was hopeless.

Blondie doused the headlights and pulled to a stop by the side of the road. He turned and watched the main road for signs of a car. We waited five minutes, then Blondie started the car and said, "Just my imagination, I guess." We drove deeper into the woods.

It finally dawned on me that these punks must be working for the organization that aided the Nazis and that they had been ordered to pick me up before the police got to me. They wanted the list that I carried in my coat pocket. Somehow, I would have to get rid of it. I remembered only three names. Townsend, Chambers, and the attorney, Cullen. I feared the worst. They were probably taking us to a remote place in the woods to be searched and interrogated. Then, they probably intended to do away with us. They surely would have blindfolded us if they had intended for us to live.

I should have known better than to let Maria meet me in Santa Cruz. It was obvious that they had followed her, and she led them right to me. Maria was right. All I had been thinking about was a good bottle of wine and some abalone. I had to find a way to get her out of this, no matter what it took. First I would unload the list, then wait for an opportunity to escape, but that wouldn't be easy. College boy was keeping his eyes on us while holding the gun in his right hand. I needed to do something and soon. Time was running out.

We were about four miles from the coast road in an area surrounded by redwood trees and dense foliage when Blondie turned right onto a narrow dirt road going deeper into the La Honda woods. The head-lights bore into the dark creating a tunnel of light. I considered my options. I could make a try at College Boy now to get his gun, but that would be too dangerous with Maria sitting between us. We could jump out of the car and make a run for it. In the dark woods maybe we could elude them, but one or both of us would probably get shot in the process. Probably better to wait and see where they were taking us and bide my time.

I reached into my left-hand coat pocket for my cigarettes. College boy raised his gun and snapped, "Hold it! What are you doing?"

"I'm getting a cigarette. You don't mind if I smoke, do you?"

"Go ahead but make it quick. We're almost there."

I took the pack out of my pocket, tipped it sideways, removed a cigarette and put it in my mouth. I made a show of searching for a match. Reaching into my inside coat pocket, I felt the matches and the folded piece of paper containing the list. I removed the paper and the matches at the same time. Maria took the matches and lit my cigarette, while I kept the paper hidden in my hand.

As I drew smoke deep into my lungs, I wondered if this might be my last cigarette. I tried to analyze our situation. Blondie and the College boy had to be on the payroll of Mister Big, the guy who called the shots in San Francisco. He was probably one of the names on the list and he must think Maria and I had seen those names and could jeopardize their operation. The discouraging fact was, list or no list, they wanted us out of the picture... permanently.

Blondie slowed down as we took several sharp turns on the narrow dirt road. Then the road straightened out and a large structure was illuminated by the headlights. As we got closer, I could make out a huge stone wall that trailed off into the darkness on either side of a weird-looking iron gate. The stone walls towered above us, reminding me of a medieval fortress. The car stopped at the gate. The place was strange looking and I knew that if we were going to make a run for it, it better be before we got inside those walls.

Blondie turned around in the front seat and said to College boy, "I'm going to call in to open the gates. You can take them the rest of the way on foot while I park the car."

As Blondie got out, I opened the lid of the ash tray on the back of the front seat and snubbed my cigarette out. I also stuffed the folded piece of paper containing the list into the ash tray then closed the lid. At least they wouldn't find the list on me.

College boy opened the rear door, got out and waved for us to follow. I whispered to Maria, "Get ready to make a run for it."

Blondie was standing at the gate talking on a telephone. College boy watched Maria and me as we stepped out of the car. His gun was leveled at me, but it was now or never. I lurched forward and slammed my fist down on his wrist. The kid dropped his gun and I backhanded him across the face. He dropped to the ground, and I yelled, "Run, Maria!"

College boy lay stunned for a moment then frantically reached for the gun on the ground. I stepped on it with my left foot and gave him a quick kick to the head with my right one. I reached down for the .38, just as I heard Blondie's voice behind me. "Don't try it, DeLucca!"

I turned looked up to see Blondie was standing over me pointing a long-barreled .45 at my head. At least I had accomplished one thing: Maria had disappeared into the woods and would be safe.

Blondie reached down and grabbed me by the hair, pulling my head back and jammed the barrel of the gun against my throat. then yelled, "Come back, little lady, or your boyfriend has had it!"

I knew he was bluffing. Their orders were to bring me back alive. I hoped that Maria realized that.

Blondie yelled again, "Come back! He has twenty seconds to live."

Out of the darkness, through the trees came Maria. College boy picked up his gun and eyed me with hatred as he grabbed Maria roughly by the arm and pulled her toward the open gate.

Blondie relaxed the hammer on the .45. "Get up and start walking. No more tricks."

My attempt to get Maria clear of danger had failed. I had to figure another way out of this predicament, but for now I could only wait and find out more about our abductors and their intentions.

I walked through the open double gates behind College boy and Maria with Blondie and his gun held ready close behind. For a brief instant, I thought I saw a light close to the road we had just traveled. I wondered if this small ray of hope was real or just in my imagination.

The long driveway wound its way through the trees then straightened out where we came up to a rise. Beyond that was a small valley where the driveway was flanked by cypress trees with lights sparkling through them. As we came to the end of the line of trees, I gaped at the sight. Looming in front of us was a dark stone castle right out of the Middle Ages. To the left of the castle was a large ranch-style house, the source of the lights. The driveway led past the entrance of the castle and curved in a circle in front of the house. As we got closer, I could tell that the ancient-looking structure was built of the same large stones as the walls that enclosed the grounds. Above the castle's portal on either side were two turrets with jagged parapets that rose up into the night sky. We stopped in front of the castle's huge wooden door with massive iron hinges. College boy slid an iron bar aside and pushed open the door. A dim light came from within. Maria and I were pushed inside, then the door was slammed shut with a thud and barred from the outside.

The dark closed in around us. The only light came from a candle mounted on an iron torchier to the right of the doorway. Maria took my hand and stared at the flickering candle flame. "DeLucca! What is this place? Why have they taken us here?"

I put my arm around her. "We've run across some of the boys on the list. I've got an idea that number one is the owner of this place. Let's see if we can find a way out of here. We might not have much time."

"What do you mean, DeLucca? Are you saying that they intend to kill us?"

"Well, I wouldn't say that, but I'm sure they have something un-pleasant planned for us."

She had hit it right the first time. Unless we could find a way to escape, I was sure our lives weren't worth a plugged nickel.

"Maria, if only you had kept going once you got into the woods."

"And leave you all alone in this mess? Not a chance, DeLucca."

I removed the candle from the stand and started to inspect the large room. It looked like a great hall. It was about forty feet wide and twice as deep, with the floor and walls made of big stones. We walked together along the side of the right wall and, as I held the candle overhead, we could see several tapestries hanging against the rough stones. There were suits of armor standing in stone niches along the wall. Above them, shields, swords and spears were mounted on iron brackets too high to reach. At the end of the hall was a stone fireplace, maybe fourteen feet wide and over eight feet high, with giant fire irons in the hearth. On the opposite wall we found another door. made of heavy wooden planks and covered with crude, hammered iron ornament. There was no latch or handle I could find, but I figured it opened into the part of the ranch house that I'd seen up built up next to the castle wall. We couldn't see the ceiling in the dim candlelight, but thirty feet up, there were several arched windows with bars. Through those bars we could see the night sky but saw no way out. We walked back to the front entrance and noticed openings on either side of the door at the base of the turrets. Closer inspection showed us archways to spiral stone stairs leading up inside the turrets. The pair of the archways were identical and spaced about twenty feet on either side of the main door. I decided to check one out.

"DeLucca, where are you going?" Maria asked as I poked the candle deeper into the darkness at the base of the stairs. "Don't leave me alone in here. I'm coming with you."

"Look, Maria." I held the candle over my head. "These stairs must go to the top of the turret. There's probably no way out up there, but we might as well have a look."

I hoped that the candle wouldn't blow out as we started up the dark, narrow steps. The long winding climb forced us to stop and rest halfway up. After we caught our breath, I gave her the candle then took her hand and led her the rest of the way to the top. As we reached the end of the stairs, I felt the cool night air on my face and saw the sky.

We stepped out onto the top of the turret where a stone walkway bridged the front of the castle, crossing from turret to turret around the top of the castle. I stepped up to the parapet and looked down over the edge. We were damn near eighty feet up. There was no way we could get off the top of this castle without wings.

We were in a tight fix, trapped on the turret of a twelfth century castle somewhere in the La Honda woods, with no place to go but down. Our host was taking his time introducing himself, which probably meant he hadn't decided yet how to dispose of us. The faint light that I thought I had seen in the woods could be our only hope. It could mean that someone had followed us, but who?

"DeLucca! I hope you have some matches. The candle just blew out."

"Damn!" I searched through my pockets. "I had a book of matches, but now I can't find them."

Maria looked into her handbag and found a lighter. Unfortunately, the thing didn't work. She stepped close to me and put her head against my chest. "It doesn't look good, does it, DeLucca?"

"Hell, Maria, we've been in tighter squeezes than this. We'll get out, somehow. Right now, let's see if we can get back down to the main floor."

I walked to the edge of the staircase and could see the first five steps spiraling down into pitch darkness. Without the candle, it would be dangerous. One slip and we'd tumble eighty feet to the floor below. We'd have to sit down on the steps and take them one at a time.

"Maria. I'll go first, you stay close behind me. Just take it slow."

I sat down on the first step and slowly lowered myself to the next step below. Maria followed my every move, feeling the way in total darkness.

"DeLucca! I can't see a thing."

"We're about halfway down. Just take it one at a..." At that moment the inside of the turret illuminated with light. Set into the stones about every six feet were electrical light fixtures which were all lit up now.

I stood up. "Christ! The place is wired for electricity." I took Maria's hand and we continued down the narrow stairs. When we reached the bottom, we stepped out into the now brightly-lit hall. Overhead, hanging from a chain attached to thick wooden timbers a great chandelier lit up the room revealing deep red tapestries depicting hunting and battle scenes hanging on the towering gray walls. We could see the shields now with their coat of arms and iron helmets mounted between the tapestries. The only piece of furniture was a large wooden table to the right of the fireplace. Whoever built this place must have copied it from some old castle in Europe.

"DeLucca. What do you think is going to happen now?"

"I suspect that very soon, Maria, we will meet our host, and I wouldn't be at all surprised if he isn't someone we know."

TWENTY-TWO

We didn't have long to wait. From the wooden door on the left wall, we heard sounds, then a crack of light appeared as the heavy door swung inward. A tall man in a suit and tie stepped through the doorway.

Maria whispered, "My God, DeLucca, it's Townsend, the president of the Board of Trustees at the opera."

"It figures, Maria. He's the one behind all of this."

Townsend was slightly bald, with gray sideburns. His large, hooked nose protruded from his narrow face. He tapped the stone floor with a bone-handled walking cane. His two flunkies, Blondie and College boy stepped forward and stood by his side. College boy had his .38 clenched in his fist.

Townsend said, "Put the gun away. I'm sure Mister DeLucca won't do anything foolish." Townsend raised his cane and pointed it at me. "Come closer, Mister DeLucca. Let me look at the man who caused me all this trouble. Since you and your little Jewish friend, Kotchman, have been on the scene, you have presented a threat that must be dealt with." His penetrating blue eyes turned to Maria. "And this must be Maria Martinelli, the office girl who obviously supplied you with the information which enabled you to penetrate my organization. It's most unfortunate that you've meddled into matters that do not concern you." He tapped his cane on the floor again as he stared at me. "Most unfortunate indeed."

I'd heard enough about how unfortunate everything was and started to say my piece when he smiled and waved his cane out in front of me and said, "How do you like my castle?"

He waited for my answer, expecting me to be amazed I suppose. "It's OK, as far as castles go."

"Mister DeLucca, you obviously know nothing about castles of the Middle Ages. This one was brought piece by piece from the Rhine in Germany and erected just as it was in the twelfth century. Of course, it's not finished. There is still the second floor to be done and all of the furniture to be delivered. It will be completed early next year." His mild expression changed to grim determination. "Now we must proceed. My informants tell me that you possess certain information that I must have."

"Oh yeah? What information would that be?"

"Mister DeLucca. I am going to ask you a series of questions and I expect you to answer them truthfully."

"And if I don't choose to answer them at all?"

"You will, Mister DeLucca. Believe me, you will."

"Well, let's find out. Go ahead, ask me a question."

"Fist I want to know where the little brown book is."

"What little brown book?"

"Where is your friend Kotchman?"

"I don't know."

"Where is Carl Hessler?"

"Hessler? You mean the butcher of Belzec? I haven't the slightest idea."

Townsend looked over at Blondie and smiled. "Well, Mister DeLucca, you have failed on all three questions. I know you are lying. Shall we ask them again?"

"Go ahead. You'll get the same answers."

"That's not at all cooperative, Mister DeLucca. You see, we already know that you found the book in the shoe brush. We know that the book was recovered at Pier 29 during that unfortunate incident. We also assume that you made a copy of the book. We also know that Hessler's flight did not arrive at its destination. All of these facts we already know. Now, you see how you can help us? Just fill in the missing answers."

"Not a chance in hell."

"In hell, it may very well be. You see, we have means of persuasion."

I laughed. "You mean these two juveniles here? Christ! Those two punks couldn't persuade a doughnut to give up its hole."

"Possibly you are right, but I have someone else in mind." Townsend turned to the doorway and called, "Elsa! Would you come out here please and bring your friend."

Maria and I looked at one another, then watched the corridor beyond the door. Soon we heard heavy footsteps approaching. A large, big-boned, hard-looking woman appeared and stood next to Townsend glaring at Maria. Her straight brown hair was swept back from her broad forehead, and fat lips resembled moist sausages. To me she looked like a sadistic lesbian.

Townsend beamed with pride. "This is Elsa, my secretary and housekeeper. Elsa, I want you to take the woman and find out how much she knows."

Elsa started forward. Maria moved behind me as I slowly backed away. "She's not going anywhere." Elsa stopped. She seemed disappointed.

Townsend tapped his cane and said, "Mister DeLucca. It's useless to resist."

Blondie and College boy tensed, anticipating action. Then there was another noise in the corridor. A giant figure filled the doorway. It was Gunther Mueller. His bald head was sticking out of a turtleneck sweater and his small eyes were fixed on me as he slowly moved forward, dragging his wounded leg.

Townsend held his cane in front of Mueller. "You remember this fellow, don't you, Mister DeLucca? While recuperating from a nasty wound he received at the opera house, he has generously offered to assist me. I will leave you two in Elsa's and Gunther's capable hands. They have a most interesting way of securing answers. Believe me, Mister DeLucca, it won't be pleasant."

Horrified, Maria backed away from the two monsters. I tried desperately to think of a way out. I could make a fight of it while Maria ran to the stairs in the turret, but that would only prolong the inevitable. I could make them chase us, draw them away from the door, and then run by them and lock all of them in the castle. But things like that only succeeded in the movies, so I decided that my only alternative was to talk, tell Townsend some half-truths to get him off my back. I couldn't permit Maria to be subjected to torture and I damn sure didn't want that big German ape to get his hands on me.

Townsend impatiently tapped his cane on the floor. "Well, what will it be, Mister DeLucca? Are you ready to answer my questions now? Or must we indulge in this unpleasant business?"

I had to tell him something, anything... I needed to stall for time.

"OK, Townsend, I'll answer your questions, but believe me, you won't like my answers. First, the book. Hell! You already know where it is. Hessler has it, but you don't know where Hessler is." I waited for his reaction.

"You are starting to irritate me, Mister DeLucca. Get on with it."

"All right. The next question. Where is my friend Kotchman?" I looked at my watch. "By now he's in Miami, Florida. And the last question. Where is Carl Hessler?"

Townsend's impatience was nearing the boiling point. "Yes! Where is Carl Hessler?"

"In Miami with Kotchman and the Israeli Secret Service."

Townsend looked at Gunther, then back at me. "Miami! How could that be? We know that Hessler chartered a flight from San Jose to Santa Fe. Are you telling me that he was forcibly put on a flight to Miami?"

"That's what I'm telling you."

Gunther roared, "Impossible! Herr Hessler could never be taken by the Jewish pigs." He started toward me. "You lie."

Townsend held out his cane. "Calm yourself, Gunther. Mister DeLucca. We know that your car was left in the parking lot at the San Jose Airport. Were you with Kotchman when he and Hessler boarded the flight to Miami?"

"Yes."

"Was there another passenger with Hessler?"

"You mean Julie Koslo? Yeah, she was with him."

"How did Kotchman get Hessler on the plane?"

"I have no knowledge of that. Kotchman made all of the arrangements."

Gunther clenched his fists and snarled, "You lie, DeLucca. I will choke the truth out of you."

Townsend said, "Wait! We will listen to what else he has to say. So far, what we have heard will be very easy to check."

I figured it was time for me to drop the bomb. "You said that you thought I had made a copy of the book. Well, you're right, I did." Maria looked worried and touched my arm as I continued. "Since ten o'clock yesterday, the F.B.I. has been in possession of the copy. I wouldn't be surprised if you won't have visitors pretty soon."

Townsend's eyes narrowed and his face looked grim. Then I dropped the final bomb. "And another thing. We were followed here from Santa Cruz. This place is probably surrounded by the F.B.I. right now."

Townsend turned quickly to Gunther. "Inspect the grounds and report back to me."

Gunther limped off through the doorway, then Townsend faced Blondie. "What about it? Were you followed?"

"No, we weren't followed, Mister Townsend. There was a car on the road behind us for a while, but when we turned off, it went on by."

Now that I had them worried, I thought I'd add one more little barb. "That was a pro following us. Your boys led them right to your front door."

Townsend pounded his cane on the floor. "Enough of this. Put them both in the hole, then call Cullen and have him check with the F.B.I."

"But it's four in the morning, sir," said College boy.

"I don't care what time it is. Call him and tell him to start working on it. Don't delay! Put them below and when you're through, come to the main house." Townsend scowled as he turned and walked back through the doorway.

College boy pulled out his .38 and told us to move over to the big table by the fireplace. He gave Elsa his gun to point at us, then he and

Blondie slid the heavy table across the stones. Under the table was a large stone slab with an iron ring on one end. Overhead, hanging from a beam was a chain hoist with a hook. College boy lowered the hook and Blondie slipped it into the ring attached it to the stone, and then they hoisted up the stone on one end.

The stone rose like a trap door revealing stone stairs leading downward. College boy took the gun from Elsa, pointed to the opening and said, "Go down."

Having no choice, Maria and I started down the stairs. There was a light below. When we reached the bottom we were about ten feet below the floor above us. A dim light bulb hung on a cord from overhead. The huge stone lowered and slammed into its closed position. I felt we'd been entombed, never to see daylight again.

Maria shivered. "It's cold down here, DeLucca. Come keep me warm."

I put my arm around her and gave the dungeon the once over. The room was about twenty feet long and ten feet wide. The walls and floor were made of stone and there wasn't even a bench to sit on. It must have been specially built for some purpose, but I couldn't figure out what, unless it served as a prison cell at some time before. It felt like a tomb, and I hoped that it wouldn't be our last resting place. At least there were no skulls, or human bones lying on the floor. I scanned the walls. On the far end, opposite the stairs, I saw an iron grill set into the stones. I went over to take a look. Solid iron bars covered a dark hole three feet in diameter. Maybe the hole was a drainpipe or an air vent. I didn't know what is was for, but after close inspection and some determined tugs, I knew the iron grill couldn't be removed without a blow torch or explosives. Sewer rats might be able to get through it, but not us.

Maria lowered herself to the floor and leaned against the wall. "DeLucca, I'm so tired. What's going to happen to us?"

"Well, from the looks of it, we don't have a chance in hell of getting out of here right now, but there's always hope that will change."

"What hope, DeLucca? They mean to kill us. I know it."

Maria had started to lose faith, but then again, why shouldn't she? We seemed to be in an impossible situation. I reached for my cigarettes. There were only two left in the pack. Then I remembered I lost the matches.

I sat down next to Maria, put my arm around her and gave her a squeeze. "It'll be OK. We're not licked yet."

She looked up into my eyes and sobbed, "It could have been great for us, DeLucca, if only you had brought the police or the F.B.I. into this. But no! You had to do it Kotchman's way. Now Kotchman has left you holding the bag while he's safe with his prisoner on his way to Israel."

TWENTY-THREE

Maria was right. I could have played things differently. It was my fault that we were here at Townsend's mercy. I had to come up with something. I couldn't take my eyes off the grill covering the drainpipe. If there was a way out of here, that would be it. I stood up and walked over to it again. I smelled fresh air coming from the dark hole which meant it must be open to the outside somewhere. I figured that the pipe must be going underground for some distance then open to the outside, maybe even beyond the castle walls. If only this grill could be removed. I wrapped my hand around one of the bars and gave it several hard tugs, grunting with effort. It was useless. The grill was fully embedded in the stones and cement. The only way out would have to be up the stairs past the big stone that sealed us in.

I sat there in the semi-darkness thinking hard about our options. Maria was frightened and tired of playing the game. She wanted to go home and so did I. Was it possible Townsend had no intention of killing us? Maybe he figured that we were no real threat to him and his powerful organization. Then again, why would he take the chance? If he could silence us for good, it would be to his advantage.

I doubted that we'd really been followed but had almost started to believe it because I wanted so badly for it to be true. Looking around at our stone prison, I decided tThe place looked like a large septic tank. Maybe that's what it really was. Townsend had said that the building of this castle wasn't complete. This sure wasn't a very glorious way to go out, starving to death in a septic tank.

Maria hadn't spoken for over twenty minutes. She'd rested her head on my shoulder and fallen asleep.

Suddenly, the floor overhead rumbled as the big stone slowly raised out of its opening. A shaft of light illuminated the stairs.

Maria jarred from her sleep and grabbed my arm. "What is it, DeLucca!"

"They're raising the stone. Now I guess we'll find out what the hell they're going to do with us."

We stood up and moved back away from the stairs. Someone was at the top of the stairs. There was no mistaking Gunther's angry voice. "Go down!"

A man slowly started down the stairs, then he was pushed from behind and tumbled to the floor below. The man tried to raise himself and seemed to be in pain. As the stone lowered, I stepped forward to help him. The man raised his head and looked at me. "DeLucca! Christ! Is that you?"

I was looking down at the bloody face of Ace Conlin. "Yeah. It's me, Ace. Let me help you up. How badly are you hurt?"

Conlin stood up. "I'm OK. It's just my head. That big ape upstairs damn near knocked my brains out."

Maria stepped closer. "DeLucca, do you know this man?"

"Yeah. This is Ace Conlin, the pilot who flew Hessler to El Paso. Ace, this is Maria. It looks like we're all in the same boat." Maria inspected Conlin's head. The skin was split on the forehead, just above his right eye. She wiped the blood away with her handkerchief.

"Thanks, I guess I'll live." Ace turned to me. "What are you doing here? Where the hell are we?"

"Somewhere in the La Honda woods, about twenty miles from San Francisco. Maria and I were brought here at gunpoint and thrown into this hole."

Conlin thought for a moment. "These guys upstairs have something to do with the German war criminals, right?"

"You hit it on the nose. The big boy up there is the head of an organization that provides the Nazis with protection. How do you happen to be here, Ace?"

"Hell! That's a very short story. After delivering Hessler and the girl to Kotchman's people in El Paso, I refueled and flew back home. When I landed, I had a reception committee waiting for me. An hour or so later I was standing in the middle of a castle with some tall geek asking me a lot of questions, while a big bald-headed kraut stood by to rough me up. Believe me. I've been in better places."

"What did Townsend want to know?"

"Townsend! Is that the tall guy in the suit?"

"Yeah, he's the one. What did he ask you?"

"Well, for starters, he wanted to know why I didn't fly to Santa Fe with my passengers. I told him to go to hell and that I wasn't going to answer any of his questions. That's when baldy pulls out a pair of pruning shears and says for every question I don't answer truthfully he's going to cut off one of my fingers. Needless to say, I answered his questions. I told him that Kotchman had paid me to fly Hessler and the girl to a small field just outside of El Paso, that friends of Kotchman's met the plane and took Hessler and the girl away in a car. Then he asked where they were taking them. I told him I wasn't told where they were taking them. Then he wanted to know where Kotchman was. I said all I knew was that Kotchman had a flight out of San Jose to Houston. In short, I spilled my guts. It's a good thing I didn't know any more. At least I didn't mention you and they didn't ask. Then the big kraut puts down the pruning shears, smacks me across the head and says I better be telling the truth. Then those two fags hoist up a stone in the floor, the kraut throws me down the stairs and here I am. The way I see it, your little friend, Kotchman, has put all of us in a hell of a bind. I figured we'd see one another again for that drink some day, but this is ridiculous."

I thought over Conlin's story. Now Townsend knew that I lied about Kotchman going to Miami. He knew Hessler was in the hands of the Israeli secret service, but he didn't know where Hessler was to be taken. That would be his next question. The thought of Gunther and his pruning shears made me think of three-fingered Julie. Cold chills ran up my spine.

I reached for my cigarettes then asked Ace if he had any matches. He handed me a pack. I lit up and wondered when the krauts would come for me. I had the answers to their questions, and they knew it.

Conlin walked around the room and ended up at the grill. "What about using this to get out of here?"

I joined him at the grill. "I tried to move it, but it's no use."

Conlin pulled on the bars with both hands. "Yeah, it's solid all right. Is there any rope or cable down here?"

"No. I looked. There's nothing."

"Too bad. I have an idea that might work, but it would take about twenty feet of rope. Well, DeLucca, what's our next move? It looks like they've got us in a hole."

"You're right. It doesn't look good. I think, very soon now, they are going to call me up for more questioning. If only we had a weapon.

When they raise the stone, maybe we could take on the one by the entrance."

Conlin kept looking around. "Yeah, but we don't have a weapon. Are you sure there's no rope or anything in here?"

"I'm sure. If we did have a rope, what the hell would we do with it?"

Conlin smiled. "I was thinking we could tie it to the iron bars on the grill and attach it to the stone door. When they hoist up the stone, it could pull the grill right out of the wall."

"That's a brilliant idea, Ace. All we'd need is a way to attach it. Let's take a look at the bottom of the stone."

We climbed the stairs and after a close inspection, we found that the stone was a huge cement block. The stones on the other side that matched the castle floor must have been inlaid in the cement. The iron eye used to hoist the block went all the way through the cement and stuck six inches out of the bottom.

"Your idea would work, if only we had some rope."

Conlin started down the stairs. "Yeah, well it was something to think about anyway. I've only been here a little while and I'm already starting to go nuts. We've got to find a way out of here."

We no more than stepped off the bottom of the stairs, when the large block overhead started to move upward. The three of us stood at the base of the stairs and watched. Then, Gunther's booming voice bounced off the walls of the dungeon. "DeLucca! You come up."

Maria grabbed my arm. "Don't go, DeLucca! I'm afraid something terrible is going to happen."

"It's all right, Maria. They're just going to ask me some more questions."

Conlin said, "You better tell them what they want to know."

"We'll see how it goes, Ace."

As I got to the top of the stairs I heard Ace say, "Good luck, pal."

Gunther met me head on as I stepped out onto the castle floor. Blondie and College boy lowered the stone, while Gunther pushed me toward the table. Townsend was sitting in a high-backed chair nervously tapping his fingers on the wooden planks of the table.

"This is the last time we will talk. No more cute little games this time. I want the truth. I know you lied about going to the F.B.I. I was just informed that the bureau has no record of having talked to you. I seriously doubt that you made a copy of the list, and you lied when you said you were being followed. You lied when you said Kotchman and Hessler flew to Miami. I know Kotchman took a flight from San Jose to Houston. I also know Hessler was highjacked to El Paso, Texas. Now, I want to know where Kotchman's agents took Hessler and the girl, and why did Kotchman go to Houston? It's obvious to me that they are trying to take Hessler and the girl out of the country without extradition papers. It occurred to me that a ship would be the only way, and Galveston is the closest port to Houston. That's it, isn't it, DeLucca?"

So far, this guy was answering his own questions. I smiled and remained silent. I wondered why he was so intent on knowing where Hessler was. Townsend leaned back in his chair and motioned to Gunther. "I want answers and I want them now."

Gunther grabbed my left hand and pinned it to the table. In his other hand was a pair of pruning shears. This was the moment of truth. He already had his answer, so I nodded, "Yes! They went to Galveston."

Gunther withdrew the shears. Townsend smiled. "Now we're getting somewhere. One more question and you can go back to your friends. I want to know the name of the ship and its destination, also the date and time of its departure."

I knew that question would come up. If he knew the ship and when it was leaving, then he had all of the answers he needed. I found it hard to believe that he could rescue Hessler from the Israeli agents, but then Hessler had escaped justice before. I decided to hold off giving the answer as long as I could.

"I don't know the name of the ship or where it's going."

Townsend's eyes widened. "Wrong answer, DeLucca. Gunther!"

Once again, Gunther slammed my hand down on the table and held it like a vise. This time he was going to do it. I threw my weight against him catching him off guard. He released my hand and I moved quickly with a back hand slam to his throat. He fell back, momentarily stunned, then his big fist caught me high on the cheek bone. As I staggered backwards, he came back in fast and gave me another crushing blow that damn near tore my head off. Gunther still wasn't through with me. He was about to pound me into the floor when Townsend yelled, "Enough! Bring him back to the table and hold him."

Blondie put an arm lock around my neck and College boy held my midsection as Gunther once again pinned my hand to the table. I tried to speak, but the throat hold was too tight.

Townsend raised his hand. "Let him talk. I'm waiting, DeLucca."

"If I knew the answers, I would tell you. I wasn't told anything about the ship."

"Gunther! Take off his little finger."

The next thing I remember was screaming in pain as I felt the blades of the shears and heard the crack of bones. The three of them held me as I stared down at my bloody finger and its dismembered tip inches from my hand. I gritted my teeth as the pain overtook my body. I felt like vomiting. Everything was a blur.

Townsend's voice sounded like it was in an echo chamber. "The answer, DeLucca!" I couldn't speak. I realized this had gone too far.

"Take off his second finger!" cried Townsend.

Gunther opened the blood-spattered shears and enclosed my finger. I yelled, "No! No more, you bastards. I'll tell you!"

Gunther pulled back the shears. Townsend leaned forward and looked into my pain-filled eyes. "I'm waiting, DeLucca."

Blondie released his hold on my neck. I coughed and tried to comprehend what had just happened. Gunther stood close to me, snapping the blades of the shears like a pair of scissors and looking at the blood on the table.

I'd had it. Like Ace Conlin, I spilled my guts. "It's the Erasmus! A Greek tanker. It leaves Galveston Thursday morning at 6:00 a.m."

Townsend smiled. "Good. Now you may keep your other three fingers. Wrap up his finger and take him below. We have work to do."

Blondie tied a rag around my hand, then he and College boy raised the stone and Gunther shoved me toward the opening.

I turned and faced Townsend. "Hold it a minute! I answered all of your damn questions. Now I have a question for you."

Gunther snarled and was about to push me down the stairs, when Townsend said, "Wait. Let him ask his question."

"Why would you go through all of this for a bunch of Nazi war criminals? You're a respected member of the opera board. You have power, money, land and position. Why would you jeopardize it all for a guy like Hessler? What is he to you?"

Townsend paused for a moment. "To answer that question properly, it would take more time than we have, for it is a lengthy and perplexing story. But as for my relationship with Hessler? He is my brother." Townsend turned and quickly walked off as Gunther spun me around and slung me down the stairs like a bag of laundry. I caught my balance halfway down and stumbled to the bottom as the big stone closed above me.

Maria and Conlin rushed to my side. "My God, DeLucca! What did they do to you?"

Conlin led me to the wall. "Sit down over here. It looks like the bastards roughed you up quite a bit."

I lowered myself to the floor. The pain in my hand was killing me. Maria looked at the blood-soaked cloth wrapped around my finger. "Did they...?

"Yes, I'm afraid they did. Gunther and his shears...he took off my little finger."

Conlin grimaced. "Jesus! You let them do it? Why the hell didn't you tell them what they wanted to know?"

"I did tell them. If I hadn't, I wouldn't have any fingers left."

Maria lifted my hand. "You need medical attention. If only we had something to bandage it with."

I reached down toward my feet. "Maria, help me take off my shoe. We can use the laces to tie a sock around the wound to stop the bleeding."

Twenty-Four

The three of us sat on the floor with our backs against the wall. We had been down in this hole for six hours, but it seemed like days. I couldn't remember the last time I had eaten or had anything to drink. Maria was leaning against me sound asleep, while Conlin fingered the dirt and threw pebbles against the far wall.

"Christ, DeLucca. You must have had some pretty important information for them to cut off your finger."

"Yeah. I told them about the ship and when it leaves from Galveston, but I found out that Townsend is Hessler's brother. That's the German connection at the opera house."

Conlin picked up a handful of dirt and let it sift through his fingers. "What the hell are they going to do with us now?"

I looked at Maria and saw she was still asleep. I whispered, "Expect the worst, Ace. I believe they have no intention of letting us live. Unless we do something, and soon, we've had it."

"You paint a pretty dim picture, DeLucca. Looks like we won't be having that drink together after all."

At that moment, I heard a noise. It seemed to be coming from behind the grill in the drainpipe. "Hear that?"

Maria opened her eyes. "What is it, DeLucca?"

"I think someone's in the pipe."

We stood up, went to the iron grill and listened. Conlin put his head next to the bars. "You're right, DeLucca. There's someone or something down there. Look! I see light. It's got to be a flashlight."

It was then that I heard my name being called. I leaned closer to the grill. "Yes! It's DeLucca."

The beam of light got closer, and I could see a figure crawling toward us. Then a small ferret-like face appeared on the other side of the grill. At first, I thought it was Kotchman, but the voice was different and he spoke with a only slight accent. "Are you DeLucca?"

"Yes! I'm DeLucca. Who the hell are you?"

"My name is Ronen Eliud. Kotchman sent me to find you. Where is this place?"

"We're locked in a chamber under the castle floor. Were you the one who was following us in a car?"

"Yes. Kotchman called me in El Paso yesterday morning. I met with him at the San Jose Airport, and he told me to follow you. He suspected trouble."

"What did you say your name was?"

"You can call me Ronnie."

"OK, Ronnie. We don't have much time. How can you help us? There's no way out of here, except by the entrance above us and it's sealed with a large block of cement. These iron bars can't be moved, unless you happen to have some plastic explosives. Do you?"

"No. I'm sorry. I do not."

"Do you have any weapons you could slip through the bars?"

"I have two. One is a Colt .45 I could let you have, but I must keep my other gun."

"Good enough. How many extra rounds do you have?"

"Just one clip."

"OK. Let's have it. At least we'll go down fighting."

Conlin reached up through the bars, took the gun and said, "Too bad you can't slip us a machine gun. Then we could really give the bastards a fight. Listen, Ronnie. Do you have any rope? We need about twenty or thirty feet of it."

"No. I have no rope. What would you use it for?"

I said, "Conlin here has an idea of how to pull the grill out of the wall."

"That's good. Would forty feet of airplane cable do?"

"It damn sure would," said Conlin. "You have some?"

"I have it in my car. I'm parked on the other side of the south wall and used a length of it to climb over the wall, then at daybreak, I found this open drainpipe about fifty feet from the wall and decided to see if I could use it to get inside the castle. I didn't expect to find you at the end. Okay, I'll go now and be back with the extra cable from my car as soon as I can." Ronnie started crawling back out through the pipe.

Conlin smiled at me. "Hey, old pal. Looks like we may get to have that drink yet."

Maria's spirits perked up. "DeLucca, do you really think we can escape from here?"

"Sure we can. As soon as Ronnie comes back with the cable, we'll get it all rigged up, then wait for them to raise the stone."

"What if they don't raise the stone?" asked Maria.

"Then it won't make much difference one way or the other. Ace, let me have the gun."

"Are you sure you can handle it with that bad hand?"

"Don't worry. I'll manage."

Conlin handed me the gun and I tucked it into my belt. I started to formulate a plan to get Maria and Conlin out. Someone had to stay behind and hold off the krauts when the stone was lifted, otherwise they would follow us through the drainpipe and if they knew we escaped through the pipe, they would seal off the outside exit.

TWENTY-FIVE

O nce again we played the waiting game. I feared that they would come for us before Ronnie came back with the cable. If that happened, I figured we'd go along with them until I had a chance to open fire at close range. Maybe I could get lucky and drop all of them. Then again, the whole thing could turn sour. My hand wasn't in the greatest shape. Conlin could be right; maybe I wouldn't be able to handle the gun well enough to pull it off.

I wondered about Townsend and his story. Where and when did it all start? Probably during the rise of the Third Reich in Germany. He must have left the country, changed his name and made his fortune in America while his brother, Hessler, stayed behind and became an SS man. After the war, Townsend's position with the San Francisco Opera enabled him to help his brother and his comrades. I had a hard time believing anyone living in America could sympathize with the Nazi cause, but he had used Nazi tactics on me. Maybe I would never know the full story.

There was movement in the pipe again and Conlin stood up. "DeLucca, he's back."

We went to the grill. Ronnie pushed the cable through the bars and said, "There is a lot of activity up there. The entrance to the castle is heavily guarded and men are patrolling the grounds. It's as though they suspect something is about to happen."

"It's just a precaution," I said. "I told them we were followed and that the F.B.I. was probably surrounding the place. I wanted to make them sweat a bit."

Conlin took the end of the cable, climbed up the stairs and wrapped it several times around the iron bolt that stuck out of the cement block. He tied it off with a couple of half hitches, then pulled the cable tight at the grill. Ronnie helped tie it securely to the iron bars.

"There it is," said Conlin. "I hope this works. It's as tight as we can get it."

I checked the cable and found no slack. If the cable didn't snap, I believed it would work.

I stepped close to the bars and looked at Ronnie. "OK. Now we come to the business of getting out of here. Ronnie, how far is your car from the outside wall?"

"It is parked in the trees about fifty yards beyond the wall."

"Is there an easy way over it?"

"I have a grappling hook and cable to climb up. It should be easy for a man or a woman... with two arms." He was looking at my missing one.

"You said the wall is about fifty yards from the drainpipe?"

"Yes."

"Is there any cover on the way to the wall?"

"Not much. A few shrubs and trees."

"That will have to do. Here's the plan. When and if they raise the stone and it pulls the grill cover out, Maria and Ace will follow you through the pipe. I want you to get over the wall and make it to the car. As soon as you can, contact Kotchman and tell him they know everything about the ship and its departure."

Maria looked at me with sad eyes. "Oh, DeLucca, I hope you're not going to say what I think you're going to say."

"It's the only way, Maria. I'll hold them off as long as I can. There is no other way. Otherwise, we all go down together."

"DeLucca, please don't do this. There has to be another way."

Ronnie put his head next to the bars. "Two guns will be better than one, DeLucca. This is more my fight than yours and I am trained for it. I'll stay with you and the two of us will make them pay."

I couldn't erase the doubts I had about the final outcome. What if they decided to leave us down here to rot? If they did come to take us out, would the cable hold? Would the raising of the stone be powerful enough to pull the grill out of the wall? And then there was my mangled hand. Would I be able to handle the gun? I looked over at Maria sitting against the wall with Conlin. She had been through enough. I hoped at least she and Conlin could escape to safety. I figured I'd have to play it like I lived and take one thing at a time.

Ronnie was hunched down in the drainpipe waiting patiently. He called to me. "DeLucca. How many of them are we up against? What are the odds?"

"I only saw five. Townsend, the woman, the two kids, and Mueller. I don't know how many others there are."

Ronnie slammed a clip into his automatic. "I saw four men outside. Two of them might have been the kid ones who drove you from Santa Cruz. Leaving two more, that means there are at least seven to deal with. How many are armed?"

"Blondie and College boy both have hand guns. The big kraut, Gunther, wasn't carrying a gun, but I'm sure he must have one."

Unlike Kotchman who never smiled, Ronnie did. "That's not such bad odds, DeLucca. We hold the element of surprise. They won't know that there are two of us and that we are armed. If we work it right, we may be able to cut the odds down a bit more."

I tried to make out Ronnie's features, but his face was hidden in the shadows behind the bars. "It sounds like you have something in mind."

"I do. When the iron grill is pulled from the wall."

"You mean, 'if' the grill is pulled from the wall?"

"Yes, there is always that 'if', but if it all goes well, I will come out of the drainpipe and join you while the woman and Conlin crawl in and make their way to the outside. It would be better if we were in position over there to the side and below the stairs. They'll probably hear the grill when it hits the floor and send someone down to investigate. That's when we cut the odds. Do you like my plan?"

"Yeah. It just might work."

"How is your hand? Will you have trouble handling the gun?"

I shook my hand and the bloody sock fell off and landed on the floor. The finger was still bleeding but not as much. I lifted the gun from my belt and painfully put my trigger finger in place. "No, I can handle it."

"That is good. Now, my friend. We wait for the battle."

Maria looked like she was going to cry as she watched me put the gun back into my belt. "Oh, how I wish this was over, DeLucca. Why can't we all go out through the drainpipe?"

"Then they would be waiting for us at the other end. Believe me, this is the best way. Try not to worry. It's about time we had a little luck."

It was then that we heard the grating noise of stone against stone as they started to raise the block.

"Quick! Maria, Ace, get away from the grill. As soon as Ronnie comes out, climb in and go like hell through the pipe."

The cable became as tight as a violin string as the stone was slowly raised. Then we heard the rock and cement crumbling as the grill was coming loose.

"Get ready!" I said. "It's going to work."

The cable held strong and the grill pulled out of the wall and crashed to the floor. Ronnie bounded out of the pipe, gun in hand. Conlin took Maria by the arm and helped her into the opened hole.

He turned and said, "Good luck, pal. Be seeing you." then disappeared into the dark tunnel.

Ronnie joined me at the base of the stairs. The stone kept moving up, loudly dragging the grill across the floor. I took the .45 out of my belt, positioned my trigger finger and stood ready.

Daylight flooded into the dark chamber. Ronnie and I crouched in the shadows beside the stairs and listened.

Gunther's gruff voice exploded, "Vot is dis?"

I could see the cable being yanked back and forth.

"Vot is wrong? Go down! Find out."

There was movement at the top of the stairs. The shadow of a man fell across the stairs as he slowly came down. It was College Boy carrying a gun in his right hand. When he got halfway down, Ronnie reached up and grabbed his leg making him to lose his balance. With a cry of surprise, College boy fell, firing his gun twice into the darkness, before he slammed onto the ground. His crumpled form lay still at the bottom of the stairs.

Ronnie motioned for me to stay where I was, then he crept along the base of the stone stairs toward the prone kid. College boy was playing possum. He slid his gun hand under his body and fired at Ronnie. The bullet barely missed and careened off the wall as Ronnie returned the fire. College boy screamed, dropped his gun and fell back. A hail of gunfire came from the top of the stairs. The rapid rounds ricocheted off the floor. Ronnie threw himself back against the side of the stairs out of the line of fire. His eyes flashed at me with excitement.

"It's started, DeLucca! Now it's their move."

This was the first time I'd had a chance to see Ronen Eliud up close. He was a wiry little guy who reminded me of Kotchman in many ways, but there was a youthful innocence about him Kotchman didn't have. He moved like spring steel and his courage could not be denied. I figured if we got out of this alive, I would be proud to buy the little guy a drink.

It was all quiet above. They probably knew now that the grill had been pulled out. I hoped we'd given Maria and Conlin enough time to get through the pipe and over the wall.

Ronnie lifted his head up to get a glimpse of the top of the stairs. "There's no activity up there. Should we try for the top?"

"Christ, Ronnie! No, they'd pick us off like ducks."

"But, DeLucca, we may have the upper hand and don't know it. I'm going to see if I can draw their fire."

He stood up and leaned over the stairs. He drew back hearing the cocking sound of a machine pistol, then another hail of bullets sprayed the dungeon. Chips of splintered stone scattered around us. Next a metal object bounced down the stairs and the overhead stone started to close.

Ronnie yelled, "Tear gas! Quick, DeLucca, out through the pipe. It's all we can do."

Ronnie disappeared into the pipe. I quickly followed but tripped over the body of College boy. He was still alive and looked up at me with tear-filled eyes.

"Help me! I don't want to die."

Ronnie's voice echoed through the drainpipe. "DeLucca! Hurry."

I looked down at College boy and said, "Sorry kid, you got in with the wrong crowd."

I rushed to the opening and threw myself into the dark hole. I found it difficult to keep up with Ronnie, but I could see daylight at the end of the pipe. Another thirty feet and I would be out. Ronnie knelt on the ground waiting for me. As I reached the opening, I heard two shots. Ronnie dropped to the ground, holding his knee. I shoved myself out of the pipe, rolled twice on the ground, turned and raised my gun as three more bullets kicked up dirt around us.

I couldn't see where the shots were coming from. "Ronnie! How bad are you hit?"

"In the leg. I can't walk. You go, try to make it over the wall and I'll hold them up."

I looked behind me and saw the stone wall. It was about fifty yards away, mostly open ground, except for some rocks and a few poplar trees. Two more bullets kicked into the dirt, too close for comfort.

I stood up, put the gun in my belt and grabbed Ronnie's coat. I jerked him to his feet and put his arm over my shoulder. "Come on! We'll head for those rocks. It's the only cover."

We started for the rocks and heard another barrage of gunfire. I felt something hot tear into my right side. "Christ!" I knew I'd been hit. We fell forward and crawled into the rocks, like two wounded lizards.

I hadn't even fired my gun yet. This was a one-sided war. We were both shot up and it didn't look good. Ronnie tightened his belt around his thigh to stop the bleeding, but my wound was pumping blood like an oil derrick and my vision was failing. I felt like I was going to pass out, but I didn't think Ronnie knew that I was wounded. He looked up over the rocks and said, "DeLucca, there are three of them, coming from different directions. You cover the one on the right. I'll keep an eye on the other two." I lifted my arm and laid it on top of the rock, pointing the gun at the three men walking towards us. The one in the middle was Blondie and he was carrying a sub-machine gun. They were about twenty yards away when Ronnie fired, missing the man on our left as he ducked behind a tree. I took aim and fired a pattern of three rounds. Blondie took cover. The man to my right ran forward and threw himself on the ground firing at will with an automatic rifle. Two of the bullets hit Ronnie in the right side and knocked to the ground. For a moment Ronnie clawed at the dirt then rolled over staring up at the sky.

I could see he was dead, and I was losing strength. I didn't think it would end this way, but there wasn't a chance in hell of my getting out of this alive. It was like we'd been shooting blanks, and they knew it. I checked for the guy to my right. He was gone. Where the hell did he go? I looked ahead and saw Blondie walking right at me. I imagined a smile on his smug face. It was now or never. I stood up and raised the gun but before I could fire, I felt another stinging pain. The bullet hit me high on the right leg, just below the hip. The impact knocked me down. I lay there and heard footsteps approaching.

Play dead," I said to myself and didn't move.

I heard Blondie say, "It's over. Bring the car and we'll bury them in the woods."

Two men walked away, leaving Blondie alone. He walked up to where I lay face down, put his foot under my body and turned me over. He had a look of disbelief in his eyes as I fired three times hitting him squarely in the chest. He slammed backwards onto the ground. The two men he had sent for the car turned and started back toward me on the run. I could barely see them, but I rapidly squeezed the trigger. I only heard one shot go off, then clicks. The gun was empty. I fell back to the ground. It felt like I was floating in my own blood. My eyes closed. I had no more strength left to fight. Before I completely lost consciousness, I thought I heard sirens.

I figured I must be hallucinating. I saw Kotchman's face close to mine as he kept saying, "Make it, DeLucca. Make it." And then I saw Maria and heard myself say, "Maybe the next time around, kid."

TWENTY-SIX

What followed had to be what happens just before death. I had visions of weird, distorted faces as if I were in a test tube looking out at throngs of people peering at me through a glass wall. I floated in a void with no sound and the viewers seemed to pass by as if they were actors in a silent movie. It was strange how I knew all of the performers. I saw the bartender at the Courtroom Bar, but he wasn't wearing his usual short red jacket. There was Joe Bender, the business agent of Local 16, but he didn't have his cigar. Earl 'Mac' McGuire and his bunch of stagehands paraded by, but they were dressed up as if going to a funeral. I also saw Al Ferrigno, the doorman, but he was without his hat. And there was Bruno Guffanti, Phil Cohen, Big Jer, and finally Tommy Doyle wearing his trench coat with the Bogart hat pulled down over his eyes. Maria floated by, smiling at me, but with tears falling from her eyes. Ace Conlin appeared and gave me a smile, with a thumbs up gesture. I saw Julian Bagely with his red carnation in the lapel of his worn dark suit. There were Mr. and Mrs. Koslo looking at me too and they seemed to be very sad. Then, I saw Wolf Kotchman.

He sneered at me, as if to say, I had cheated life and found the perfect solution. And there was Maria again and again, always Maria.

There were some other players I didn't recognize, at least four of them. They appeared to be very tall and their heads seemed to float in space. They looked mean and didn't seem to like me. I was glad to be safe in my test tube. But then came the damned dreams I couldn't escape. These weren't like the silent movies. These were nightmares filled with pain and blood. Gunther Mueller had the leading role. I liked the sad silent films which took the morbid taste of death out of my mouth. I recalled the movie, "The Big Sleep" with Humphrey Bogart, and wondered if this was my big sleep just as I fell into another blood-soaked nightmare...

The goddamned machine guns slowed down our advance. We'd knock one out, and another would pick up the constant firing. My head was pressed against the ground and my rifle had gotten wet during the landing and covered with sand. The mortars had zeroed in on us and relentless machine gun fire kept us pinned down behind a sandy bluff about five hundred yards from the beach. Sergeant Driscoll crawled up behind me, slapped my back and yelled, "Move out! We've got to get off the beach."

A long wave of troops started to move forward. A mortar struck to my right and took out three of my buddies. Its cordite smoke filled my lungs, and I couldn't breathe. I reached the top of the bluff, threw myself on the ground and closed my eyes as mortar shells burst and bullets kicked up sand all around me.

Then suddenly, it was all quiet. The deafening sounds of war were replaced with music. I had heard this music before, a full orchestra playing an opera. I found myself lying face down on wet cement in my battle gear. It was dark except for a dim light that shone at the end of a long, narrow corridor. I realized I was in the basement of the San

Francisco Opera House. I raised my head and fixed my eyes on the light at the end of the dark tunnel. I stood up, held my rifle ready and slowly moved forward. I was drawn toward the light like a fragment of metal being pulled by a magnet.

The tunnel seemed to close in on me as I approached a large iron door in a cement wall. The orchestra thundered overhead. Lightning flashed as the iron door swung open. A German soldier, his face shadowed by a steel helmet, was sitting behind a heavy caliber machine gun. His face slowly materialized. It was Gunther Mueller. I tried to raise my rifle, but my arms wouldn't move. The gun belched fire. Hot chunks of steel tore into my body and knocked me backwards to the floor. The sounds of drums, cymbals and the frantic cry, "Medic!" filled my head.

Then there was a floating sensation as if I were flying low over the ground. I forced my eyes open. The sky and clouds moved overhead. The music had stopped and once again I heard the sounds of war. I raised my head and found myself strapped tight to a stretcher. I was being moved down the beach by the bearers. My combat jacket had been cut away from my right shoulder and what was once my arm, had turned into a bloody mass of flesh and bone. I lowered my head, bit my lip and uttered a muffled cry.

The scene changed to a large white room. Bright lights overhead blinded my eyes. At the foot of my bed three men dressed in white stood with their backs to me, speaking in whispers. I heard one of them say, "There is nothing else we can do." Another said, "I agree. We'll have to take it off." Then the big one in the center turned toward me. In a menacing guttural voice, he said, "I will take it off!" and his face came into focus. It was Gunther Mueller and in his hand he flexed a pair of pruning shears. I tried to move, but something held me fast to the bed. I strained against the bonds and heard myself yell.

I opened my eyes.

I was flat on my back in a bed. The room was dark and cool. To my right was an open door, and beyond it was a dimly lit hallway. I wondered if this was a continuation of the nightmare or if it was real. I looked down and could see a leather strap across my chest holding me firmly to the bed. My left hand was bandaged, and I had pain in my right side and leg. The pain was definitely real at least and I remembered the gun battle at the castle. I'd been shot twice, and my hand...that was the work of Gunther Mueller. It appeared I was still in one piece...what there was left of me. I felt weak and very tired. It must have been the middle of the night because no one was around.

Suddenly, the room lights went on. Standing in the doorway was a large colored nurse. "Is that you making all that racket, Mister DeLucca?" She came up to the bed, stuck a thermometer in my mouth and wrapped a rubber tube around my arm. "You been having more of those nightmares? I swear, they must be something, the noises you been making."

I tried to talk with the thermometer in my mouth. She shoved it back under my tongue and said, "Don't talk! I'll go tell your lady friend that you're awake. She's been here the last two nights." She pulled the thing out of my mouth and held it up to the light, then unwrapped my arm. "How is your pain? Do you need something?"

"No. I can get by without it, but I'd like to know how long I've been here, and what this strap is doing across my chest?"

"That strap is to keep you from falling off of the bed. When you got out of the operating room, you kept moving around, so the doctor ordered a restraint to hold you still."

"Operation?"

"Yes, Mister DeLucca. We almost lost you. The doctor will be in to see you in the morning."

"Did you say Maria is here?"

"Yes, I'll go get her and bring you some fresh water." She turned and left the room.

So, I was still alive, all patched up, minus an arm as usual, and now a little finger. Maria would answer all of my questions. Things were looking up, I thought, then realized I should have taken the pain pills when the nurse had offered them.

I heard the click of high heels in the hallway. The nurse entered the room followed by Maria who rushed to the bed. "DeLucca." She kissed me and reached for my bandaged hand. Tears were in her eyes. "DeLucca, you're back." She sat down on the bed and held my hand to her cheek.

The big nurse looked down at me and smiled. I wondered how long she was going to stay there hovering. "What is your name, nurse?"

"My name is Lotta."

Well, Lotta, you can take this damn strap off of my chest now. I won't be falling out of bed."

"Sorry, no can do without orders from your doctor. You can talk to him tomorrow." She picked up the tray and left the room.

I looked into Maria's face. "I'm glad you're here. I can't think of anyone I'd rather see than you."

Maria brushed away her tears. "I'm so thankful that you are going to be all right. For a time there, it was touch and go, but my prayers were answered."

"Maria. Tell me what happened. Where am I? How long have I been here? I don't remember anything but being all shot up and having a lot of bad dreams. Maria, what—."

She put her fingers to my lips. "Don't talk, just rest and I'll tell you everything. You're in San Francisco General Hospital. You were half-dead when they operated on you. That was Tuesday afternoon. This is Sunday."

"I've been here for five days? Jesus! I must have been out of it. How the hell did I get here?"

"When Ace Conlin and I climbed over the wall, we took Ronnie's car and drove to La Honda where Ace called the police and an ambulance. They arrived just in time. You were in bad shape. Ronnie was dead and also the man you called Blondie. The F.B.I. arrived on the scene just as we left in the ambulance. Thank God we got you here in time."

I held her hand. "Maria. Have you been with me this whole time?"

She leaned forward and gave me a kiss. "All the time, my darling, and now you must rest. I'll come back in the morning."

My eyes already started to close as Maria smiled and threw me a kiss from the doorway. I hoped that the nightmares would not return as I fell off to sleep.

At dawn, the big nurse woke me up. She took my temperature and blood pressure, then gave me a pain pill. I fell back to sleep and, around 9:00 in the morning, I opened my eyes again to find Maria sitting by the bed.

"Good morning. How are you feeling?"

This was the first time I was able to separate reality from my visions and dreams. I managed to unbuckle the strap across my chest. Since I was entertaining the thought of having a cigarette, I knew I was on the mend.

"I'm doing OK. Just seeing you makes me feel a lot better. The last time we talked, I was a bit groggy, but now I think I've got my wits about me. Tell me, Maria, did I have any visitors when I was brought in here? I don't know if I was just dreaming or if it really did happen."

"Yes, DeLucca. You had visitors. The whole opera crew was here. You also had a visit from a police inspector and two F.B.I. agents. They insisted on talking to you and forced their way into the recovery room. The doctors ushered them out and told them it would be a few days before you could talk to anyone. I guess they still have no idea what happened."

"Yeah, I suppose I'll have to tell them everything. What about Kotchman? I remember seeing him."

"No. Kotchman wasn't here. That must have been a dream. You probably won't see Kotchman again."

Maria looked very tired. I knew that she must have worn herself out worrying about me these last five days. I told her to go home and get some rest, that I was doing all right and would be up and around in no time.

She was about to leave when the doctor came in to inspect his handy work. The guy seemed too young to be a surgeon, but I figured he knew his business. Maria waved goodbye as the doctor started to remove my bandages.

"You're a very lucky fellow, Mister DeLucca. If we hadn't got to you when we did, I'm afraid you would have ended up a statistic." He stood over me and mumbled, "Yes, the side seems to be coming along just fine." He pressed his fingers close to the wound. "Does that hurt?"

It did, but I said, "No."

A nurse came in and started to put a clean dressing on my side while the young doctor stood at the foot of the bed and studied his clipboard. He looked up and smiled. "You know, I think we can let you go home in a few days. Nurse, you can remove the IV. I think Mister DeLucca is ready for some solid food now. The wound in the thigh will heal quickly. There will be some discomfort for a short while, but it will pass. Your side may cause you some pain when you walk, but that also will eventually disappear. I'm afraid there is nothing we can do about your finger. Just keep it clean and it will heal over in time. You can try to walk if you like. Just don't overdo it. We'll order you a wheelchair. You can go out and get some fresh air. How would that be?"

This was my chance to smoke a cigarette. I said, "That would be fine, doctor. Thank you for putting me back together."

He started for the door, then turned. "Oh, I almost forgot. A police inspector and two F.B.I. agents will be coming to see you this afternoon at 1:00. I told them you were well enough to answer questions. I'll be looking in on you tomorrow. Maybe then we'll decide when you can leave." He put his pen in his pocket, the clipboard under his arm and walked out into the hallway followed by the nurse.

I'd used a wheelchair once before when I was in the Army hospital. I didn't like it. It was always bumping into something or somebody. You damn sure couldn't use the stairs and trying to get into a crowded elevator was a problem. I thought I'd make an effort to walk, so I slid to the edge of the bed, raised myself to a sitting position and lowered my legs to the floor pushing with my arm until I was standing. There was pain, but nothing I couldn't live with. I slowly walked to the locker against the wall, opened it and searched through my pockets for a cigarette. My pockets were empty. I went to the bathroom and then back to bed. After taking a couple of pain pills, I lay back to take a nap. The thought of the interview with the police and the F.B.I. didn't thrill me, but it had to be done. I faded off to sleep.

TWENTY-SEVEN

It seemed like only minutes later that someone was touching my shoulder. "Mr. DeLucca, wake up. There are people here waiting to talk to you."

I looked up at the nurse. "You mean, it's 1:00 already?"

"Yes it is." She raised the bed to an upright position. "Is that more comfortable?"

"Yes. Thank you."

Three tall men in dark suits stood at the foot of my bed. They all looked alike, except that the one on my right had a mustache. Three angry faces glared at me with impatience. The one with the mustache stepped closer and said, "DeLucca, I'm Inspector Arnold, S.F.P.D. and these gentlemen are agents Rawlings and Turner with the F.B.I."

I was going to ask for their identification, but thought, the hell with it. What reason would they have to lie? Besides, all three of them looked official as hell.

The inspector pulled up a chair and sat down. "This is the first time that we have been able to question you since you came out of the operating room. The doctor said it would be OK. We need a lot of answers. Are you ready to assist us?"

"Yes. I'm ready. What do you want to know?"

The inspector looked up at the two agents and smiled, then turned to me. "All right. Now we're getting somewhere. Let me tell you what we know and you can fill in the missing links." He reached into his coat pocket, took out a notebook and opened it. "Last Sunday, the eighteenth at 8:50 P.M. we received a call from a Julian Bagely, informing us that there had been a gun battle in the basement of the opera house. We responded immediately and found several shell casings and a considerable amount of fresh blood on the floor of the passageway under the stage. We questioned Mr. Bagely and he said he had been hiding in the trash room during the gunfire. He thought there were three men involved. The signs of blood ended at the end of the passageway in front of a door. Mr. Bagely had the key and unlocked it. We inspected the building and found no further signs of blood. We questioned the night doorman, Peterson. He had just arrived on duty and knew nothing about the incident. Monday, the morning of the nineteenth, we questioned the day doorman, a Mr. Al Ferrigno. He supported Mr. Bagely's account of the gunshots and said that two men left the building by the stage door. He didn't know how they got in. He thought probably through the War Memorial building and down through the basement. He gave us the names of the two men. One of them was you, DeLucca. The other was a Wolf Kotchman. He said he was an Israeli agent tracking a Nazi war criminal. That's when I called in the F.B.I. We went to your apartment in North Beach. It was a wreck. Your car was not there and neither were you. We put out a bulletin on you and waited. Tuesday the twentieth, the San Jose police identified your car in the airport parking lot. We checked the car rentals and knew you rented a car the night before. Santa Cruz police found the rental in the parking lot of the Dream Inn." The inspector took a breath, then continued. "Wednesday the twenty-first, about 11:40 A.M., we receive a call about another gun battle at the Townsend estate in the La Honda woods. Units were sent out immediately along with agents Rawlings and Turner. When we arrived, we found you wounded and two dead bodies lying beside you. One was identified as Terrance Jenson and the other, Ronen Eliud. He was carrying Israeli identification. We searched the grounds and the house and found it empty, except for another dead body in the basement of the castle. He was identified as James Cullen, the son of a wel-known attorney. Then we came back to the hospital to find out if you had survived the gunshot wounds. Frankly, DeLucca, I was ready to book you on breaking and entering and assault with a deadly weapon. I'm expecting you to come up with some pretty good answers to this mystery. Oh yes, I almost forgot. We found a list of names in the ashtray of the Pontiac at the Townsend estate."

"You found the list? How did you know where to look?"

"An anonymous caller gave us the tip."

"Was it a woman?"

"Yes. I believe it was. These past few days, the bureau has come up with some very interesting findings concerning the list of names. Most of these people are wealthy and prominent. Another strange thing is that none of them can be located. It's as if someone had warned them that trouble was on the way." He leaned back and sighed. "That's what we know to date. Now, DeLucca. It's your turn. What have you got for us?"

Rawlings and Turner grabbed a couple of chairs and sat down. I wasn't sure where to begin. It was so damn complicated. I leaned forward and asked, "Do you have a cigarette?"

The inspector said, "You can't smoke in here."

Rawlings reached into his pocket and pulled out a pack and threw it on the bed. "What the hell. Let him have a cigarette."

I lit up and started to tell the whole story. "It all began when I was called in to investigate the death of Ben Koslo, a prop man at the opera. I found out that he had been murdered by a Nazi war criminal who had been identified by Koslo's wife, Julie. The Nazi's name was Carl Hessler. He was one of the commanders at a death camp in Poland called Belzec. The more I looked into it, the more evidence I found confirming my suspicions of Nazi infiltration at the opera. At that time, I had no idea that there was a powerful organization supporting and protecting them. I found that out later when I tied in with Kotchman."

Rawlings leaned forward in the chair and said, "Tell us about Wolf Kotchman. You say he is an Israeli agent?"

"Yes. He knew about Hessler and his henchmen and was closing in on them. That's when he discovered that I was working on the same case. What I had uncovered was way over my head, so I was somewhat relieved when Kotchman asked for my assistance."

Agent Turner asked, "What did Kotchman intend to do with the Nazis?"

"He had a plan to kidnap all three of them and take them back to Israel for trial."

Inspector Arnold held out his hand. "Wait a minute. You said three of them. Were there two others besides Hessler?"

"Yes. There were Heitman and Mueller. Both of them had been SS men and had worked for Hessler at Belzec."

"Go on." said Arnold.

"Kotchman had made arrangements to transport the three of them by rail to Galveston where they would be put on a Greek tanker and taken to Haifa in Israel. Abe Shoiket was Kotchman's man here in

San Francisco. The three of us planned to kidnap the Nazis from the opera house and move them to Pier 29 where Kotchman had secured a temporary hiding place."

Inspector Arnold scratched his head. "Wait a minute. I know that name, Abe Shoiket. Yes, now I have it. He was fished out of the bay next to Pier 29. You're saying that those so-called gang land killings at the pier have something to do with all of this?"

"Yes. It's all the same case. The three Germans were locked in a store room at the end of the pier. I had found the notebook in Hessler's briefcase just after we kidnapped them. I copied the names from the book and hid the list, then I took the book to Kotchman at the pier. After I left, the three Germans escaped with the help of outside assistance. Abe Shoiket was killed and Kotchman narrowly escaped with his life before killing Heitman."

"That's not the name of the unidentified stiff we've got down at the morgue, is it?" asked Arnold.

"Yes. He was one of Hessler's boys."

Rawlings shifted his weight in the chair and asked, "Where is this fellow Kotchman now?"

"He's probably on his way to Israel with Hessler and Julie Koslo."

"Is she the eyewitness that the Germans held prisoner?" asked Arnold.

"Yes, she is."

"What about the third German?" asked Rawlings. "What did you say his name was?"

"I was just about to ask you about him. Gunther Mueller is his name. He's the one that left his blood in the basement of the opera and he's the one that took off my finger with pruning shears. I take it, you didn't find him at the Townsend estate?"

"No," said Arnold. "This guy Gunther must have flown the coop with Townsend." Inspector Arnold stood up. "There is one other thing that remains a mystery to me. What were you, Ace Conlin and the girl doing at Townsend's estate?"

"We were all kidnapped and brought to the estate. Townsend desperately needed the information we had."

Agent Rawlings stood up and stepped forward. "I'd like to know why?"

"Because it pertained to the whereabouts of Hessler. He wanted to rescue Hessler from the Israelis."

"Why would he take such a chance?"

"I asked Townsend that same question. He told me that Carl Hessler was his brother."

Rawlings was surprised. "His Brother! So Townsend's name was Hessler before he changed it. We'll have to put a check on him and find out when he left Germany. It's highly possible that he was sent here by the Nazis before the war to spy. It all makes sense. You, Conlin and the girl were put down in the dungeon for safe keeping, while Townsend alerted his contacts and tried to rescue his brother."

"That's about it."

"How the hell did you escape? And where did the other Israeli agent come from?"

"Kotchman had Ronnie tail us. He knew there would be trouble. He helped us escape. Ace and Maria got away, but Townsend's goons killed Ronnie and damn near killed me. You know the rest."

I leaned back in the bed and took a drink of water. My whole body was perspiring. Reviewing the events of the last two weeks had exhausted me. I looked up at the three men. They looked quite different than they had when they'd first entered. Their faces had softened and in their eyes I could detect a glint of understanding.

Inspector Arnold reached over and touched my shoulder. "You've been through a lot, DeLucca. Better get some rest. We won't be bothering you again."

Agent Rawlings said, "With the information you've given us, we should be able to break up this Nazi ring and its supporters. Thanks, DeLucca."

As they prepared to leave, a nurse came in to take my blood pressure. She was carrying a small white box. "This was delivered at the desk for you, Mr. DeLucca."

"Would you open it please, nurse?"

The box had a string around it. A card was slipped under the string with the name, DeLucca, written on it. The nurse untied the string and lifted the top of the box. She looked into it and gasped. Turning her face away, she held the box in front of me. The inspector and the two agents craned their necks to inspect the contents of the box. My left hand twinged with pain. I had seen it before. It was the tip of my little finger covered with black dried blood. Beside the finger tip, was a bloody pair of pruning shears.

Agent Rawlings exclaimed, "Christ! Who the hell would send a thing like that?"

I replied, "Only one person I know. It has to be Gunther Mueller."

Rawlings addressed the nurse. "Do you know who delivered this package?"

"No, Sir. It was left at the desk."

Rawlings turned to his fellow agent. "Turner, go to the desk and find out who delivered the package." He faced the inspector. "It's obvious that Townsend has put out a contract on DeLucca and the contractor is Gunther Mueller. You better put a plainclothes man by the door around the clock. It's not unlikely that DeLucca might have an unwanted visitor."

"I'll have a man stationed outside the door right away," said Inspector Arnold.

Agent Turner entered the room. "The box was delivered about twenty minutes ago by a boy around the age of twelve."

Rawlings snapped, "What did he look like?"

"The nurse at the desk could only remember that he was white and wore a baseball cap."

"All right! You go out and see if you can find the kid. DeLucca, can you give us a description of Mueller?"

"Sure. He's a huge man with a bald head, small eyes and he walks with a limp."

"Someone like that shouldn't be hard to spot," said Rawlings. "Inspector, put a bulletin out on him. He's probably armed and he's definitely dangerous. I think it best to station some men around the hospital. If he intends to make his threat good, we may be able to nab him on the outside. We'll be leaving now, DeLucca. There will be a man at the door day and night. You'll be all right. Don't worry, we'll have this guy in custody in a matter of hours."

Agent Rawlings and the inspector hurried out of the room. The white box was tucked under the inspector's right arm.

The guy said, "Don't worry." What the hell else could I do, but worry? It looked like the big German was after my ass. I had no place to go and no place to hide. I hoped that Rawlings hadn't underestimated the big kraut. He didn't seem too bright, but he was very dangerous, especially when he was carrying out his orders. I wondered what Maria would say when she found out that it wasn't over yet. Someone once said, "It's never over till it's over." I supposed that, for Kotchman, it was never over. For the first time, I started to understand Kotchman's way of life. To hunt and to be hunted. It went on and on, until the end and if you lived through it, there was no end. In the last two weeks I had been threatened, chased, hit on the head, knifed, shot twice, and had lost the tip of my finger. Somehow, I felt that Kotchman had used me to good advantage. Now, there wasn't much left of me to use and I wanted out.

TWENTY-EIGHT

At four o'clock, the nurse came in, gave me the usual blood pressure check and handed me some pills in a paper cup. "The doctor said you could have these. One is for pain, the other is a sleeping pill. You should get some sleep."

I knew I wouldn't be taking the sleeping pill, not as long as Gunther Mueller was still out there. Ten minutes later, Maria arrived carrying a bathrobe and a pair of slippers. I knew she was upset. She gave me a quick kiss and sat down on the bed.

"DeLucca. I heard what happened."

"What did you hear?"

"For God's sake! It's common knowledge in the hospital, the box with your finger and the shears. Police are all over downstairs and I see you have a bodyguard at the door." She took my hand. "It's not going to end, is it?"

"It's going to end, Maria and damn soon. Today the doctor said I could go home in a couple of days. If you help me, I might be able to get out of here a lot sooner. We could go back to the cabin on the beach. Remember what you said there? You wished it would never end. Well, I think it would be a good place to go until all of this blows over. What do you say?"

"I don't know, DeLucca. You haven't had enough time to recover. It might do you more harm than good."

"Nonsense, it's just what I need: some sea air, a lot of rest and you." She smiled. "Are you sure you'll get any rest?"

"No, seriously, I believe it would do me a world of good. A few days by the sea and I'd be up and around in no time. Think about it. I'll talk to the doctor tomorrow morning and see what he says. Will you think about it?"

"All right, DeLucca, but I don't think you're well enough yet to travel."

"You just let me and the doctor be the judges of that."

Maria stayed with me the rest of the day. After a bland dinner, I lay back on the bed and we talked about everything, except what was really on our minds. I couldn't shake the vision of those damned pruning shears. I didn't feel safe in the hospital even though I had a guard at the door. I knew that the sooner I left, the better my chances. I had to talk to Rawlings.

I tried to stay awake, but my body ached for rest. I awoke in the middle of the night. Maria was gone and the lights were turned off. A dim glow came through the open doorway from the hall. It was too quiet for my liking and I wondered if the guard was still outside my door. I slid off the bed, put my feet into the slippers, threw on the robe and limped toward the door. I peeked around the door jam and noticed that the guard was not there. The hallway was empty and the ward looked abandoned. I knew it was late, but there ought to be someone around. I slowly picked my way down the hall and, as I rounded a corner, I heard voices. It sounded like agent Rawlings talking to someone. I stopped and listened.

"I guess the bastard isn't going to show. We'll keep a man on the exit stairs to the floor and make sure DeLucca's room is guarded. I'm calling it a night."

Rawlings started to walk my way. He turned the corner and reached for his shoulder holster in surprise.

"Jesus Christ, DeLucca. What are you doing out of bed?"

"I thought I'd take a walk. I found no guard at the door and not a living soul in the hall. Now, I start to get the picture. You're using me as bait, hoping that Mueller would make his move. You emptied out the floor to make it appear safe for him to come up here and do his dirty work."

"You were safe all the time, DeLucca. We have the floor and all of the exits and stairs covered. We were ready for him."

"Listen, Rawlings. This guy, Mueller, is not so dumb as to send me his calling card then show up the same night."

"Maybe you're right, DeLucca, but I thought we'd give it a try. Go back to sleep. Everything is secure."

"Back to sleep? Christ! I may never sleep again." I hobbled back to my room, dying for a cigarette.

I stayed awake the rest of the night. Nothing happened, except the repeated visits from the nurse. At 9:00 the next morning, the doctor stopped by to see how I was doing. After a lot of fast talking, I convinced him to release me. He said I could leave the hospital at 1:30 P.M., providing I had someone to drive me home and help change my dressings. He made me an appointment to visit his office in nine days and told me to use the crutch until I was stronger.

As soon as the doctor left the room, I grabbed the phone and called Maria.

"DeLucca. What's wrong? Are you all right?"

"Sure, I'm fine and getting better all the time."

"I was worried that something had happened last night. Did you get any sleep?"

"No, I didn't. Listen, Maria. They're going to release me at 1:30 today. Could you go to my apartment and pick up a couple of shirts and my shaving gear? Why don't you pack a small bag with the things you'll need for a few days. When you pick me up, we'll head straight for the beach. How does that sound?"

"It sounds wonderful, but are you sure the doctor said you could go home?"

"He did."

"OK, I'll be there at 1:00. Oh, I almost forgot. I have tickets for the final performance of the Flying Dutchman, on Thursday night. Can we go?"

"Hell, I don't know. I guess so."

"Wonderful! And another thing...the boys at the opera are throwing a party on stage after the performance and they would like you to be there."

"Why would they want me to be there?"

"I suppose it's because they want to pay their respects. I'll see you at 1:00."

"Hold it, Maria! I'd appreciate it if you picked me up a pack of cigarettes."

At one o'clock, Maria arrived with my clothes. I changed and said goodbye to the hospital. I was escorted down the elevator in a wheelchair, loaded down with bandages, pills and a crutch. Maria met me at the curb with the car and ten minutes later I was sitting back in the front seat, smoking a cigarette, and heading for the coast highway.

From the time we left the front entrance of the hospital, I was aware of a light gray sedan following us. I had a chance to see the driver and wasn't worried. It was the same guard who had stood outside my door in the hospital. Police Inspector Arnold probably told him to tail me when I left. He was far too obvious and made a lousy tail. I didn't mention it to Maria. There was no sense in having anything upsetting our little vacation.

Halfway to Rockaway Beach, Maria said with alarm, "DeLucca! We're being followed."

"You're right."

"You knew?"

"Yes. Nothing to worry about. It's one of the inspector's boys keeping an eye on us. I'm ready for some solid food. Where would you like to go to dinner?"

The next three days went by much too fast. We enjoyed candlelit dinners overlooking the sea, fresh shrimp and wine on the beach, lots of fresh air, and I slept like a log for the first time in weeks. In those few days I had gained some of my strength back and was able to get around quite well without the crutch.

Thursday afternoon, we packed up, cleaned the cabin and bade farewell to our Shangri-La by the sea. On the way back to the city I thought about the future. Where was I going with my private eye business? I had a hell of a time paying my bills and I damn sure didn't live high on the hog. One more case like this last one and I'd either be a nervous wreck or six feet under. The chances were a million to one of running across another case like this one. The idea that I had uncovered a bunch of war criminals at the opera was fantastic. Even though I had Kotchman's help, I had done most of the investigative work. I must have done something right. I thought possibly Maria and I working together could make it.

"DeLucca. You're a thousand miles off. What's on your mind? Let me in on it."

"I was just thinking, Maria. Maybe it's about time I had a good-looking secretary with a pair of gorgeous legs. Do you know where I can find a gal like that?"

At a quarter to five, Maria dropped me off at my apartment, then she went home to get all primped up for the opera. She was to pick me up at seven. After climbing the stairs, I was all worn out. My wounds were healing, but it would take time for me to regain my strength. I was surprised to see the apartment all cleaned up. I figured that somehow Maria had found time to straighten out the wreckage. After cleaning up and changing clothes, I sat down with a cognac and waited for Maria. I wondered if Rawlings and his agents had caught up with Townsend and Gunther Mueller. I remembered what Rawlings had said to me four days ago in the hospital. "Don't worry. We'll have the guy in custody in a matter of hours."

Maria was right on time and looked like a million dollars. Her hair was different and she wore a low cut gown that clung to her slender body like a second skin. At seven-thirty, we parked in the lot and joined the opera crowd making its way to the entrance. It was slow going, but we finally found our seats in the dress circle. The drone of the crowd and the musicians tuning their instruments put me into a trance. My eyes were starting to close.

As the house lights dimmed, Maria nudged me and announced with excitement, "DeLucca. It's going to start."

I had a difficult time staying awake through the first two acts. My head kept bobbing up and down. During the third act, I forced myself to stay awake. I was particularly interested in the Dutchman's ship. After it was all over, there were several curtain calls, lots of applause and bravos with standing ovations.

Maria enjoyed it immensely. When she asked me how I liked it, I replied, "It was OK."

We waited until the throngs of people had cleared out, then we started down to the stage to attend the party to end all parties.

The elevator dropped us off on the main floor and Maria led me through the doors and down the aisle to the orchestra pit. The main curtain was up and the janitors had already started to clean the seats. My leg was killing me as I climbed up a ramp following Maria to the stage apron. The stage crew was putting a final wrap to another performance at the opera. I looked up and could see part of the Dutchman's ghost ship. The masts and rigging with the blood-red sails draped in black gauze were hanging overhead. The other ships, the rocks and the cyclorama had been removed. Only the black masking wings that framed the last act remained. It was as though all of the magic had been turned off leaving a bare stage all the way to the back wall of the theatre. It was then that things started to happen. Denny, the prop man and his crew emerged from the left stage wings rolling a large gold throne chair and placed it center stage. Denny smiled and said, "There you are, Vince. Have a seat. Glad to see you up and around."

From the grid overhead, a large banner was lowered. Red-glittered letters on a white field read: "Bravo, DeLucca." A long table loaded with ice, mix and booze was rolled in from right stage. Earl 'Mac' McGuire and his crew greeted me, along with Big Jer and the scenic crew. There was Al Ferrigno, Irv the elevator engineer, and the custodian Julian Bagely. Joe Bender, the business agent, joined the group, and Ace Conlin was there, too. I was surrounded by all the people who had a hand in helping me during my investigation. All but Kotchman. I was overwhelmed. Maria looked down at me and squeezed my hand. Mac raised his voice above the din of conversation. "OK! Let the party begin. What are you drinking, Vince?"

TWENTY-NINE

An hour later, the party was in full swing. Tommy Doyle and Bruno Guffanti were swapping war stories with Ace Conlin at the bar. Some of the girls from the chorus had been invited and the music and dancing had begun. I was watching Big Jer dance with Maria from my chair on the apron when Joe Bender came over and handed me a check for two thousand dollars.

"Joe. This is much more than we agreed upon."

"I know, Vince. But you damn sure earned it. Call it a little extra bonus and don't worry about the hospital bills. They'll be taken care of." He headed back to the bar chewing his cigar with a smile on his face. I was surprised to see Inspector Arnold walking towards me.

"Inspector. Is this an official visit?"

"No, DeLucca. I just thought I'd drop by and see how you were doing and bring you some news. The F.B.I. is holding Townsend on a charge of kidnapping and conspiracy. It looks like they can make it stick."

"What about Mueller? Did they pick him up?"

"No. I'm afraid not. There's no sign of him, but I wouldn't worry. He's probably out of the state by now. Have a nice night, DeLucca. You deserve it."

Al the doorman came over and knelt by my chair. "Vince. I wanted to tell you that I am sorry I had to put you on the spot by mentioning your name to the police about that affair down in the basement. They came to my home and questioned me. I could have lied, but they would have found out later."

"It's OK, Al. You did the right thing. If it wasn't for you, we never would have caught up with Hessler."

At that moment, a loud bell rang several times. "Jesus!" said Al. "Who could that be?"

"What bell is that, Al?" I asked.

"It's the night bell at the stage door. I'll check and see who it is."

A minute later, Al was walking toward me followed by two men. The tall one I recognized as F.B.I. agent Rawlings. The other guy strutted in like a rooster with a plaster cast on his right arm. It was Wolf Kotchman. Now the group was complete.

Al approached me and said with a grin, "You know this guy, Vince?"

Kotchman stepped forward and looked down at me. His expression never changed. It was the same look he had given me when I first met him in my office. "Well, DeLucca. I see you managed to come through this ordeal alive. Even though a few parts are missing."

"What the hell are you doing here, Wolf? I figured I'd never see you again. Are you planning World War Three? If so, count me out."

Kotchman forced a smile from his twisted lips. "No, DeLucca. Just a bit of unfinished business. That's all. I wanted to tell you that making a copy of the list and not telling me about it put me at a disadvantage."

"You didn't get the book from Hessler?"

"No. He must have destroyed it or given it to someone before my people searched him."

"And this unfinished business, Wolf. It couldn't be Mueller, could it?"

"That is possible, DeLucca."

"Did Rawlings tell you Mueller can't be found?"

"Yes. Agent Rawlings filled me in on everything there is to know, except where Mueller is hiding."

"Christ, Wolf! You got Hessler and your witness Julie Koslo. Isn't that enough?"

"It's never enough, DeLucca. Yes, Hessler is safely on his way to Haifa and will be tried and punished by Israeli justice but so must Mueller."

"What will happen to Julie Koslo?"

"She will be taken to a hospital in Tel Aviv and cared for until the trial. Agent Rawlings has agreed to work with the Israeli government on the war criminal matter. I am more optimistic now about the final outcome."

"Well, Wolf, I'm happy to hear that. I wish you good hunting, but right now, let's have a drink together. It's been a rough battle. Maybe someday you will have the chance to win the war."

The party started to wind down and most of the stagehands went home. Tommy Doyle and Ace Conlin remained at the bar. Al had stationed himself at the stage door and Rawlings, Kotchman and Inspector Arnold were still involved in conversation.

Maria leaned down, gave me a kiss and said, "It's after 2:00. Aren't you ready to leave? You must be awfully tired."

"Yeah, I am. You're right, it's about time. I'll be right with you as soon as I go to the bathroom."

I walked up to the bar. Conlin was three sheets to the wind and so was Doyle. Ace smiled, "Well Vince, we had that drink together after all."

Doyle gulped down the last of his drink, set the glass on the bar and grinned. "Vince, old buddy, anytime you need help capturing Nazi bastards, I'm your man. If there's anything I can do, just ask."

"There is one more thing you can do for me, Doyle."

"Name it."

"Which way is the can?"

Doyle pointed the way and his directions took me across stage, through a pair of doors next to the prop room and to the left into an empty hallway. I noticed a mop handle sticking out of a bucket in front of the bathroom door. I pushed the door open and headed for the urinal. A noise came from one of the stalls to my right. I looked under the door of the center stall and saw a pair of shoes. I thought it might be one of the stagehands who had tipped a few too many and fallen asleep.

I called out, "Are you OK, fella?" There was no answer. I knocked on the door. There was no response. The door was unlocked, so I pushed it open. Sitting on the commode was a janitor, fallen sideways leaning against the wall of the stall. His face was distorted: his mouth hung open and his eyes bulged from their sockets. On his neck were large bruises. He had obviously been choked to death.

I stepped back from the stall and turned toward the door. I sensed movement behind me and, before I could turn, an arm lashed out and encircled my neck in a death lock. In my weakened state I had no defense. I tried to jab my elbow into his ribs, but it had no effect so I lifted both my legs up and kicked against the stall. Our bodies spun around facing the mirror. The reflection in the mirror confirmed my worst fear. It was Gunther Mueller. His bald head glistened and there was madness in his eyes. His left arm tightened the neck lock as he held a pistol to my temple. My windpipe was blocked and I felt close to falling unconscious.

The bathroom door opened. It was Ace Conlin. "What the hell's going on?"

Gunther dropped me to the floor and fired two shots narrowly missing Conlin. Ace slammed the door and ducked behind the wall. I raised my head up from the floor and watched Gunther rapidly move to the door. Suddenly, he stopped, turned around and looked at me. Uttering a growl, he raised the pistol at me and fired. I rolled on the floor as the bullet shattered the tile behind me. He opened the door and disappeared.

Conlin rushed back in and knelt beside me. "DeLucca! Are you OK?"

I had difficulty speaking. "Yeah, I think so."

Rawlings, Inspector Arnold and Kotchman came rushing in. Rawlings shouted, "What happened in here?"

Kotchman moved up next to me and said, "It was Mueller, wasn't it, DeLucca?"

"Yes. It was Mueller."

"Which way did he go?"

"I don't know. I just saw him go through the door."

"I know where he went," said Ace. "He got into the elevator." Rawlings and Kotchman ran out of the bathroom, followed by Inspector Arnold.

Ace helped me to my feet. "That was a close one, DeLucca. When I heard that last shot, I thought he had killed you."

"He damn near did, Ace. Maybe my luck has finally changed for the better. Let's get the hell out of this bathroom."

Maria met me at the door. Her face was white as a sheet. "My God! DeLucca. Not again. When will this—."

"It's all right, Maria. It's about to end now."

We walked out onto the stage and were met by a very excited Tommy Doyle. "Vince! It looks like they've got the bastard trapped up on 4F."

"Where is that?"

"All the way up, just below the grid. Rawlings and the inspector went up the same elevator Mueller took and Kotchman used the other elevator on right stage. They'll be coming at the kraut from both directions. There's no place he can go. Listen! You can hear them up on the catwalk over us."

I looked up into the darkness and could hear footsteps on the metal catwalk. If Mueller was trapped up there, there would be a fight. Kotchman wanted to take Mueller alive, but this time it might not be possible.

Suddenly, gun shots resounded from the grid. Maria grabbed my arm. The dark overhead transformed with the fireworks of a blazing gun battle. When the shooting stopped, we heard a falling metal object hitting the pipes on the way down.

Doyle yelled, "Get out from under. Something's coming down."

We retreated to the safety of the wings. There were a few more clangs and the object hit the deck. It was a pistol, but whose gun was it? We waited and listened. Then something else banged against the pipes on its way down. This was no gun. I looked up from the wings and saw a body falling. It hit the hanging Dutchman's ship, tore the rigging, ripped through the sails, and finally dropped with a thud onto the stage floor. We approached to see who it was. There, wrapped in fragments of the blood red sails and tangled in a black net shroud lay Gunther Mueller, dead at last.

Maria took my hand and looked at me. "DeLucca, is it finally over?"

"Yes." I put my arm around her. "It's over."

As we walked to the exit, I could hear the droning of the electric motor lowering the grand drape to the stage floor.

THE END

EPILOGUE

W hen I was publishing my late husband's novel *Witness In The Wings*, I was reminded of my own encounter with a Nazi. This is the story of that event.

The SS Anti-Partisan Squadron Commander And The Silver Slippers

By

Catherine Hand

My mother was a handsome woman with classic Semitic features and shining black hair. Despite the hardships of her life, she carried herself with great dignity, but her large, muscular, work-worn hands showed she had not led a life of leisure. It was those capable hands that I admired most about her.

She had escaped the holocaust at thirteen, gone from New York sweatshops to union organizing, then on to Europe, Russia, and Spain where she met the revolutionaries of her day, but to achieve American respectability, she had settled for security, a life that became for her a slow death. After twenty years of marriage, freed at last by divorce from her pretentious husband, and from raising three children—one about to graduate daughter (me), one son gone to the father, and only her brooding ten-year-old left—she was ready to declare her independence. She finally had her own bank account and, though not knowing how to drive, she threw caution to the winds and bought herself a twenty-year-old black Cadillac sedan. My mother, the revolutionary, was ready to revolt.

On the eve of my high school graduation, I brought home scholarships. Amazed by the unexpected windfall, she announced, "Kids, we're going to Mexico. We leave in a week." Then she turned to me and said, "You will drive."

Since I had my new driver's license, my mother's declaration of personal independence included me as her chauffeur. We would travel from sleepy Orange County through the Sonora desert into the heart of Mexico. A week later, I took the wheel of my mother's Cadillac to drive the fifteen-hundred miles through the Sonora desert all the way to Mexico City. The hot dusty roads through long stretches of scorching desert played havoc with Mamma's high blood pressure. Without air conditioning in 120 degree heat, she fell unconscious on the seat by my side. Those last twenty miles I drove to reach Hermosillo were the fastest I ever drove in my life. With the challenges of our trip just beginning, I realized the weight of my responsibility and wondered if I was up to it.

Seeing the sparse palms of Hermosillo, I sped to a screeching halt in front of a rundown motel, jumped out, and ran into the lobby, calling for help. There we found a doctor, who proceeded to nurse my Mamma back to health, then attempt to woo her. When I saw her flutter her eyelashes, I breathed a sigh of relief knowing she'd recovered. The doctor's flirtatious attentions gave her new strength, and we drove on to the next stop on our journey.

After a three-month course in Guadalajara, we headed to Mexico City, where we toured the capital. We hired a guide to take us to Taxco, Mexico's famous silver center, where my mother hoped to purchase some fine silver jewelry. Jorge, our unctuous guide, was all over himself, flattering her. He mentioned her excellent taste in jewelry, commenting that gold befitted her more than silver.

When he discovered her European Jewish origin, Jorge struck on the ultimate way to cater to her taste. He drove us to a Jewish delicatessen outside the capital. The proprietor surprised my mother by welcoming her in Yiddish. To avoid speaking her mother tongue in the presence of her American children, she answered in English. She had made a great effort to achieve almost perfect English with only the trace of an accent, and she took no pride in her original language.

After we left the delicatessen, our oily guide proclaimed, "The dinner was such a success and you and your children are so charming that I must invite you all to join me this evening to a private party in the Capital hosted by some of my most cultivated friends." He said the hostess was a famed European ballerina and he would like to introduce my mother, who could be a countess in her own right to this distinguished group. How could she refuse such an invitation?

Mother donned her best gold jewelry, wore her black velvet stole, and changed handbags, transferring some bills from the worn leather one to the petit point opera bag she had embroidered herself. Jorge drove us through the alleyways of a gloomy Spanish baroque neighborhood. The apartment was in a dark building. We walked through a long, narrow, carpeted corridor to reach the apartment. A heavily made-up woman of about sixty who reeked of strong perfume opened the door. Her tightly permed, flaming red hair matched her lipstick. She wore a draped eggshell satin blouse with dolman sleeves that floated around her slack arms. Her long black crepe skirt was slit up the side, revealing her bulked dancer's calves, her smoke gray hose, and shiny silver sequined slippers. She spoke with a thick German accent.

"Willkommen, Countess! Do come in." She motioned us to a small dimly lit bedroom and indicated that my mother should leave her stole and her bag on the bed and then follow her to the salon to meet her other distinguished European guests. We were seated on a gray velvet overstuffed sofa. Old-fashioned flowery wallpaper covered the walls bordered by heavy mahogany moldings. Thick oriental carpets littered the floor, and a curvaceous side table was laden with decanters of brandy and Bohemian crystal apéritif glasses. Our hostess ceremoniously offered my mother a brandy, which, although I'd never known her to drink, she accepted. Dim light came from a dark brass chandelier hanging from the middle of the peeling coved ceiling, and floor lamps lit the corners of the room through shades of what looked like yellowing animal skin.

I felt swallowed in the formless soft seat of the sofa and found it hard to breathe in the oppressive grayness and mustiness of the room, where the eerie light filtered through the smoke of strong cigarettes. As my little brother seemed to disappear into the cushions, through the kitchen's swinging door strode an apparition - a tall, gaunt, hollow-cheeked man with slicked back steel gray hair, wearing a paisley ascot and striped trousers and vest.

The man towered over us with his snifter of brandy dangling over our heads. Across his chest, he wore a bandolier with a medal pinned to it, a silver medallion which depicted a sword hilt plunging down into a skull. Its acanthus leaf oval frame surrounding the center motif provided the base for three entwining two-headed snakes. One of those tails twisted up the sword shaft to the circle a swastika in its center. My little brother stared, mesmerized by the ghoulish image of the medal hanging on the ribbon stretched across the man's chest. I do not think he knew its meaning, but I did.

"Herr General!" croaked the ballerina in her mannish voice, "Allow me to introduce you to our new friend, the Countess Berta and her pretty little children. Dear Madam, do have another brandy," she said as she lifted the decanter to refill my mother's Bohemian crystal glass. "This is General Meinhof of the Third Reich, famous in the old country for his service during the var."

The general sat on the sofa next to me, too close for my comfort, and stretched his arm across the high back so that I felt even more dwarfed as I sank into the cushions. I felt his heavily alcohol-laden breath on my neck as he said, "Ah yah, those ver vanderful times den. Vat use vee made of everything vee had in those days. Even the lampshades vee made, and nothing vas ever gone to vaste. The gold from all those teeth has provided very vell for us, has it not, Hilke?" He laughed as he tossed down the whole snifter of brandy in one gulp, and I felt my mother's trembling through my skirt as our thighs touched.

When I started to ask what he meant about the lampshades, Momma pinched my thigh and stood up, announcing to our hostess, "It has been a terribly long hot day for my children, and we really must be going. I do not want to overtire them."

She grabbed my arm and pulled me up. I grabbed my little brother's arm and did the same. Momma turned to Jorge. "Please be so kind as to take us back now to the hotel." She ushered us like chicks to the bedroom down the hall, grabbed her fur stole and petit point opera bag, muttering under her breath. "I hope they left us enough to pay the hotel bill. Don't say a word. We're getting out of here right now. Then she shoved us down the hallway and out into the dark street, leaving behind the Nazi expatriates with their memories of the good old days, and the hundred dollars they had removed from her wallet.

The next morning, we packed before dawn and left Mexico City in a hurry.

Momma ordered me, "Don't stop, don't look back, just drive!"

www.ingramcontent.com/pod-product-compliance
Lightning Source LLC
Chambersburg PA
CBHW070311260626
47160CB00003B/802